# The Girl from Raven Island

Glenn Burwell

Somewhat Grumpy Press

Published by arrangement with Somewhat Grumpy Press Inc. Halifax, Nova Scotia, Canada. The Somewhat Grumpy Press name and Pallas' cat logo are registered trademarks.

ISBN 978-1-7380743-8-9 (paperback)
ISBN 978-1-7380743-7-2 (eBook)

September 2024 v4

# Cast of Characters

**Family**

Robert Lui......Detective, Vancouver Police Department
Sophie and Robin Lui......Robert's children
Ethan & Mary Lui......Robert's parents
Rose Esmeraldo......Sophie's friend

**Protesters and others**

Allo Foot......Bella Kind
Mary Tinlit......Bella Kind
George Tinlit......Mary's father
Andy Dhillon......protestor
Anne Leforet......Architect, Hummingbird Architects
Nancy Brick......Project Manager, City of Vancouver
Ricardo Remuda......Director Housing, City of Vancouver
Arby Knutson
......Site Superintendent, Tornado Housing Co-op
Bernard Lily......CBC reporter
Gilberto......Cafe Paulo owner
Carmelita......barista

Yuko......barista
Fiona Hamilton......wife of Archie Hamilton
Gary Hamilton......son of Archie Hamilton
Sandra Kour......chef at Arnott Bay Lodge, Bella Kind
Roger......Beaver pilot
Bobbi Atwal......ex-gang member
Safa Atwal......Bobbi's sister

**Police**

Thomas Harrow
......Head of Investigations, Special Constable, VPD
David McKnight
......Deputy Chief, Investigation Division, VPD
Ranit......Assistant to the chiefs
Archie Hamilton......officer, VPD
Walter Gray......Sergeant, RCMP, Bella Kind
Rodney Fister......sergeant detective, VPD
Tony Bortolo......detective constable, VPD
Finn Black......detective constable, VPD
Norma van Kleet......Admin for Thomas Harrow
Troy Geelham......RCMP, Richmond
Vito Cotoni......detective, VPD
Rory......cyber crime officer, VPD, group leader

If you need to fly and have a choice, take a real plane.

# Chapter 1

Five young women and men circled a ceremonial fire set smack in the middle of the traffic intersection. They trotted with arms out, ratty blankets drifting behind them as though they were down-at-heel raptors, floating on the thermals. The blankets rose and lowered as their owners wafted around the flames, imitating the ravens or hawks a few of them had known from the coastal communities they hailed from. The syncopated beat of a drum echoed off the walls of the buildings at the corners of the two main thoroughfares. Depending on your perspective or knowledge, it could be mistaken for a war drum. Evening had descended, lending focus to the fire and the protesters surrounding it.

Another small group of women and men sat huddled around the drum, a few metres from the fire, several of them pounding the diaphanous skin. Not all of them were native born, but the ones with European backgrounds had been attracted to the clannish feel of the group. A larger circle of protesters stood, slightly removed, as though they hadn't achieved the necessary status to join the inner group. Some held signs, but most were empty-handed. Beyond them, other hangers-on as well as police officers belonging to the City of Vancouver watched the action.

So far, the protest was following the script of just about every other recent demonstration in the city: shut down a major transportation route until the police decided that the group's point had been made. At some indeterminate time, the officers would move in and break up the affair, detaining anyone who didn't feel like calling it a day peacefully.

A couple of television crews from competing stations had shown up to document the scene for the late evening news, interviewing spokespeople who could provide the expected rant about the issue of the moment. It was usually enough to get the viewers' heart rates to elevate slightly. A young journalist, fairly new to the broadcast business, was having a conversation with Mary Tinlit, one of the inner group members around the fire. She had agreed to step away from the fire for the conversation. Mary's pert face was framed by short, black hair. Ragged bangs hung above dark eyes, eyebrows not styled. Her body was compact, but not skinny. She didn't seem to have missed any meals recently.

"Hello. I am Bernard Lily, with the CBC. What is your name, and why are you blocking this intersection?" His cameraman was filming.

"I'm Mary, and like, we are going to be here until the city provides real homes for us and all the others who desperately need housing."

"Well, that could take a while I suspect." Bernard countered with a hint of logic, to see what the reaction would be.

"Like, we don't care. We're going to do whatever it takes to like, get our rights."

"What rights are those, specifically?"

"The right to have a home at a price we can like, afford."

"Not really sure if that's a right, Mary."

"Fucking right it is, you asshole."

Not everything caught on tape could be used, Bernard was quickly learning. He looked at his cameraman, who was grinning back at him.

He tried another tack. "Are you in charge of all these people?"

"Why don't you go screw yourself?"

Bernard came up with a few things he could say, but went with neutral. "Is there someone else I could talk with?"

Instead of answering, Mary curved her lips in apparent distaste, turned, and tromped away in her monster black boots. He watched as she went over to one of the demonstrators standing by the fire and had a few words. She looked around, eventually walking over to another young man standing alone, watching the police officers.

The first man looked at Bernard and casually sauntered over, as though he had better things to do than speak to the media, when really, the whole point of the protest was to get the media's attention. An earnest face framed with longish black locks topped a skinny body. He wasn't bad looking, to Bernard, anyway.

He spoke first. "You want to talk with me?"

"That would be nice. But if all you are going to do is swear at us, like young Mary over there, then possibly not." Bernard laid it out.

"Okay."

"What is your name?"

"Allo Foot."

"Unusual. Where do you hail from?"

"Haida Gwaii."

"And are you visiting, or do you live here?"

"I live in East Vancouver, in a squat. I can't afford the price to rent a home here."

At this point, a bottle from somewhere beyond the fire went flying high over their heads. Bernard turned to watch its arc as it rotated end over end, dropping, finally hitting a police officer on her chest. Bernard knew immediately that this was not helpful for his interview. Sure enough, the officers started to gather together, readying for action.

Bernard said to Allo, "Perhaps we'll talk another time." He and his cameraman took a few steps back, waiting for the action to start. It was obvious to Bernard that the protest group was not of a single mind. Allo quickly returned to the fire where a few of the youngsters were suddenly talking amongst themselves, worry evident on their faces. A couple more bottles went flying towards the police, but these came from the outer circle of protesters, the unholy. Shields were produced, helmets adjusted, and a cadre of about twenty officers started their advance on the outer group. More bottles and some bricks went the officers' way. The police evidently decided they had had enough and launched a charge.

Off to the side, Bernard watched as more cars and trucks arrived, officers spilling out in riot gear with shields. They had obviously been held in reserve somewhere close by. In under a minute, the scene became chaotic. Six officers led a separate charge at the central group, kicking the fire apart as they ran through it, somehow avoiding lighting up as they danced through the flames. Most of the protesters were running away at this point, but not without hurling some more ordinance upon the police, some of whom seemed intent on catching the misbehavers. People scattered in all directions, the protest seemingly winding down of its own accord, but not willingly.

When there was nothing left to film, Bernard and his cameraman went back to their van, stowed their equipment and waited in the front seats, just in case anything else remotely newsworthy took place.

"That it?" Bernard asked.

"S'pose. Might be some shit happening in the back alleys, though."

"I'm fine here. Don't fancy getting knifed, do we?" Bernard responded.

After fifteen minutes of nothing, they called it a night and headed back to the CBC studios, known as the mothership. Bernard knew they should have been hot footing it through the back streets chasing the action, but after covering several local protests, he was already slightly lazy and jaded, not a good combination for a young reporter with ambitions. He had noticed that none of the other news teams were chasing the action either, so he felt relaxed about leaving.

Early the next morning, at the Cambie Street headquarters of the Vancouver Police Department, Detective Robert Lui slid into his work desk out in the central pod farm — the work area with no view of the outside world. He sat, stretched, then looked around for an accomplice for his daily run up the street to fuel his caffeine addiction. As his eye wandered across the workstations, he couldn't avoid seeing his old office, where Rodney Fister was roosting these days.

It wasn't Rodney's fault that Robert had trouble with suspensions, subsequently losing his private office, but it sure felt like it. Robert's animosity towards Rodney stemmed from a gang kidnapping of Robert's son over a year earlier. Rodney was put in charge of the case and proceeded to do little to affect any possible good outcome, seemingly only concerned with his reputation. Rodney for his part, thought Robert was obstructing his case, but the only reason the boy was eventually rescued was due to Robert's 'outside the rule book' efforts.

His recently-minted detective buddy, Tony, was absent, so he looked over and beckoned Finn Black to join him. Not having been previously indoctrinated, Finn didn't know the drill, but he nodded in reply as he rose.

The pair made their way up Cambie Street, south towards Cafe Paulo. It was officially autumn, and leaves were changing colours on the street trees, some dropping prematurely from the deficit of water through the late summer. The drenching rains had yet to arrive, unnatural for Vancouver, Robert considered.

Finn was a member from the Haida Gwaii First Nation, and had endured a rough process similar to Robert's, who was half-Asian, as Finn rose to become an investigator. He was a large man with an open, weathered face, earned honestly by spending his youth working the fishing boats around the islands and straights of Haida Gwaii. When Robert had asked Finn why he wasn't doing his law enforcement back up in his home community, Finn had grinned. "Have you been up there? It is beautiful and all, but I'd be dead asleep if I was in Massett. Vancouver is way more exciting."

"Anything interesting in your caseload, Finn?" Robert asked, as they drew close to the cafe.

"Not really." Giving the lie to his statement about Vancouver's action. Finn had inherited the west side of Vancouver from a previous detective who had resigned and left town. If there were overt crimes, they tended to be the white-collar type, and theft. Violent crime was a rarity.

Robert was going to be handed the east side of Vancouver to cover, but the switchover hadn't occurred yet. He had endured an extensive in-house review of his work on a previous case, which had effectively ended in the suburb of Langley, with a few people dead, hence the investigation. In addition, a group called the Independent Investigations Office poked around the case. This civilian led group looked into every death or serious injury that occurred in a police action in the entire province. Robert had come out of the process relatively unscathed, but it had taken time for the verdicts to be rendered.

The detective presently tasked to the east side was Rodney Fister, a role he felt was far beneath his capabilities, so he had recently asked his boss to be transferred to the Gang Task-force. The man running the investigative group, Thomas Harrow, had acquiesced to Rod's request so that he could play cops and robbers with various gangs that called the Lower Mainland home. Rodney couldn't appreciate it yet, but because of Robert Lui's efforts, the gang front was going to be quieter for the next year or two. It took Rodney time to realize anything, but by giving up the hated east side, he was once again going to leave himself out of the coming action.

The pair entered the cafe, Robert yelling his customary greetings at Gilberto standing behind his espresso machine, before sitting at his favourite table, facing the street.

Robert started kvetching. "Wish I was back chasing those gangsters."

"No, you don't. You just think you do. None of that turned out particularly well for you. And I seem to recall you spending more time on suspension than actually working." Finn looked down at Robert's less than perfect right hand. "Couldn't they straighten those things out?"

He followed Finn's eyes, his two smallest fingers still akimbo and aching from his last interaction with a particular thug. "They did. You should have seen them before."

Giberto himself brought two espressos over to the table, service unheard of at Cafe Paulo, unless you were Robert Lui. He smiled back at Gilberto, accepting the proffered cups. "Maybe it's time for a holiday."

Finn looked at Robert, shaking his head. He had never known Robert to have taken time off, unless it was forced because of some perceived infringement of Vancouver Police Department regulations. There was plenty of that, he realized. Perhaps that was why Robert didn't take vacations.

"Hawaii? Or Mexico?" The options from Vancouver were somewhat limited, in Finn's view.

"Don't know. Maybe I'll ask Norma where she'd like to go."

Finn smiled. He'd heard that something was going on between the two. Norma worked as the administrative assistant to their boss, Thomas. Robert and Norma had tried valiantly to keep it professional in the workplace, but everyone knew something was up.

Robert's phone rang. He reached inside his jacket while placing his cup onto the table.

Finn watched as Robert's eyes narrowed. "Be right back." Robert put his phone away, grabbed his cup and drained it. "Got to go. Missing cop from last evenings' hijinks out at Hastings and Clark. Not sure if it is my case or not. Don't think Rod has been given his marching orders as yet."

Finn choked back his coffee, joining Robert as he waved goodbye to Gilberto. "How come we're only hearing about this now?" Finn asked.

"Don't know. You'd think someone missing at the end of a shift would be noticed."

"Well, maybe it was noticed, but someone didn't care."

"There is always that possibility."

When they returned to their floor, Finn went back to his uninteresting work, while Robert rapped on Thomas's door frame, angling his head to see if his boss was in. He was indeed sitting behind his desk. Rodney Fister slumped in a guest chair across from him.

"Come in, Robert." Thomas didn't waste any time. "A search has been mounted in the area around the site of yesterday's protest at Clark and Hastings. The missing officer has been identified as Archie Hamilton. Didn't return to the precinct after all the shenanigans had died down. You might want to get out there and take a look around. Check on who saw him last as well."

"That's my beat." Rodney raised his voice, put out at the perceived slight.

"You are being transferred to the gang detail as per your request, so it's better if Robert attends. You aren't going to be around for the end of this, anyway."

Rodney stared at Robert with a look that Medusa would have been proud of, if he had that power. Robert nodded in return, his smirk impossible to hide.

"Okay, Thomas." Robert hadn't even sat down. He turned and left, heading down to the basement to get a car for the drive east. Rodney spluttered a few curses to no one in particular as he left Thomas's office.

This assignment was unusual. Cops generally were able to take care of themselves, even in a riot situation. Robert snaked his way north down to Hastings Street, then headed east until he reached Clark, parking on a side street twenty minutes after leaving Cambie.

Walking back to the site of the protest, Robert saw little to indicate it had ever taken place. City crews had removed all the debris. Only a few black marks remained in the middle of the intersection where the fire had been kicked over onto the tarmac. A seemingly endless procession of semi-trucks hauling shipping containers rumbled by, either entering or leaving the Port of Vancouver via Clark Drive.

Robert noticed several more VPD cars parked on Clark, left by officers making their enquiries of the local businesses. He started walking around to get a feel for the area. The immediate buildings seemed to be industrial or commercial affairs in an obviously low rent area; car shops and furniture makers being the trades of choice. Robert doubted whether any of the bourgeois brought their sedans and coupes here for repair. He went up to an officer who was leaving one of the body shops. The vehicles parked in the lane alongside appeared to be products of inbreeding amongst farm machinery. Robert asked how the search was going.

"This place is dead in the evening, it appears. No one I've talked to was even around last night when the riot happened. Big bunch of nothing so far," the officer said. "But I have been trying for any security video that is available. Some companies have cameras, but many don't. Probably not overly concerned with what happens to most of these vehicles."

"Well, keep at it. Never know what may turn up." It was a pretty lame attempt at rallying the troops. Better to keep his mouth shut, so he saluted briefly and kept walking. After an hour of uselessly walking the streets, he remembered that a locally famous restaurant was only a couple of blocks away. Its specialty was dim sum, and even though it was early, and Robert only a party of one, he headed over. Robert was a noodle hound, and if he wouldn't sample too many of the dishes on the rolling carts which were meant for larger parties, he could always order a plate of *chow mien* and get his fix.

The place was surprisingly busy for a weekday. After the hostess directed him to a small table near the kitchen, he settled in and started to eat after a few carts rolled by. He'd do some research into Archie once he got back to Cambie Street, see what he was dealing with. Perhaps the guy had simply gone absent without leave. Unlikely, but stranger things had happened.

An hour passed. Robert was feeling immensely full, and happy. Time to get back. He kept an eye out for other officers as he returned to his car, but they all seemed to be still busy interviewing business owners.

Robert returned to Cambie Street headquarters and walked back onto his floor, nodding to Norma with a small grin as he approached her station. She had been mysteriously absent earlier, so he was happy to see her back.

"Norma." He just liked saying her name.

"Yes?"

"Could you, perchance, pull the personnel file on an Archie Hamilton for me?"

"Perchance? Where are we, merry olde England?" Norma van Kleet was of resolutely Dutch heritage, and had no problem with reminding people of that.

Robert smiled and kept moving, not wanting to start something that might turn out inappropriately in an office setting. He went to his desk, looked at his in-tray and reluctantly started to peruse the files he had now inherited, documenting other east side cases. Murders were relatively rare in any part of Vancouver, but assaults were ever present in this area. Fortunately, or unfortunately, depending on how you looked at things, solving the cases didn't require much brainpower. His comment that morning to Finn was real; he missed the gang action, even though it had almost resulted in his death a few months earlier. He shook his head. He still was a father to two teenagers, so a drop in action wasn't a bad thing. He just missed it.

The more he read his files, the sleepier he became. Two things then happened. Norma came up to him. "Hey handsome, here is your file." Dropping it in front of him, she said, "Friday?" Robert smiled and nodded. They had a standing date most every Friday.

The second thing was the arrival of his former protégé, Tony Bortolo, to his desk beside Robert's. Robert waved at Tony as he pulled open the dossier of Archie Hamilton. A quick overview revealed nothing unexpected. A drinking problem, a divorce when he had been with the RCMP, a career stalled out, all told a tale of failed ambitions or perhaps baggage that had not resolved itself.

Archie had come over from the RCMP a few years earlier. Mention of a suspension for some incident while with the horsemen was unremarkable. Robert had lost his job once, returned, then had been on desk duties earlier this year, and he was relatively young. Archie was similar to so many on the force without a hint as to why he would go missing. Robert closed the file and his mind wandered to what he was going to come up with as dinner for his children.

Just after 7:30 the next morning, at Lee's Automotive on Frances Street, one of the workers needed some fresh paint for the coming day's work. Lee's body shop was a couple of blocks south of where the protest action had happened a day and a half earlier. After joking around with one of his co-workers, he swung into action and opened the door to the storage room. He was face to face with a naked man, hanging by his neck from one of the steel joists overhead. An expletive in his native Vietnamese escaped his mouth. He turned and fled, yelling as he went, "Dead man, dead man!" The owner looked up from his desk as the man ran into his office, obviously distraught.

"Calm down, Tong. Where is he?"

"Paint storage."

By this time, the other three employees had gathered in front of the storage room door to see for themselves, their phones out. A quick glance by the owner was all he needed to make the call to 911.

After looking again, he confirmed there was not a stitch of clothing on the body, and it was covered in red welts. He stepped back and closed the door quickly. There wouldn't be much work done this day. He was about to send his workers home when he thought better of it. Perhaps the police would want to talk with everybody. He was unsure. He felt ill. This was the worst kind of thing for his business. How was he going to rid his shop of this bad luck?

He looked over at his workforce and, sure enough, they were already staring at their cellphones, letting the world know what had happened, before he could stop them — as if he even could.

# CHAPTER 2

That same morning, Robert had just arrived at the office when Thomas bellowed from his office. "Robert!"

*What the heck happened to protocol?* Usually, when Robert was summoned, the chain of command went through Norma in a dignified manner. Robert wasn't a big fan of change in any part of his life. "Coming," he responded.

Once in Thomas's office, door closed, Thomas laid it out. "A body has been discovered in a body shop near that protest. Don't say it."

Robert couldn't help himself. "Sounds about right."

Thomas shook his head. "Get out there. It's on Frances Street. Norma has the address. I hope it's not the missing Archie, but...."

"Shit." Robert's reply was succinct as he left the office. He headed down to get a car, after a short visit with Norma. He drove the route he already knew and pulled up to the address, leaving his car in the middle of the street amongst several cruisers, their lights flashing the basic red and blue colour palette relentlessly. Yellow tape was already up, with officers walking around, none looking pleased.

Robert strode the cracked tarmac up through the raised garage door. He met with a scene of three prepped but unpainted cars, a workbench along the entire back wall supporting various tools, metal parts, and dust — yellow dust everywhere. A couple of officers were talking with what Robert assumed to be employees. The coroner was already present and pulled Robert aside before he could talk to anyone.

"We have left him for you as he was found. Appears to be the missing cop. One of the officers here made the identification. It also looks like he was attacked with a Taser, multiple times, like torture, I would say. There are burn marks all over his body. They didn't spare anything. And I mean anything." She stared at Robert squarely in the eyes.

"How do you know it was a Taser?"

"Just a wild guess, but there is a Taser on the floor."

"So planned and pre-meditated." He moved towards the closed door. "Not that it matters. An officer is dead, so it's murder one anyway."

She nodded. "That is your area of expertise. We'll get the body back home and do our examinations. I'll let you know the results maybe by the end of day, or more probably tomorrow."

Robert entered the storage room and gently closed the door. He didn't move, taking in the brutality of what he was viewing. Archie's hands were taped behind his back, his head tilted slightly to one side, feet a few inches above the concrete floor. Whoever had done this had paid particular attention to Archie's genitals. The rope around his neck looked old, but it was also fashioned into a genuine hangman's noose.

Robert noticed dried blood on the neck and shoulder. He moved around the body but didn't learn anything further. The stench of decomposition was beginning to bloom.

He scanned the small room. In the corner, next to some plastic paint pails, was the discarded Taser laying close-by. Archie's clothes were strewn by the shelving. His service belt seemed to be missing, presumably with his weapon. The light was dim. It would not have been a pleasant place to die. This was revenge for something. He stood still for a while longer, then turned and walked out into the shop area, softly closing the door behind him.

Robert knew none of this was sitting well with the officers in the garage. It wouldn't take very long before the whole force would be out for blood, literally. If they were smart, those protesters would keep their heads out of sight for a time until a cause for the murder was established. Some of the VPD would not be on their best manners shortly. Robert was certain the officers present would jump to the conclusion that the protesters were behind this. His preference was to wait on evidence, which was why he was the detective, and they weren't.

An officer was interviewing Mr. Lee in his office, but Robert left him to it, deciding to get back to Cambie Street. It was time to review that dossier more closely. As he left the front door, a news van pulled up, the media circus already starting. He looked at the crew as they exited the van, but didn't see anyone he knew and no one recognized him, so he was left alone as they fanned out, looking for targets to speak with.

Back at Cambie, once Robert dumped his car, he returned to his floor and nodded to Norma as he went straight into Thomas's office. Thomas looked up, expectantly.

"It was Archie all right. And he wasn't treated very well. Looks as though someone had it in for him, or cops in general. Hard to say right now."

Thomas's eyes tightened. "I'm sure you will figure it out, right? I don't have to tell you how top of mind this will be around here."

Robert nodded and left the room, heading to his desk. He re-opened the file on top of his desk but stared blankly at it. He thought back to the news van that had arrived at the scene, and what he had seen on the CBC News the previous evening about the protest. He knew one of the reporters there, the one who had interviewed the young man at the protest. It wasn't a very long news clip, but maybe there was more to the story.

He called Bernard Lily. "Hey, guess who?"

"Robert? It's been some time since we last spoke. To what do I owe the pleasure? Wait, forget that. I just heard that a cop was found dead out by Clark Street. Is this it?"

"Yes, in a way. I wondered if you could tell me anything about two nights ago. The protest? I saw you on the news."

Robert waited while Bernard was evidently hesitating, wondering if he would spill what he knew to Robert.

"I interviewed a woman that night before the piece that aired. A Mary Tinlit, but she had such a foul mouth, we couldn't use any of the footage, so it was a short conversation. She seemed pretty hopped up about something. After, she went over to a second young man, not the one we interviewed. We probably have footage of him, but never got a chance to talk with anyone else other than that Foot fellow before the riot started."

"Well, it is now a murder investigation, so that footage would be helpful, if your mothership wouldn't mind." Fat chance, he thought. The media would bend over backwards not to help the police, or especially, to appear to be doing so. Bernard, he felt, might have a different view.

"I'll see what I can find. USB okay?"

"Thanks Bernard. This deserves lunch soon. I'll be in touch." Robert smiled inwardly. Playing fast with the rules sometimes had advantages. They were both well aware that each was using each the other for their own purposes. Few people knew of the arrangement, and so far, it had worked to their mutual benefit.

Tony spoke from the next workstation. "Looks like I just got tasked to join you for this hunt." He rolled his chair back and stuck his head around the low wall, grinning. "Like old times."

Robert nodded, "Sort of." He was pondering where Tony could start. And this consideration deserved someplace other than the office. He signed his coffee question and the two immediately vacated the floor. The previous spring, some ad hoc meetings had taken place at Cafe Paulo with Thomas leading the way, so this was not something new or forbidden, even if it was unorthodox.

Robert and Tony entered the cafe and Gilberto looked up, an instant grin breaking out. "I knew you were too quick a while ago." He was shaking his head. Robert had been in earlier for a shot before work, which he took standing at the bar. Robert shook his head and went over to Carmelita to order his Americanos.

"Ah, now you are angry that I spoke the truth."

Robert grinned back at him, remaining quiet. Tony had a hard time with all the drama over a simple cup of coffee, but remained silent as well. They sat down.

Robert started. "I have Archie Hamilton's personnel file. I've given it the once over, but it obviously needs a more detailed look, which I'd like you to do. I would say that Archie's death looks like a bad case of retribution."

"How old was he?"

"I didn't check, but seemed to be in his late forties, maybe? He was RCMP before he came on here. I suggest looking at that part of his history first." Gilberto's helper brought their coffees over.

"Also, we might get some additional television footage of the night in question."

"CBC?" asked Tony.

"Yup. I'll look at that. You can go through the security video from businesses near Lee's Automotive."

"Gee, thanks."

"Don't mention it. If you're feeling put out, don't. I'm the one with the responsibilities on this case. You're sitting easy."

"Guess you are right. We should get back soon. Don't want to appear like we aren't taking this seriously," said Tony.

"Good point. I wonder what other news crews were at the demonstration that evening. Maybe you could chase that down as well."

As Robert and Tony settled in back at their desks, Rodney walked out of his office, sneered at Robert and kept going.

"Did Rod just give me the stink-eye?" Robert asked.

"He's probably angry about our case. Poor Rod." Tony replied.

Robert rolled his chair into Tony's work area so he could talk quietly. "Yeah, Thomas has given him his transfer. Don't think he's very happy now, even though he was the one asking for it."

Robert switched to the case. "What bothers me is how did Archie get nabbed? I mean, it must have been a chaotic scene, and nighttime as well. Was it all planned? Or was chance involved? And how did they get him alone? I'm assuming that more than one person was involved, but maybe not."

"Those are a lot of questions, Robert. Good thing we are detectives, experts at just this type of problem."

Robert shook his head slowly. "This isn't helping, Tony." After a moment, he continued. "Maybe they used a rabbit."

"Yes, that's what I'd do, I think."

"We should talk with whoever was the last officer to see Archie. Can you find out who that was and let me know? *Grazie*." With that, Robert rolled back into his cell. Since information from the coroner wouldn't be arriving any time soon, he started to think about lunch. While he was considering this, he received a text from Bernard Lily.

**'I've got the USB, can you send someone?'**

This required some delicacy. Bernard couldn't be seen to be openly dealing with the devil, so Robert answered,

**'I'll send a woman down. Meet outside the north entry to the city library concourse at 3:00 pm. She'll have her hair in a ponytail. Can you wear a scarf or something?'**

From Robert's observations about on-air talent, every single one of them had a scarf or three as part of their on-air getup. He assumed Bernard was no different.

Bernard responded,

**'Scarf - sure.'**

Now all he had to do was to get Norma to 'pony-up' and head downtown. He knew he shouldn't do what he was about to do, but he couldn't help himself. He went over to Norma's desk.

"Lunch?"

This was unusual, as in, they had never eaten lunch together at work to date. "Okay, sure."

"Great, I'll swing by in about an hour?"

Norma nodded and looked down at her work.

# CHAPTER 3

While Robert made lunch plans, a project meeting was taking place on a construction site down East Hastings Street. The project was a mid-rise tower, named Tornado House, and was intended for social housing, one of only a few to escape the clutches of the interminable Vancouver planning process and actually proceed to construction. The building was in its early stages. The concrete structure was rising slowly, mere metres from the sidewalk.

Inside the construction trailer, which featured muddy floors, a long, scarred plastic table with a dozen metal chairs, and a water cooler, the project manager representing the general contractor, Bamboo Construction, was chairing the meeting. Also in attendance was Nancy Brick, a project manager from the City of Vancouver, a structural engineer, whose firm worked for the architects, and Anne Leforet, the architect for the project. Anne was expounding rather loudly on the advantages of the latest changes she had made to the project, which no one else in the room seemed happy about.

"I've added these items back to the roof-top garden because those people deserve the best. Why should they have to put up with second-rate things just because they aren't wealthy?" Anne laid it out, taking the moral high ground. A taupe pantsuit and jacket framed a brilliant white blouse — audacious clothing for a construction site visit. Her auburn hair was cut short and swept back behind her ears in a no-nonsense way. Her eyes were firing darts at everyone they passed over as she spoke.

"That is not the issue here, is it? The problem is making expensive changes to the project after the contract has been signed, and building has started." Nancy Brick wasn't having any of this fancy designer malarky. "All those items were removed from the documents before it went to tender, so we could be on budget. Now you are adding them back in, and they'll cost twice as much at this stage."

"I'm sticking with the changes. You can use your precious contingency fund."

"And what is with the redesign to the front building entry? This canopy is way over the top." Nancy wasn't finished.

"So, are you saying that the residents shouldn't feel proud about entering their own building?" Anne wasn't letting up.

"Again, this isn't the issue, as you well know."

The site superintendent, Arby Knutsen, who worked for Bamboo, displayed a hint of a smile, enjoying the banter between people he had little respect for. He sat in on all meetings as it was his responsibility to coordinate the trades and get the building built per the documents. Arby was large and could be intimidating if he found it useful. He knew that any expensive changes made to the contract at this stage would be passed along to the owner, who happened to be the City of Vancouver. He was also aware that a ton of extra costs had already been sent to the owner because of unexpected soil conditions. He guessed that whatever contingency the city had was getting thin, but it was just a guess, as the owner would never let on what reserves they had for a project. It was up to the contractor to get as much money out of the owner as humanly possible on each project, and design changes helped facilitate this. Mistakes or oversights were another cause of changes, but the items being championed by the architect in this meeting didn't fit into that category.

The structural engineer piped up, "There will be some more change documents coming because of the issues caused by the clay found on site."

Even Anne was unaware of this. The rest of the participants stared at the engineer.

"We had to redo some calculations and a fair amount of rebar was added to the shear walls. The documents outlining these changes are almost ready to issue. The rebar has already been added, in case you are worried about the walls." He smiled thinly.

Anne fixed a withering glare at her engineer. Nancy couldn't say much about this news; nobody wanted a building to fall down, and more specifically, nobody wanted to be the party responsible for such a calamity. It also sounded like the work had already taken place, not exactly how the process was supposed to work. The meeting devolved to the minutiae of managing other construction issues, but Nancy was concerned about the project budget and not at all happy with her design team. It was time to talk to one of her superiors, once she returned to City Hall.

At police headquarters on Cambie Street, Robert retrieved Norma and walked her up to his favourite noodle palace on Broadway.

"What's up Robert? I thought we were going to keep it cool at work," Norma asked, as they sat down in the restaurant.

"This is business, Norma." He smiled. "I need you to do a courier task. A reporter at the CBC has a thumb drive with some footage on it that may be useful for the murdered cop case I'm looking at. Thought lunch might be appropriate."

"Why can't you or Tony get it?" She was puzzled.

"We're the enemy. Reporters can't be seen cavorting with the police."

Norma nodded while Robert waved at a waiter and ordered a plate of spicy noodles with some sliced vegetables for both of them. "All you have to do is take the train downtown. Three o'clock, outside the north entry to the library concourse with your hair in a ponytail. Bernard is a young reporter, he'll be wearing a scarf of some kind. He's actually been on TV recently, doing news clips. That's it, easy peasy."

"Well, since it's for you, okay. But I think I should get a raise for this undercover work. Could I at least get a trench coat?"

Robert smiled at the suggested extravagance. Their lunch plates arrived, and Robert served some food into each of their bowls. "You'll have to take the raise up with Thomas."

Silence ensued as they started eating, Robert with chopsticks, Norma with a fork.

"Would you like me to give a seminar?" He said, nodding at Norma's utensil.

She tilted her head. "How about this Friday? I could order in."

"Hmmm, will you pay attention?"

"Maybe, depends on what to." Her smile widened. They exhausted all the food and reluctantly headed back to the precinct, where Robert settled back into his chair and waited for the autopsy results, puzzling about Archie and his apparent foe.

Just after half-past three, Norma bounced into Robert's cubicle and laid the USB on his desk. "You were correct. It was easy. I might apply to the Canadian Spy Agency. I seem to be cut out for this business."

Robert shook his head and thanked her, putting the USB into the side of his laptop. Norma didn't hang around, returning to her workstation. Robert proceeded to review the footage of the protest sent by Bernard. There wasn't much to it. The clip that he had seen on the news was there; the short interview with Allo Foot, then the beginnings of the riot. The scene grew chaotic quickly, then ended. The only other piece was the aborted interview with Mary Tinlit.

Bernard was correct. Mary seemed to have a few problems. The camera had followed Mary after her discussion with Bernard. Robert saw her talk briefly to Allo, then she went over towards another man, but when she reached him, they were hidden by an intervening group of demonstrators. That was it. Not exactly a fountain of clues. He reviewed all the footage once again, but didn't learn anything more. He wasn't sure about Mary, but from his comments, apparently Allo was First Nation. Maybe he'd ask Thomas to put Finn on their team as well. Couldn't hurt to have that perspective and experience on their side.

Robert looked at his watch and decided to call the coroner's service.

"Sorry, Robert, I'll be working late on this one. You'll have my report on your desk when you arrive tomorrow, okay?"

"Sure. I'll call if I have questions." With that he looked around the divider, but Tony was nowhere to be seen, so his next thought was dinner. Being the sole cook in the household that had two teenagers was a challenge almost as big as any he faced at work. After a few minutes of ruminating, he decided to go up to the local high-end grocery store and wander the aisles, hoping for inspiration.

The first section he meandered through was the meat and fish area. Nothing twigged his interest, so he went over to the international aisles. Bingo, he was face to face with boxes of taco shells. He retraced his steps to pick up some ground beef, then some salsa, and added all the other extra garnishes he would need to round out the meal.

When he finally pulled into the carport at the rear of his east-side townhouse, he could see the lights on. Good. At least one of the kids was home. He walked in, announcing his arrival with a yell to the upstairs where Robin and Sophie theoretically were. He heard some responses, so he relaxed, then spread the groceries onto the counter. He went to his whisky sideboard and opened its door slowly. While he pondered the countries represented, he also recalled where it had almost led him several months earlier when he was making a determined effort at alcoholism. He shook his head before fixing himself a glass — today, visiting Ireland.

Once the tacos were served, silence reigned, broken only by the sound of crisp taco shells meeting their doom. As dinner eventually wound down, taco mess everywhere, Robert made an attempt at conversation. "Anything new with you two?"

"Are you going on another date with Norma this Friday?" Sophie stared back at her dad.

"Yes." Answering a question with a question seemed like something a politician might try. Robert studied his daughter with narrowed eyes.

Robin tried a different tack as he wiped his mouth. "I have a game tomorrow evening. Riley Park, I think." Robin was back playing Bantam house hockey after taking a year away from the game.

Robert hadn't been able to get to many games so far. "How is the team doing? I'll try to attend, but you better line up a ride in case I'm still at work. Don't know whether you heard, but an officer got murdered the other night at that protest. It's my case."

Robin answered. "We're doing just fine. Only one loss so far."

Both teenagers knew all about how dangerous police work was from firsthand experience with Robert's involvement on the Gang Taskforce. "Be careful, Dad, okay?" Sophie pleaded.

"I intend to." That wrapped up another successful dinner, mixed with an unsuccessful try at penetrating his kid's social lives. All in all, life as it should be, Robert concluded.

Next morning was Thursday. The coroner's report was lying on Robert's desk when he arrived, so after sitting down, he studied the envelope before gingerly opening it. Not his optimum choice for starting a day. He went right to the cause of death, and, despite the presence of a rope around Archie's neck, he apparently died of heart failure, likely the result of trauma caused from repeated application of a Taser weapon. The burn count was thirty-seven.

It seemed that the killer had put something under Archie's feet so that he wouldn't die of strangulation before having to suffer through the electric shocks. The blood that Robert had noticed came from a contusion to the skull. Archie had been struck by something circular, but this had not been the cause of death. Added information included the presence of a fair amount of alcohol in his blood, which could seem surprising given that Archie was on duty, but really, maybe not. Archie's liver wasn't in pristine condition either, only a couple of steps from being unusable. Not even a pawnshop would have taken it.

Robert pondered the scant information available from the report while he waited for Tony's appearance. Perhaps the knock on the head had rendered Archie unconscious, enabling Archie's foe or foes to get the upper hand.

Norma yelled out, to no one in particular, "Sounds like a demonstration on the Cambie Bridge. Climate related, according to their signage. They've closed it down. We already have some officers on scene."

This announcement caught everyone's attention, for obvious reasons. Previously, protests had been generally benign affairs. Now, not so much. Robert went over to Thomas's office and rapped on his doorframe. "Think I'm going to wander up the street, see if any of the people from the Clark Drive protest are stupid enough to join this one. Might get lucky."

"Okay. Just make sure you are not alone out there, that's all."

Robert nodded and left to grab his jacket before heading north to the bridge. Traffic was choked in the area as drivers sought an alternative way to enter downtown. The lanes up to the bridge deck that spanned False Creek started right outside the precinct offices, so it took all of two minutes for Robert to reach deck level. The protest wasn't a marching one, but something similar to the Clark Drive fiasco.

Robert walked past the traffic barriers set up to stop the public from venturing any closer to the centre of the protesters and came up to what seemed to be the core group. Several uniformed police officers were keeping an eye on the action. Behind the group, maybe about another hundred people were standing round, some with signs, many with nothing. Beyond them stood Yaletown's grey wall of bland condominium towers on False Creek's north shore, hiding the downtown core.

He recognized Mary Tinlit, who was yelling something at the police standing in a line about nine metres away. Robert went up to one of the uniformed officers and pointed at Mary. "She was at the protest the other night. I want a word with her to see what she knows and who she is" Robert knew this might offend the protesters. Tough, he thought.

Mary noticed Robert pointing at her and started aiming her rants at him. Not being in uniform didn't seem to be an impediment to receiving abuse. She was so caught up in her expletive laced tirade that she failed to comprehend what was going to happen to her until it did. Two officers had her by the arms and after Mary exploded, they tried to cuff her. Robert's smiles at this loss of control didn't help matters in the least. Well, he thought, if they didn't get anywhere with the Archie angle, it looked like resisting arrest could be used to keep her in custody. Mary was acting like a crazed sea otter, definitely not going quietly. Robert hoped she wouldn't get injured from all the gyrations she seemed capable of. As the only protester he immediately recognized from the other night, she was as good as anyone to start asking questions of.

Robert stood for a while, searching the rest of the crowd. Unfortunately, he was not as up to speed on who had attended Clark Drive as he should have been. He failed to recognize anyone else and was about to turn when.... was that his daughter? He stared at the larger group well behind the front lines, and yes, it was Sophie. She didn't seem to notice him, speaking to another girl beside her. He wondered what to do.

Everything seemed peaceful enough after Mary had been led away, but he pulled an officer aside, pointed Sophie out to him and told him her protection was in his hands — nothing else mattered if things went sideways. The officer nodded. Robert waited a few seconds longer, surveying the crowd, then walked back down the traffic lanes to the office to grab Tony for a trip up to Cafe Paulo. He needed some sustenance before interviewing Mary.

Tony was indeed at his desk, so Robert signalled him. "Breaking news Tony, we snagged one of the protesters from the other night. We'll talk to her after some coffee."

Tony seemed impressed at the speed with which Robert had penetrated the case. "Nice work." He smiled as he rose to join Robert.

At the door to his office, Rodney Fister stood, watching the pair leave the floor. He had a pretty good idea about what they were going to do, so he decided he would tail them, and maybe let the rest of the rank and file know how Vancouver's finest detective was handling the case of their murdered brethren.

Rodney didn't have to do much. He followed Tony and Robert and watched as they entered their cafe. He crossed the street, took his phone out, and snapped a close-up shot of the two laughing it up at their table by the window. Perfect.

Rodney was going to make their life hell. Which was only fitting, he thought.

# Chapter 4

After sitting down with their coffees and a sweet pastry, Robert told Tony, "My daughter was on the bridge, part of the demonstration." He shook his head.

"Shouldn't she be in school?"

"As far as I know. Maybe they're studying protests this week, or doing a course section on climate? I foresee a small discussion will be in order this evening."

"What if violence breaks out?" asked Tony.

"That might be the real learning moment. I tasked an officer to watch out for her, but everything seemed calm when I left."

"Glad I don't have kids."

Robert shook his head again. "I'll admit, I'm a bit worried, but they're a source of a lot of joy as well, Tony. It's a fine balance, figuring out how much leeway to give a teenager these days." He took a bite of the pastry. "Learned anything yet from the video?"

"I have been looking at everything on offer for the businesses close to Lee's. As a result, my eyes are wonky. Night video is hard to follow, I'll tell you that for free."

"This sounds suspiciously like complaining, but I'm sure it isn't, is it?"

Tony shook his head. "So far, not much to report. A few people running by two of the cameras, but not Archie, and not that girl. I haven't looked at all the available footage yet."

"I'm thinking that we need to know more about Mary Tinlit before we interview her. Let's concentrate on that this afternoon and talk to her tomorrow. Let her spend a night in a cell. Maybe she'll cool down a tad." Robert smiled. "Fat chance, from what I've seen so far." After another moment, he asked, "Made any progress with Archie's dossier yet?"

Tony didn't respond, but looked out the window. "Isn't that Rod across the street? What's he up to? Is he taking a shot of us with his phone?"

"Well, if Rod is involved, it can't be good." Robert answered. Then he switched back to the previous subject. "I think I'll take a look at Archie's file again. I'll use my RCMP contacts." Robert could sense some unhappiness from Tony. "It takes time, Tony, to make all the useful connections that eventually help to find out things. Don't be impatient. Soon enough you'll have your own cases, with juniors helping you out, and your own stool pigeons, okay?"

Tony nodded, but Robert could see ambition in his eyes, chafing at the seeming restraints. Silence ensued as the two ate their pastries, sipping on their coffees, wondering where this case would lead them.

"Rod still out there?" Robert asked.

"No. Looks like he went back to the station."

"I have a good idea what Rod will do with his photos, but let's see what happens." They finished up, yelled their goodbyes at Gilberto, and returned to the office.

Before Robert sat down, he thought he'd have some fun. He went over to his former office and rapped on the doorframe. "Hey Rod, saw you outside the cafe. Why didn't you come in and join us?" He waited a beat, then, "Or were you too busy concentrating on your limited photographic skills?" He walked away before Rodney had a chance to say a word. He was sure that Rod's intentions were to make Robert and Tony look bad. Not much he could do about that now, so his mind slipped into research mode, with Mary as the target.

Before he started that, however, he went over to Norma, "Think you could let me know when that protest winds down? My daughter is up there. I've got someone watching out for her."

Norma nodded. "I'll keep you updated."

Robert returned to his desk. "Tony, can you see if Mary has a record? I'll do a net search." With that, he concentrated on his computer screen for a while. The only things he could find were a reference to her once living in Bella Kind up the coast, and attending an architecture school in Winnipeg, at the University of Manitoba. So, possibly First Nations. He looked up Bella Kind and found it located on the eastern edge of Raven Island. There was also a reference to her being a member of a Marxist-Leninist group in Vancouver. She seemed to have no fixed address, so his guess was that she was living in one of the tent cities populating the local area, or in a squat, like Allo Foot. He estimated that she was in her early thirties. Not a lot to go on.

Half an hour later, Tony rolled his chair into Robert's space. "Our Mary has been detained a couple of times in Vancouver but not charged. She seems to be a social disturber, and maybe a professional protester, if such a thing exists. She was taken in at a rally to stop an oil pipeline being built two years ago, a scene at a tent city last spring, then there was the housing thing from a couple of days ago, now the climate protest."

"Definitely seems to have found her niche." Robert commented. "I wonder if she is driven by her own convictions, or put up to it by others?"

Tony shrugged and rolled back into his space. "You can ponder that. I've got more footage to look at."

Robert had a suspicion that the upcoming interview with Mary was going to produce nothing, but he'd try at least. Maybe she would spill something inadvertently.

Robert opened Archie's file. Archie had joined the VPD seven years earlier, but there was nothing to indicate when he had left the RCMP. Archie's Vancouver career seemed relatively clean, excluding one reprimand for being intoxicated while on the job. His home address was listed as being at the eastern edge of Vancouver proper, near Boundary Road. Nothing to indicate run-ins with anyone while on duty, but that didn't mean it couldn't have happened.

He called the RCMP, starting with an officer he had worked with over a year earlier, Troy Geelham, who commanded a detachment in Richmond, south of Vancouver.

"Troy? Robert Lui here."

"Robert, it's been a while. How are you after all that nonsense last spring? I heard that Manny bought the farm."

"I'm fine Troy, thanks. I may have helped Manny with the purchase, but don't let that get very far."

Troy laughed briefly. "What can I do for you?"

"I'm looking into a murder here in town, and I'm interested in what the RCMP can tell me about Archie Hamilton. He worked for you lot somewhere in the past. He was the one killed the other day, if you didn't know already."

"We heard. Not good. Let me see what I can find and get back to you."

"Thanks Troy." He hung up and while he waited, he'd try to find out who the last officer was to see Archie alive. He called up the Tactical squad leader who said he'd get back to Robert. More waiting. Robert sighed, then called the University of Manitoba to find out about Mary's supposed architectural career.

Once again, whoever it was he talked with said they'd have to check and get back to him. At first, they didn't want to reveal anything, but Robert pulled the murder investigation card and magically, they became cooperative. Or so it seemed. Robert wasn't very trustful with anyone he dealt with and preferred to wait on results before rendering a verdict.

He sat, thinking. Usually, when he had a few problems to solve, he'd head down to False Creek and take a walk along the seawall, but he didn't even have the basics in the case yet, so his mind wandered to his other cases.

Much later, after lunch, Tony hooted a small shout, "Got her!" Robert rolled his chair into Tony's space to watch the replay. "This is down the street from Lee's. Here Mary comes, running, wait, then here comes Archie, about twenty metres behind her. That's pretty much it so far."

"Not much, but our guess was correct. A rabbit." Robert concluded.

"Yeah, but as far as I know, being a rabbit is not a crime."

"So far." Robert responded. "However, aiding and abetting is something a rabbit might try if they were hip-hoppity enough."

"She must have had some help somehow. I doubt whether Mary could get the best of Archie, even if he was winded. It doesn't look like running was Archie's favourite pastime."

"Do you have the information from the scene?" Robert asked.

"Yes," said Tony. What are you looking for?"

"How they got into the body shop."

Tony looked down at the written notes from the processing team. "The man-door to the lane was found to have been opened by someone without a key, forced entry."

"So, lane footage, then. Do you have any?"

"No. The camera above the garage door to the lane had been destroyed, presumably by our murderers, but that is uncertain. Mr. Lee couldn't remember the last time he saw it in one piece. And there doesn't appear to be any other cameras in that lane."

"Not a bunch to help us with our Mary interview. We'll have to wing it." With that, Robert slid back to his desk and called it a day. He remembered his son was playing hockey that evening. He decided to go watch and give his mind something else to concentrate on, but only after a discussion with his daughter.

At home, Robert stood at the kitchen island watching as Sophie pulled leftovers from the fridge. "How was school today, Sophie?"

She looked back over at her father, eyebrows scrunched up, "Good, Dad. How was work?"

"Work was fine, Sophie, except for the part where I was watching a demonstration on the Cambie Bridge." Sophie's face changed colour from pale to scarlet in mere seconds. It was a wonder to behold. "I don't mind at all that you have beliefs, and causes to support, but I must insist that you use your brain and assess who you are doing these things with. We arrested a possible murder suspect on the bridge, one of the protesters. I need you to use your discretion, understand?"

"Oh."

"Yes, oh! I don't want you hanging around with criminals, Sophie. It's dangerous, so if one of your friends got you into this, better have a talk with them, okay?"

"Okay. I didn't know. How would I tell if someone is a criminal, Dad?"

Now this was the kind of question that science fiction is made for, Robert thought as he stared at Sophie. And something an adult might ask. "Sophie, if I knew the answer to that, I'd probably be in charge of the whole police force.

So far, there is no easy answer to that one. Your question is an excellent one, however, and maybe I've been a little hard on you, but for good reason. And when police officers get killed, everyone is on edge."

She nodded. "I'll have a word with my friend."

"You didn't by any chance talk to this woman that we arrested, did you? Her name is Mary Tinlit."

Sophie hesitated. "No one was giving out their names and there were a lot of people there, Dad. I didn't talk to any of them."

"Good, let's get this stuff warmed up."

The next morning, Robert called down to the holding cells to have Mary put into an interview room. Then he signalled Tony for a trip up the street. When they had their coffees, Robert stared into the middle distance, not drinking. "What's up?" Tony asked.

"This will be more of a reconnoitre than anything. I want to get a sense of Mary. We can always get her back again." At this moment, Robert's cell rang.

"Robert."

"Hi, it's Troy. I have some info here on Archie Hamilton. I'll send it on to you by e-mail."

"Great. Where was he stationed?"

"A few places on the west coast up north, but his last posting was at Bella Kind on Raven Island."

"Really? This helps. Is there a contact at Bella Kind? Someone I can ask a few questions of?"

"It's in the notes. If you need anything else, call me."

"Okay, many thanks Troy." He looked at Tony with a hint of a smile. "We have a second connection between Archie and Mary. They both spent time in Bella Kind up the coast." He finally started sipping his Americano.

"Mary seems extremely guilty already." Tony said.

"I concur."

"Concur? What are you, a doctor now?"

"Maybe." He smiled at the very thought. He didn't like blood. No way could he ever be a doctor. "I suppose we should mosey back." As he took another small sip of his coffee, he looked out the window — still no rain. What was going on? He knew he shouldn't pray for rain, because once it started, he'd be praying all the harder for it to stop.

"Okay, show time." They walked back down the street slowly, giving time for Mary's anger to build. Robert was counting on emotions to trigger a mistake. He didn't have much else up his sleeve.

The detectives stood for a moment, looking through the one-way glass at Mary, fidgeting as she waited. "Let's go, Tony." They entered the room, introducing themselves as they sat.

Robert started. "Do you want a lawyer present?"

"I haven't done anything, assholes. Like, why would I want a lawyer?"

Robert waited, silence filling the space.

Mary finally cracked. "It was a peaceful protest. We have the right to demonstrate. Why was I, like, arrested?"

"Do you know an Archie Hamilton?"

"No."

"You are from Bella Kind."

"Like, so what?" Mary's eyes were glinting.

"Archie spent time in Bella Kind with the RCMP. Sure you don't know him?"

"I hate having to repeat myself to morons."

"Are you native born?"

"Like it's any of your business."

"Fair enough, but Bella Kind is a small community, the type where everyone knows everyone else. The night of the housing protest, we have you on camera being chased by Archie Hamilton during the riot. Then we found him dead. Which is why you are here."

Mary's eyes started to shift around. Her right index finger drummed on the table. She didn't say anything. Robert was mildly impressed with her silence.

"Do you know an Allo Foot?" Robert pressed on.

She hesitated, then, "No."

"We have you on camera talking to Mr. Foot."

"I just met him that night. Like, I don't know anything about him."

"Where do you live?" Tony tried switching topics.

"None of your business."

Tony smiled. "Actually, it has become our business. How would you fancy a new home? Comes complete with a metal door and three meals a day."

"I want out of here."

Tony smiled, "Sure. As soon as you tell us where you can be found. Otherwise, we'll file charges of resisting arrest from your antics yesterday and you can remain locked up. I believe you've been here before, correct?" Then he and Robert sat back, watching as Mary mulled over her options.

After a couple of moments, Mary relented. "I live in a squat."

"Address?" Robert asked.

"I don't know. It's like Oxford Street, I think. East Side."

"Fine. An officer will escort you back to your place so we can verify where you are living. You are to remain in Vancouver until we tell you otherwise."

Mary started to complain, then thought better of it, conceding defeat.

Robert and Tony left the room, giving their instructions to the attending officer. They made their way back upstairs.

"She lies quite well, don't you think?" Robert asked. "Talks like a teenager. Wonder where she got her education?"

"My guess is that she'll change locales pretty quickly," Tony answered.

Robert nodded as they sat down in their workstations. He looked around. Still no view of the outside world. Once you had the office with windows on the outside wall, it was tough to go back. He decided he'd had enough, so he went over to Thomas's office.

He peeked his head around the jamb. Thomas was studying papers on his desk.

"Any chance of getting my old office back, Thomas? It's not like Rod even works with us anymore."

"Good point. He should be downstairs along with the rest of the cowboys. I'll make it happen. How is the case coming?"

"We have some leads. Wonder if we could also get Finn Black's help on this one? It seems that Bella Kind might be the start of it all." Robert declined to say more, so Thomas nodded, the conversation at an end.

# CHAPTER 5

After a short lunch, Robert returned to his desk and computer, opening the e-mail from Troy. He quickly perused it. Again, not a whole lot of information. Archie had left Bella Kind about a year before joining the VPD. There had been an inquiry involving Archie related to an incident during a logging-related protest. Robert recalled several places in British Columbia that had endured similar disturbances over the years as those trying to save the old-growth forests competed against the interests of those trying to make a living and a profit from harvesting trees. There were no further details, but a contact was included, a sergeant by the name of Walter Gray. As Robert read the remainder of the message, he felt the presence of someone behind him, then noticed the reflection in his computer screen, so he twirled his seat around. He was facing an impossibly young Sikh officer wearing an indigo turban. He waited.

"Hello. I'm Gurpal. You wanted to talk with me?"

Robert smiled, hoping to ease the officer's obvious nervousness. Then he changed his mind. "Why do I want to talk with you? I don't believe we've met before."

"No, we haven't met."

This was going well, he thought. He waited for some illumination.

"I was with Archie Hamilton the other night."

"Okay, now we're getting somewhere. Let's go to a meeting room." He beckoned Tony and they entered a small room notable for its lack of soundproofing. After sitting, and introductions, Robert started in, speaking softly.

"Were you with him the whole evening? Excluding, of course, the end."

"Pretty much. It was my first demonstration, so Archie was guiding me — telling what I should and shouldn't do."

"Keep your voice down. This room isn't exactly known for its privacy."

Gurpal nodded.

Tony started in. "We have some video of Archie chasing a young girl down Frances Street after the protest had splintered, but there was no sign of yourself."

"We had split up at that point. There was a guy and a girl that the two of us were after. The guy went one way, and I followed, being lighter on my feet than Archie. Archie kept after the girl. That was it. Never saw him again."

"Did you catch the guy?" Robert asked.

"Unfortunately not, gave me the slip."

"Would you recognize him if I showed you a picture?"

"Maybe. I saw him briefly before they turned and ran."

"Were the guy and the girl together, before they ran?"

"Yes, I believe so. They seemed to be talking."

Robert looked at Tony, eyebrows raised. Tony shook his head. "Okay, follow me back to my desk. I have some footage for you to look at."

Robert scrolled through the CBC tape on his computer, Gurpal looking over his shoulder, and came to the interview with Allo Foot. "Is this the guy?"

"Yeah, I think so." Not ironclad, Robert thought, but good enough to haul Mr. Foot in for some questions. All they had to do was to find him.

"Thanks, Gurpal, you've been a help."

Gurpal smiled, instantly relaxing. His first time dealing with detectives, Robert suspected.

Robert sat back, starting to contemplate his date with Norma that evening. He realized that he had said something about a chopstick seminar, so he figured he'd better order and pick up the food. As far as he knew, there were no Chinese restaurants in Yaletown, where Norma lived. He sent her a text.

**'I'll pick up the food for tonight. See you at 7:00?'**

It only took thirty seconds for the reply to arrive.

**'Absolutely. Hope we have time for food at some point.'**

Robert smiled. To date, their dates consisted mostly of sex, with the occasional meal added, just in case anyone asked. While Robert wasn't complaining about this, he also wondered why there wasn't more to the relationship. He couldn't seem to kickstart himself onto another level, and he couldn't discern any interest from Norma's side for something different either.

After that bit of introspection, he made one more call before he left for the day.

"Sergeant Walter Gray speaking."

"Hi, it's Robert Lui from the Vancouver Police calling. I was given your name by Troy Geelham out of the Richmond detachment. You can probably guess why I'm talking to you."

"Unfortunately, yes. We heard about Archie. Terrible news."

"I'm in charge of the investigation. Anything you can tell me would be a big help."

There was silence on the other end.

"Walter?"

"Just thinking. Can you come up here? It is not a short story. Might be good for you to understand the context of all that happened up here some years ago."

Robert had visited Williams Lake in BC's interior some years earlier for a case, but had never been up the coast as far as Bella Kind. "I'd be happy to come up. It'd be the first time to your part of the world. Any time in particular?"

"Whenever you can get here. There is a lodge at Arnott Bay you can stay at just across the water from town. Bella Kind is small and there's no hotel in town. Let me know what works for you. You should probably count on a couple of nights. Flights aren't always dependable up here despite what the schedules might say. We have an airstrip so you can take a real plane if you wish."

"I'll let you know Monday, Walter. Thanks for this." He hung up. Real plane? As opposed to what? Now all he had to do was to clear it with Thomas. But that was for later. He had the evening ahead to fantasize about.

Early Monday morning at Cambie Street headquarters, Rodney Fister was told to vacate his office and move down a floor, where he properly belonged. Robert had just arrived and watched a very unhappy Rodney carting his box of possessions across the floor to the elevator.

Rodney had a good idea who was behind his eviction, so as he passed by Robert he slowed, giving him one of his most withering looks. "It seems you have your office back, Bob." The hatred was palpable.

Robert smiled in return, not helping the situation. Robert wondered why Rodney had come up with 'Bob'. He knew it wouldn't be much longer before Rodney's cafe pictures made their way onto some social media forum for disgruntled people. Robert correctly guessed that Rodney would be sitting out in the general bullpen area, a floor below. Instead of heading over to his new/old office, Robert decided a trip up the street was in order. He crooked his finger at Tony, and they left for coffee.

After the greeting shouts and coffees poured, Robert and Tony started talking about the case.

"I didn't tell you Friday, but Gurpal confirmed Allo Foot as the other person they were chasing through the back streets. Can you get him picked up?"

"Sure. Guess you don't know where he is though, do you?"

"I'd try that squat where young Mary got dropped off at. That is, if all the rats haven't fled the ship." Robert sipped his coffee, feeling calmer and sharper all at once. "I'm going up the coast to Bella Kind, hopefully this week, talk to the RCMP."

"Sounds exotic. I've never been up there."

"Trees and water, Tony. That's what I'm thinking I'll see."

"Still, be nice to get away."

"Suppose. When you locate Mr. Foot, call me first before rounding him up. I may learn something that would bear on his questioning. Oh, and Finn is going to be helping us as well."

"Sounds like a plan. When are you going?"

"As soon as possible. Need to clear it with Thomas first, though."

"Archie's funeral may be held this Friday. We'll probably know later today."

"Well, I may be up in Bella Kind. You'll need to attend on my behalf."

"No worries."

The pair continued savouring their coffees, uninterrupted this time by anyone trying to film them from the street.

Not far away, Nancy Brick settled into her desk in the Housing Department of the City of Vancouver, placing her coffee cup beside her keyboard. She flipped on her e-mail program to scroll through the messages generated over the weekend. Nancy had several projects on the go.

She came across a missive from Hummingbird Architects. Her not so favourite architect, Anne Leforet, had attached several signed change orders to the contract for the Tornado House project. As Nancy reviewed the PDF file with the details of each change, and the monies involved, she quickly realized that Miss Anne was sending her project straight into a ditch, just as she feared.

Included in the changes were the items she had specifically ordered Anne not to continue with, at the last site meeting. Nancy had no further monies in the project budget to support these changes. *Shit*, was the most eloquent statement she could manage. This was not the best way to start a week.

Nancy recalled that she was the one who had hired Hummingbird to do the project — giving the young firm a huge boost in the process. She sent an e-mail to her boss, Ricardo Remuda, who was the head of Housing, requesting a meeting. It was time to remind Little Miss Architect about her station in life. Signing the change orders on behalf of the owner was usually a formality, after the arguing had taken place. Perhaps she wouldn't sign these ones and see what happened. Construction progress tended to slow dramatically without signed paperwork.

Robert and Tony returned to their floor and Robert went straight to his old office to check out what damage had been done to it by the interloper. Furnishings were the bare minimum, but Robert went through all the drawers of the desk and filing cabinet, smelling something foul. He finally discovered a fish sandwich in an open bag at the back of the file cabinet, no doubt intended to putrefy eventually. It had already made a good start. Robert didn't throw it away, but thought he might return it to its owner at some point in the future, depending upon how immature he might feel later. He made sure the plastic bag was firmly sealed before sticking it in his desk cupboard. After this, he carted in what few possessions he had and sat back in his less than perfect chair, contemplating the view of East Vancouver. The view hadn't changed one bit, but he had, he realized. And he wasn't going to take anything for granted anymore. A bit of decoration was called for. If he acted like it was his office, maybe it wouldn't be so easily taken from him.

Later the same morning, Nancy Brick took the stairs up to the top floor in her building to meet with Mr. Remuda. She settled into a chair across from Ricardo, and after laying out her case for getting rid of Hummingbird Architects, she waited expectantly.

"I'm not sure what you want me to do here. Firing architects in the midst of a project is not something normally even contemplated. And I don't have any more money for your project. With all the promises made by our mayor about delivering low-cost housing, cancelling the project is not on. There would be a whole bunch of money spent with nothing to show for it."

"So, there's nothing you can do for me?"

"Well, I'd tell you to toughen up, but I don't know if you have it in you. Aren't you the one who hired these monkeys?"

"Yes." Nancy realized she was on her own in this mess, something she already knew, if she was being honest with herself.

She nodded at Rick, "I'll think of something then." She returned to her office, considering her options for action. One thing she knew for sure, Anne wasn't going to get away with thumbing her nose at Nancy. She thought about her possibilities for dealing with the situation, settling upon one after further contemplation. Anne Leforet was going to regret trifling with Nancy.

Robert's taxi pulled up outside the South Terminal of the Vancouver Airport Wednesday morning. As the original passenger building for Vancouver's airport, it boasted some history, but its present use as a terminal for charters, as well as smaller airlines flying the coastal routes, suited it perfectly. Its location beside an arm of the Fraser River also allowed a float plane hub to thrive, connecting closer cities to Vancouver with a less cumbersome means of flying. As Robert's cab drove by the float docks, he realized that maybe this was what Walter Gray had been talking about. *Real planes, ha.*

Robert walked into a smaller, friendlier feeling building than Vancouver's main terminal. He already felt relaxed. He had spent the previous evening coaching his teenagers about what was in the fridge and freezer, so they wouldn't starve while he was gone.

"I'll be back by Friday," he had said. "No parties." As if. Not that he was really worried. His kids had displayed plenty of maturity over the last couple of years, but he realized they were still teenagers. Robert needed to concentrate on his case for a couple of days and couldn't worry about things going wrong at home. He had called his mother and asked her to check in with them once, to keep the chickens within sight of the coop at least. He had also called Norma, affirming his intentions to be home on Friday, no matter what. She had made the travel arrangements for him, making sure he'd be back in Vancouver in plenty of time for their weekly rendezvous.

His journey was in two stages, the first one being via a turboprop to Port Hardy, near the north tip of Vancouver Island. As he flew, Robert looked from his window seat down at the vastness of Vancouver Island and smiled. In the City of Vancouver, one needed a permit to cut down a tree. He knew that the city was trying to protect its green canopy, but it still seemed like a crock. It had to be a pure money grab from what he was seeing. British Columbia obviously had more than enough trees, and he was only flying over a tiny sliver of the province.

The Port Hardy airport was small but appeared to be a stopping off point to all places up the coast, as far as Haida Gwaii and beyond. After changing planes to something smaller and decidedly older, he finally landed on Raven Island shortly after one o'clock.

He grabbed his bag and stepped down onto the tarmac, where silence reigned. All he saw were more trees. The runway wasn't a short affair, seemingly built to handle larger planes, but it was worn and oil soaked, more than a few weeds peeking through the concrete cracks. Two taxis were idling outside a small terminal building, so it wasn't long before he arrived at the RCMP detachment in Bella Kind, located a few kilometres away, just up from the waterfront.

The town seemed utterly similar to most other small communities in BC, in that the buildings were basic, constructed of wood, and covered with wood siding without much in the way of ornamentation. The harbour below the town was the difference maker, and looked to be busy with activity.

Robert walked into the lobby, asking for Walter Gray. Less than a minute later, a large man in uniform came out around the counter to greet Robert. He sported a crew cut, speckled with grey, and friendly eyes set in an oversized, weathered face. Robert guessed that he was Indigenous.

"Robert Lui, pleased to meet you, Walter."

"Good flights?"

"Yes, thanks. How come this island is so lucky as to have a good-sized airstrip?"

"Built during World War Two. It was to be part of the coastal defences against a Japanese invasion. It has been mostly good for Raven Island over the years."

"Mostly?"

"Sometimes it makes it too easy for people to get here that maybe you don't want visiting. Not talking about you, of course." He smiled and led Robert into his office, closing the door firmly. "We'll go eat shortly, but you can start asking some of your questions."

Robert sat down, pulling out his small notepad. "Do you know a Mary Tinlit?"

Walter smiled. "Of course. Everyone knows everyone else here. She was a real fireball."

"Was she here when Archie was doing his duty?"

"Oh yes. That's part of the story."

"She said she didn't know Archie."

"Mary didn't favour the truth, more than a bit actually. Mary and her boyfriend at the time were quite the couple."

"Who was that?"

"A guy named Allo Foot — Heiltsuk Nation."

Robert stared at Walter. "Is he from Bella Kind?"

"Yup, grew up here."

"Wow. Said he was Haida from Haida Gwaii. And Mary said she didn't know him."

"That all sounds about right."

"So, these two regularly lied?"

"Yup. Don't exactly know why, but they did it."

"Maybe they are unhappy with who they are?"

Walter looked away, as though this was a new angle of thought. "Could be, Robert. More likely it's just the police they lie to. Don't take it personally."

Robert changed topics, "You were here when Archie was doing his tour?"

"I've been here with the RCMP for ten years, so yes."

"Are you from Bella Kind?"

"Grew up in Bella Coola, inland a bit. Let's go eat, I'm hungry." They left the office and sauntered south, in no hurry. Robert looked over to his left down at the harbour and spotted roughly ten bald eagles perched on tree branches alongside the road edging the water, not a sight one could see in downtown Vancouver. He watched as a few young teenagers ran by them, laughing, one on a scooter, maybe heading back to school for the afternoon, or not.

"How large is the school here?"

"All the grades. It has an excellent reputation."

"How did you end up here? I thought the RCMP was like the army, they could post you anywhere."

"That's correct, but they have grown slightly more flexible over time, not like a rubber band, but maybe like a tall spruce under a heavy windstorm, a bit of sway." Walter smiled.

The pair walked two more blocks, then came upon a small cafe looking east over the sound. The town had petered out at this point. As soon as they entered, Robert smiled as he was hit by the aroma of fresh coffee. He was already starting to like Bella Kind. All the customers in the cafe turned to look at Walter and Robert, not hiding their interest in the new guy.

After ordering, and while holding his cup of coffee, Robert started in. "So, what happened when Archie was here?"

"It was a crazy time. Nine years ago, this place was jammed with protesters from all over North America. Most of them were against the logging of the remaining original growth forests on Raven Island. The RCMP ramped up in a commensurate fashion. There was loads of tension, fights between family members, as most everyone lined up on one side or the other of the issue. You probably remember the publicized events, the court order, the blockade, the arrests. Nothing out of the ordinary for BC. Still going on today in different places. The ugly side didn't receive the publicity, however. The reporters were much more interested in the tree huggers than anything else." The server came over with their club sandwiches and french-fries. Both men tucked into their meal.

"The ugly side. I'm assuming some violence?" Robert mumbled through a mouth full of fries.

"Pretty much. A couple of boats got torched, and a home was burned to the ground. No one was hurt in those episodes and no charges were ever laid, not for want of trying. Then it got personal. Some arrests were made that weren't exactly gentle, shall we say. Bones got broken, words exchanged, revenge vowed. Archie Hamilton was right in the middle of it."

Robert looked around, trying to picture the mayhem happening years ago in what seemed like a serene town today.

Walter continued. "You have to understand that our nation was doing some of the logging. The do-gooders from away couldn't get their minds around the simple economic facts of life for our community. It has been mainly logging and fishing for us. But then again, some of the local people were resolutely against the logging, still are to this day. Not surprising really. Trees have always been important for our way of life."

Robert couldn't discern which side of the debate Walter was on. Perhaps Walter was protected by his position in the community — he didn't need to pick a side, or couldn't. Robert kept eating, the sandwich tasting like one of the best meals he had ever eaten. Maybe it was the salt air. Robert watched the seemingly never-ending small boat traffic in the harbour below, some heading up the passage, some making their slow way over to land across from town. After a second cup of coffee, they called it a meal and left, making their way back to the detachment.

"So... Archie." Robert wanting more.

"Yes, Archie. He was slightly old school. One day, he was helping with the arrests and got enthusiastic with his billy club. He broke the leg of one Tyrone Foot."

Robert looked over at Walter as they walked, so he responded. "Yes, that Foot, Allo's father. And he broke it good. Couldn't walk very well after the cast came off." Walter waited. He seemed to have some difficulty starting up again. "Then came the accident."

"Archie married a local girl, Fiona, who had a son, name of Gary, from a previous liaison. Gary took their car out one evening without Archie knowing about it. Had just received his driver's licence. The car didn't negotiate a curve very well and left the road, ending up in the woods. It was a couple of hours before Gary's absence was noticed, then he was eventually found. There are only so many roads in Bella Kind, after all. He lived but was paralyzed from the waist down. Later, it was found that the brake lines had been cut.
"

"Jesus."

"Yeah. Archie didn't take it well, to put it mildly, but he couldn't prove who had cut the lines, not for lack of trying. The wood protests continued on for weeks as the logging continued at a slow pace, the companies not backing down either. Then one day, Tyrone dragged himself back to the front lines. Archie saw him, and the first thing he did was Taser him. Hit him a couple of times, knocking him unconscious."

Robert's eyes widened at this revelation. "That is how Archie died. Multiple electric shocks to his entire body." Even as he said it, he regretted letting this information out. Too late, however.

"Sounds like retribution to me." Walter said. "I haven't finished. Tyrone passed away less than four months later. Seems he had a bad heart. Getting shocked by a Taser probably didn't help things. His family was not happy, as you can imagine. Allo and Mary started fighting all the time, sometimes openly. Things weren't going any better in Archie's home. Eventually, Archie and Fiona split up."

"What were Mary and Allo fighting about?"

"All kinds of things, but some said that Mary was pushing Allo hard to do something about his dad."

"Continue the vendetta, is that it?"

"Maybe."

"Well, it sounds like they dragged their little war to my neighbourhood." Robert said. "Are there any Foots left here?"

"Not immediate family, no. Tyrone's wife was from a band farther up the coast, so she eventually went back. Allo wasn't having it, wanted to go to the big city."

"How about Fiona? Or Gary?"

"Fiona left the island as well." Walter looked pained at the memory. Robert was puzzled at this, as if there was another un-named connection at play.

"Gary is around, but doesn't live in town. He has a place south of here up a logging road. There was some insurance money, so that is what he continues to live off. Does some fishing with a couple of buddies now and again. They rigged a boat so that he could help out, feel useful."

"Would it be possible to talk with him, maybe tomorrow?"

"I can see if he is available and willing. I'll text you if it works."

"And Mary Tinlit? Does she have family here?"

"Her parents are in town. She has a brother, but he left as well, like half of the youngsters around here. Not sure if they'll want to talk to you, but I can ask them tomorrow. You staying two nights?"

"Yes. So where is the Arnott Bay Lodge?"

Walter pointed east. "Across the water. You can get the water taxi down at the wharf. Leaves every hour on the hour." With that, Robert sensed the meeting was over.

"Thanks for your time, Walter. Think I'll take a walk around, then head over to the lodge." Robert stood up, stretching his lanky frame, and grabbed his small bag. There weren't many streets in the town, just as Walter indicated, so Robert walked most of them before heading down to the government wharf to catch the boat over to his hotel to check in.

As the taxi neared the lodge's long dock, he realized this was probably a destination for wealthy sport fishers. The building was impressive, at least from the outside. Heavy timber gables framed large expanses of glass along the main level.

After registering, he walked upstairs to the second floor and found his spartan room oddly small and unappealing, but it at least had a view of the water. He supposed people didn't come all this way to stay in their room. He dropped his bag on the floor and decided to do something he rarely did, take a nap. Two hours later, feeling refreshed, he splashed some water on his face and returned to the main floor. After taking a slow look around he entered the largely empty restaurant, taking a seat by the window. The hostess/server left him a menu before returning to the other tables to take orders.

Robert studied the dock outside the window, past a deck area where tables and stacks of chairs were sitting, testament to warmer summer evenings. A couple of fish cleaning stations occupied one end. Near the other end of the dock, a few small craft rocked gently — probably guide boats for busier times.

There were only five other guests, it seemed. His server returned, telling him that the place was usually packed in the summer months with sport fishers, but in October, things slowed considerably. Robert should have been perusing the menu, but he was having trouble taking his eyes off his server. She waited, studying Robert's face in return before finally deciding some prompting would be needed. Like many women, she seemed to find his half-Asian good looks appealing. "Would you like me to suggest something?"

Robert shook his head slightly, realizing he was making a fool of himself. He smiled. "That would help. Thank you." After ordering, Robert couldn't just let her walk away. "Arnott Bay. Is there a Mr. Arnott?"

She tilted her head. "Not certain. One legend has it that Viking hordes laid waste to this area in times past. Or more likely, it was just a Norwegian settler washing ashore, not really sure. Depends on which story you might hear during the summer evenings when the booze is flowing freely out on that deck." She smiled at the thought. Robert figured he might need to return to Arnott Bay to take up fishing after this case was done.

After an excellent meal, featuring halibut, he went outside to do some exploring. He ended up sitting on the dock, admiring the silence and watching the water gently lap at the rocks past the dock until darkness was complete. He reluctantly retired to his room, thinking about the meal and the staff, not in that order. He texted his kids to let them know he was fine, but didn't get a response. He did get one text, from Walter Gray, saying that Gary would talk with him tomorrow.

# Chapter 7

Robert woke up the next morning after eight, but lay in bed, admiring the silence, punctuated by the occasional loud calls and clicks of ravens. A few beams of sun drifted through the half open curtains. This truly felt like a vacation. Even up here, it wasn't raining yet. A couple of interviews today, then walk around some more, although he had to admit, there wasn't much to the town.

Maybe a run would be in order. He had worn his sneakers on the plane, just in case he might be tempted. He only had his jeans, but that wasn't the impediment, the locale might be. Eventually he got dressed without showering and went to the front desk to ask about it. He was happy to see his server from the previous evening behind the counter.

"Well, there is a logging road, but you are running it at your own risk. You realize that bears are getting ready to hibernate, right? They are hungry and you look like you'd make a good snack, nothing more. Too skinny." The girl was laying it out in black and white.

Robert tried to pay attention to her advice, but was distracted by her beauty. Her skin was on the dark side. Robert couldn't decide her ethnicity. Maybe native, maybe something else. She appeared to be appraising Robert in return. Whatever her heritage, she was a looker, no make-up, and none needed. Her ebony hair was gathered in an electric blue clasp at the back of her neck. Her large brown eyes were staring at Robert with interest.

Then she looked down at his hands resting on the counter, "What happened to your fingers? Bear troubles?"

"The devil tried to shake my hand. It wasn't good, but I was able to deal with it. And I doubt if the bears are as fast as me."

The girl rolled her eyes. "Can you run faster than Usain Bolt, the fastest man in the world? Because a bear can, easily. Could you please write down your next of kin?" She pushed a pad of paper over to him, a hint of a smile tugging at her lips.

Robert laughed. "Funny. See you in a while." He went outside, looked up at the now grey sky, the occasional blue hole appearing between the large cloud banks whiffing by quickly. He stretched his muscles for a few minutes before trotting off. He hadn't been out in a while, so he ran easily for a good stretch, then his fading fitness started taking its toll. After twenty minutes of breathing in the scents of cedar and hemlock, he knew he should start his return before his legs betrayed him entirely. A couple of short hills confirmed the diagnosis about his body, although it felt marvellous to be running in a forest.

He hadn't seen any wildlife other than a few ravens when he turned around, but just as he was starting back, off to the side of the road, a small bear appeared in the brush, a cub. Crap, he thought. He didn't waste any time pondering things, but lit off up the road, not wanting to be bumping into its mother. The cub looked black, so better than a grizzly, but not by much. He heard some movement in the undergrowth to his side. He picked up speed and ran by as fast as his legs would carry him. After another sixty metres or so, he slowed a tad and looked back over his shoulder. Sure enough, a larger bear was standing in the road's centre, seeming to be looking his way. Robert knew bears couldn't see very well, that they relied on their sharp sense of smell. He was gasping for air, but he slowed only slightly for a while longer until his wheezing slowed. He then jogged, trying to enjoy the silence, but it wasn't until the lodge appeared that the adrenalin surge abated, leaving his legs feeling like fossilized wood.

Robert entered the lobby slowly, smiled at the girl behind the front desk, and nodded.

"You were correct, as it turns out, but I bolted out of there."

"Good news, because we don't have any hospital beds at the lodge."

"Breakfast still being served?"

"Yes, but hurry. The kitchen shuts down in half an hour."

"You're not the chef as well?" He was well aware that in remote areas of the province, most people needed to possess several skills to make a decent living.

She smiled, but didn't answer his question, instead asking one of her own. "What are you doing up here?" already knowing who he represented.

Robert kept it simple. "Pursuing enquiries." He returned to his room, quickly showered and dressed so as not to miss a hard-earned breakfast. The omelette and sausages were heaven, much like his lunch from the day before, but the coffee less so. He figured at some point during the day he'd mosey over to the cafe he had visited the day before to get his caffeine need properly addressed.

At the detachment, Walter gave Robert directions to Mary's parents' home. He ambled that way, again admiring the serenity of Bella Kind as the stress of Vancouver slowly ebbed away. The few people he passed by were either looking at him with raised eyebrows or ignoring him completely. He was certain that the word was out as to his mission in town. He came up to the house at the western edge of town and readied himself for what was sure to be a waste of time.

A large silver pickup truck with a muddy ATV in the bed sat next to a smaller truck which lacked tires, rust eating away its body from the ground up. A fair amount of what could be considered garbage littered the clearing. A couple of larger appliances that had seen better days sat next to a grove of trees. A German Shepard was laying down but eyeing Robert as though he hadn't eaten enough for breakfast. The chain connecting him to the house's corner looked to be secure enough.

Robert knocked on the front door and waited, glancing over at the dog. After a full minute, the door finally opened a few inches, revealing a large man, clearly one who worked outdoors. His scarred hand gripped the edge of the door securely.

"Yes?"

"My name is Detective Robert Lui, of the Vancouver Police Department. I'd like to speak with you about Mary Tinlit if I may."

The door didn't open any wider. "What about? Is she in trouble again?"

"May I come in?"

"No, we can do this right here." The door opened slightly more, but Robert noticed the large boot squarely behind it.

"As you wish. When was the last time you saw Mary?"

"About a year ago. She was in town to visit."

"Does she know an Allo Foot?"

"They used to be an item. Not anymore."

"What happened?"

"None of your business. That's what happened."

"We are investigating the death of a policeman in Vancouver, name of Archie Hamilton. Mary was very near him the night he was killed."

"Archie's dead, eh?"

Robert was pretty certain Mr. Tinlit already knew this.

"Yes, dead, and tortured at that."

"Mary wouldn't do that."

"Would Allo?"

Mary's father didn't answer right away, as though he was considering the possibility. "I don't think so. Anything else?"

"Are you in regular contact with Mary?"

"Not really."

"Does Mary have a new boyfriend?"

"Not to my knowledge."

Robert's phone rang, so he snagged it from inside his coat, turning slightly. "Hello?" He listened, then, "So no flights at all tomorrow? Crap."

"Problems?" Mary's father smiled thinly.

"My flight tomorrow got cancelled, and I'd like to get out of here."

"And we'd like you to get out of here. There is always Roger's floatplane." With that, he shifted, and was about to close the door when Robert tried a different approach. He was angry with the lack of response by the father and intensely disliked coming out the loser in conversations tied to his cases.

"Do you know where Mary picked up her habit?"

"Habit? She doesn't do drugs."

"I meant her propensity for lying."

The door slammed shut. Robert stood there. Hmm.... propensity, he liked that word. Mr. Tinlit didn't seem as taken with it, or perhaps it was the other word.

Robert walked back towards the middle of town. Gary had agreed to meet with him, but not until after lunch. A floatplane, hmmm. He checked in at the detachment to find out more about Roger and his plane. The admin person gave him a number, which he called right away, wanting desperately to get back to Vancouver on Friday. Roger turned out to be amenable and agreed to get him down to Port Hardy where he could pick up the second leg of his flight at two pm. The slightly higher price didn't bother Robert as he wasn't paying out of his own pocket, so the deal was done.

As it was late morning, Robert made his way over to the cafe where he had lunched the previous day. He needed some real coffee. He looked down at the docks as he walked and saw a floatplane, maybe <u>the</u> floatplane. It looked improbably small, perhaps because it was far away?

Once inside, after being seated, Robert asked his server about the plane.

"That's Roger's Beaver. He does a good business when the flights get cancelled."

"Happen often? They didn't give me a reason."

"You were probably the only one making the flight, so they canned it. Not that they would ever tell you the real reason."

"That thing airworthy?"

"Those things are like Volkswagens. I think Roger's was one of the last to come off the line in sixty-six."

"Geeez, you mean it's almost sixty years old?"

"Pretty much, but on the upside, it's one of the newest Beavers around. I've heard they've started making a different version these days, but that's definitely not Roger's." She smiled then moved on to the next table leaving Robert to ponder whether he really needed to get off Raven Island by tomorrow. Once he left the cafe, he'd call Tony to see if anything was happening in Vancouver. As he savoured his coffee, he wondered whether he wanted to eat again, but this thought trickled away as he looked out the window at the harbour below. Eventually, he ordered some toast to fortify him until dinner, and started to consider his upcoming conversation with Gary Hamilton.

Robert's call to Tony confirmed that he had missed nothing in the day he had been away. He was standing outside the cafe, watching the harbour as he talked. Allo Foot had not been found as yet. The squat where Mary had been dropped off was found abandoned. Robert told Tony what he had learned so far about the cast of characters from Bella Kind.

"That sounds interesting, Robert."

"Not sure where that leaves us so far. Mary's father didn't reveal much at all. Kind of hostile if I had to characterize it. Also, I might have antagonized him, but what's done is done." He sighed. "Archie has a stepson here I'm going to visit shortly. It is not a simple story, but some motives are starting to appear. Lots to tell when I return tomorrow." He ended the call, waved at the cafe server through the window, and left to find one of the two town cabs to ferry him out to Gary Hamilton's place.

Once in the taxi, the driver naturally started asking Robert questions, which he answered in one-word sentences, or not at all. It was all part of the town's desire to know as much as possible about this policeman from the big city and why he was chasing the good citizens of Bella Kind. Robert was instead speculating about his upcoming meeting with a victim of past wars. Would he be obstinate, angry, defeated? Probably a combination of all that and more, he guessed. At the southwest end of Bella Kind, the road quickly regressed to a pothole filled track that would make a logging road seem like a four-lane freeway. The pace of the car dropped to a speed that Robert could have easily matched by walking. He bit his tongue, not wanting to offend the driver.

Twenty-five minutes later, the car had picked up some speed before pulling off onto a track leading gently uphill to a one-storey cabin in a large clearing. The requisite pick-up truck was parked beside the small home — something from the Land of Nippon, Robert guessed. A plywood ramp connected the ground with a porch that ran along the entire front of the cabin. Otherwise, there was nothing to indicate the state of the resident. The property looked to be several degrees tidier than the Tinlit residence. Robert arranged for his return ride, then let the cab go, hoping his conversation would last longer than the one with Mr. Tinlit. He turned around to face a vista of the sound far below through a break in the forest. Pretty nice.

The door opened and Robert looked down at a muscular man, seemingly in his twenties, sitting in a very sporty wheel-chair.

"I am Robert Lui, Vancouver Police. Thanks for agreeing to talk with me, Mr. Hamilton."

"You can come in."

So far, so good, Robert thought. "My condolences on the loss of your father, or stepfather, I understand."

"Thanks. I'm not sure what to think really. I haven't seen Archie in over five years. We kept in occasional contact, but there was a lot of guilt on his end because of what happened years back." Gary looked down at the floor before finally rolling back.

The cabin wasn't large. A bathroom sat between a basic kitchen and bedroom at the rear of the building. Living space filled the remainder of the cabin. Robert noted a couple of racks on one of the side walls; one with two fishing rods, and one empty. He speculated that a long gun would normally rest there, maybe moved out of sight for a police visit. Varnished knotty pine was the decorating theme, rendering the entire interior on the dark side. An acoustic guitar sat on a couch. A laptop resided on the dining table next to some empty beer cans, an ashtray, and the makings of fishing leaders. The faint aroma of toast and cigarettes was evident. Robert sat in an offered chair at the table.

"Walter Gray gave me the outline of what happened to you. How come you don't live in town?"

"Don't get along with some of the townsfolk. A friend of the family offered this to me at a good rate after my mother left to go back up coast. They modified it to suit my problems, so I'm fine with being out here."

"May I ask why your mother left?"

Gary eyed Robert, considering whether to answer, "She went to take care of her mother up north. I can handle myself here." A hint of defiance in the answer. "She called to tell me about Archie. She said she would try to get down for the funeral."

"I believe it is set for tomorrow." Then he shifted topics. "Mary Tinlit."

Gary's eyes sparked. "What about her?"

"We think she may have had something to do with your father's death. She was in the vicinity the night he was killed, and he was murdered, very thoroughly."

"Mary always liked taking things to the next level, no matter what she was doing."

"Would that run to murder?"

"Not likely. And if she was going to do something like that, it would have been done years ago, here."

"How about her old boyfriend, Allo?"

"I don't know. They were both a few years older than me."

"Does she have a new boyfriend?"

Gary shrugged. "No idea. They live in Vancouver. I was only there for a while, rehabbing at G.F. Strong. All before they went down there."

Robert looked around, not sure what else he could take away from the conversation. He stood up, walked over to the front window, looking over the passage southwest of Bella Kind. Not a bad view, the kind wealthy people would kill for in Vancouver.

"You seem like you're making out okay. What do you do to keep occupied?"

"Fishing with friends on occasion. It wasn't like this at first. I was pretty pissed off, some drinking, stuff not conducive to a lengthy life. Archie gave me a talking to, and after a while, the message sank in. I was lucky to get the insurance money, not that it will last much longer, but it helped set me up. Archie also sent me money when he could." Gary looked down at the coffee table, staring at nothing.

Robert thought about the possibility of police pension money, but decided to hold his tongue. He knew there should be insurance money from the coverage all officers had as part of their employment package. But who knew what Archie's last will and testament would say, or if he even had one. Then he had a thought. What if Gary was behind all this? Running out of money might be a motivation, but it would take a pretty cold-hearted bastard to be behind the killing of your own dad, or stepdad, just on the chance of receiving some cash. He parked that thought near the bottom of his brain for now.

"Want a beer? Or some coffee?"

"Coffee would be nice, thanks." Robert answered. He looked at his watch. Twenty minutes until the taxi returned, in theory. He watched as Gary rolled into the kitchen to put water on and assembled the implements. Looked like he made coffee the way Robert did. His respect for Gary instantly rose a couple of levels. Ten minutes later, Gary rolled back, holding a mug for Robert.

"You make coffee like I do. I'm impressed — not many torture themselves this way."

"Well, it's important, no?"

Robert just smiled. Fifteen minutes later, and after a discussion about fishing in the local waters, the cab pulled up.

"Thanks for your time and hospitality. Here is my card. If you remember anything else, you can contact me. Can I get your number, as well?"

Gary grabbed a small piece of paper off a pad and wrote his number down, handing it to Robert.

"Good luck Gary." With that, Robert nodded and left.

# Chapter 8

Early the next morning, Robert decided to forego the run, instead spending more time over breakfast. His legs were stiff and sore from his encounter with Yogi the Bear the previous morning. He texted his kids, his parents, then lastly Norma, saying he'd be back in Vancouver mid-afternoon. While eating, he glanced out the window of the lodge at what looked like whitecaps on the water. Must be windy. A flag on the terrace was at full attention. He wasn't sure what that meant for his flight.

After stuffing himself with another extra tasty meal, he returned to his room and grabbed his bag to go checkout. His favourite and only server was behind the desk.

"Reluctantly, I must leave, but I have quite enjoyed my short time here. You are an excellent chef."

His server smiled at the compliment. "Sure you have to leave so quickly?"

"Unfortunately. Pressing matters. Perhaps I may return — take up fishing. We'll see."

His stomach was intensely happy. He suspected that the flavours of all the food he was eating were somehow enhanced by the location and the sea air, or maybe it was because he wasn't cooking for a change. Possibly all of these.

He took the water taxi back to the government wharf to meet up with Roger. However, the boat trip over to town was rough, his meal getting jostled around, the stomach happiness fading. Fortunately, the ride wasn't long, or his breakfast might have made a second appearance. After disembarking the boat, he slung his bag over his shoulder and walked along to where the Beaver was tied up. It didn't appear to be much larger now that he was up close, more like an oversized toy. An older man who must have been Roger was talking to a middle-aged woman dressed in rough working clothes beside the plane. Maybe a veteran tree planter? Didn't they travel in clumps? Robert looked up at two eagles staring down at him from a tall cedar, as though they were contemplating a late breakfast.

Roger looked over. "You Robert Lui?"

"Exactly."

"Have you cleared airport security yet?"

Robert didn't know what to say, never having been on a floatplane before.

Roger chuckled. "No? That's fine. It's why I fly floatplanes, so we don't have to deal with that BS. Here is a life jacket. Please put it on and strap up." Wind played havoc with what hair remained on his head. He watched as both Robert and the woman struggled with their safety equipment, then helped them with adjustments. "Didn't used to have to do this either, but some pilots put their planes in the drink the last few years. This is the result."

"That thing seaworthy? Or airworthy?"

Roger looked hurt, but Robert doubted anything he said about the Beaver would bother him. Robert noted that Roger seemed to be middle-aged, a good omen he felt. He had heard a few bad stories concerning youngish pilots.

But Robert was now definitely having second thoughts. Maybe a flight home Saturday on a real plane would be just fine. Too late, however, they were being beckoned onto the plane by Roger.

"Seems kind of windy today." Robert felt the need to state the obvious as he waited for the woman to enter, then he wrangled his way up the short ladder, through the hatch behind her, and into the small cabin. A teenager slammed the door shut behind him. There were only four seats on display. It seemed some interior modifications had been done by someone in order to make more room for cargo.

"Nothing to worry about," Roger yelled, as he stepped up to his door.

Robert hated it when people said things like this. It seemed like it was just asking for trouble. The two passengers buckled in, and Robert watched as Roger settled in and went through his pre-flight check. The engine coughed into life, then settled into something sounding good, not that Robert would know good from bad. The teenager on the dock unleashed the pontoon, and the plane revved its engine, slipping sideways away from the dock.

The plane moved into the channel, away from boats, and Roger spent a few moments locating the plane where it wouldn't run into any of them as it took off. Once the engine had properly warmed up, Roger pushed the throttle forward, keeping his hand firmly on it. The plane gained speed into the wind and twenty seconds later, they were airborne, leaving the drag of the water behind them. Robert finally relaxed, slightly, looking out the window down at the strait.

The engine spluttered twice, revved up again, then lapsed into silence. This couldn't be good.

"This isn't one of those new electric plane engines, is it? Shouldn't the propeller be rotating?" Robert politely yelled.

Roger swore, then, "Brace yourselves, we're going down. I'm going to try to land it upright, but if we ditch awkwardly, we'll have to abandon ship sooner than later. Get your seatbelts off and kick the closest door open when I tell you to."

They weren't more than a hundred feet in the air, but it seemed that a gentle landing was out of the question. The nose pitched forward, and they headed down. Roger managed to even out the plane somewhat before they hit the water, but without the engine, it was a losing battle.

The waves grabbed the front of the pontoons, flipping the plane sharply forward into the water, face down. Both Robert and the woman shot forward, banging their heads on the seat backs in front of them. Robert un-buckled, landing on the seat in front. He looked over at the woman struggling with her belt. She was conscious at least, looking back at him.

"Are you okay?" Robert yelled. The pilot had disappeared.

Roger responded, "Yeah, hit my head. Are you two alive? Get the hell out, we're going down. I'll give you ten seconds before I open my door."

Robert reached over and released the woman's belt for her. He braced himself, giving the door a good kick. It sprang open, and Robert reached over to grab the woman by the waist. He angled her over to the door and pushed her out, watching as she disappeared from his view. Then he struggled to get through the hatch, kneeling precariously on the edge of the opening before jumping awkwardly into the cold water. The plane was not sinking, at least not yet, but it was pointing nose down as though it had a date with Poseidon. Robert pulled the cord on his life jacket and made sure the woman did the same. He looked for Roger. God, it was cold.

Roger finally appeared, swimming around from the other side of the plane. The Beaver started to fill with water faster after he had opened his door. All three backed away, watching as it slowly sank out of sight, the tail the last to go. White caps sloshed over their heads relentlessly, increasing the misery. They were all trying desperately not to inhale any of the salt water.

Then the engine seemed to start up again. Robert was puzzled. How could this be? He looked past where the plane had been and realized the sound came from a small boat speeding towards them. First one, then a second boat joined in the rescue, slowing, then circling the three, finally getting close and hauling the wet aviators out of the water, one by one.

All three started shivering violently as the boats swung around, heading back to the pier they had just left. An old ambulance pulled in just after they tied up to the pier. Robert stepped out of the boat, shaking, and climbed up onto the dock. He looked over at the growing crowd of people at the street end. On its edges he saw Mary Tinlit's father, staring at them. He didn't look happy. Robert then spotted the same two eagles he had seen earlier, still sitting on the top of the cedar, perhaps not as taken with wet prey. All three aviators were trembling in fits as they were given blankets and bundled into the ambulance to head to the town clinic, a trip taking all of two minutes.

After repairs to his head, fixing nothing more serious than a cut from the seat back he had landed on and a wait while his clothes dried out, Robert re-visited the RCMP station to give a statement and arrange another flight out of town the next day. His head hurt, but he assumed the pills he had been given would do their magic. He called Arnott Bay, and the lodge was more than happy to have him back for a third night. He then phoned his children and Norma with the story. They were shocked at hearing what happened but relieved to hear he was alive and not injured. As was Robert, truth be told. His bag was gone, but he still had his wallet and phone, although he didn't hold any hope for the phone working.

Walter Gray gave Robert the okay to leave Bella Kind as there wasn't much he could add to the upcoming investigation. Roger, the pilot, wouldn't be so lucky. The Transportation Safety Board would take its time assessing the crash before a hint of a reason might be found. But first, the plane would need salvaging from the seabed. The good thing was that it wasn't in small pieces.

Late that afternoon, Robert returned to the lodge in the water taxi, the trip far smoother than the morning journey to town after the winds had eased. Enroute, Robert made a silent promise to himself to stay away from water for a long time, maybe forever, after this trip was done. He studied the waves as the boat sliced through them, thinking about people who had not been as lucky as himself. Not a good way to go. They had been so fortunate that the plane had gone down close to town. He headed straight to the dining room after checking back in. The receptionist/waitress/chef noted his return by promptly bringing a large scotch over to his table. He had neglected to take the painkillers, so immediately sipped the drink.

"On the house. We heard about all the excitement. Nice to have you back," she said, grinning. Robert nodded back at her, smiling in return.

"Thanks, I'm Robert," he said, deciding introductions were in order.

"Yes, I know your name. I'm Sandra. Pleased to see you survived. Must have been scary?"

"A little, but Roger was pretty professional about the whole thing. He told us what to do and when to do it."

"Roger is good. I think this is his first accident."

"Hope that's all it was."

"What do you mean?"

Robert realized he was edging into forbidden territory. "I've learned this town has a bit of history. Let's put it that way. On another topic, I'd like the crab leg dinner, if you can do it, don't spare anything. I'm celebrating being alive tonight."

Sandra nodded, smiling. "I'll get going then and make it a night to remember." Robert watched her rear as she slowly walked back to the kitchen. He sipped his drink, something from Islay, he guessed, as relaxation finally started to take hold.

Much later, after a couple of more scotches and a dinner fit for a man escaping death, Robert was still revelling in his luck. Sandra cleared the dishes away, then returned to his table holding a bottle of one of the better reds from Oliver in the Okanagan Valley. The three other customers in the room had long since departed. She sat and took the cork out slowly, pouring two glasses. Her eyes met Robert's, not blinking. Robert started sinking, fast.

"To life, Robert! You are one fortunate guy."

"Amen." Robert answered. He had a pretty good idea where this night was heading, but he was powerless to stop it, not that he even wanted to. He had always been attracted to women with a sense of humour. "Here's to the chef." He stared back into her eyes. They seemed bottomless. Was he drowning all over again?

"Thanks, I try."

"You do more than try, you succeed. Not a common thing these days. And doing three jobs. Not many in Vancouver would measure up." He smiled. "So, you are here all winter?"

"Yes. It gets a bit slow sometimes, but not tonight."

"Not tonight." Robert answered. "I wonder if you could possibly bring a toothbrush up to my room when we are finished here. I seem to have lost most of my luggage today, and am at a loss."

"No worries, Robert. I will be up shortly after the wine is done. We provide a full service at the Arnott Bay Lodge."

"That is what I was hoping, Sandra."

Early the next morning, Robert opened his eyes. He was thirsty. He looked around. Sandra had disappeared. He supposed she had things to do, and also maybe didn't need management knowing what she got up to with the guests. Although, on reflection, maybe management was part of her duties as well.

He stretched, then reached over for the water bottle on the night table and took a long swig. He felt marvellous, if slightly fuzzy. Nothing like a brush with death to re-invigorate one's outlook on life. He lay for a while contemplating Sandra and what they had done. He couldn't put his finger on it, but something about her seemed remarkably different from anyone he had known. Was it desperation? A thanksgiving for being alive? He was unsure, but there was definitely a mutual attraction.

He eventually got up, took a long shower, then dressed in his crispy, salty clothing. His phone was dead, so he went to the front desk to ask about his flight. It wasn't Sandra at the desk, but he found that the flight was a go, so he went to have one more meal before his departure. Again, Sandra did not make an appearance in the dining room, so after he finished eating, he went looking for her in the kitchen before he departed.

"I don't like goodbyes." Sandra said. "That's why I stayed in here." She stood uncertainly in front of the range, her whites on, a large knife in her right hand. There was no one else in the kitchen.

Robert nodded. "I need to leave now, Sandra."

"If you're ever in the area ... or want to take up fishing...."

Robert nodded, went over, kissed her gently on the forehead, his hand caressing the side of her head for a long moment as he lost himself in her eyes again. Then he left.

Robert's return flights on Saturday were mercifully uneventful. He stared out the window across the rolling mountains of the island, not really seeing anything. Despite his rather abrupt departure from Arnott Bay and an attempt to cut things off, he couldn't stop thinking about Sandra. Something was up, but he was clueless as to what it was. He thought of Norma and what they got up to on a regular basis. He assumed he was smitten, but maybe he was sexually smitten, not totally attached to Norma. Was there a word for it? Was it a physical comfort that he strove for? He shook his head. Nothing seemed any clearer.

After arriving home mid-afternoon and an emotional re-connection with his children, he didn't call Norma. He was confused, he admitted to himself, after what certainly seemed like cheating.

Robert walked over to Fraser Street to purchase a new phone at his favourite small electronic store. The proprietor swapped out the sim card for him, leaving him with newer technology, most of which would likely elude or annoy him.

He decided a second good dinner wouldn't be out of order to continue celebrating his escape from death. Both of his children were out with friends, so it was up to him to choose. Then he raised the stakes by inviting his parents over. He settled on a steamed whitefish dish with some Chinese vegetables and a noodle pillow, something basic, healthy, and nourishing, but, with the correct sauces added, extremely tasty.

He went out next to buy groceries and replenish his wine collection. He noticed every detail as he first shopped, then prepared for dinner. His brush with death definitely had repercussions. As he chopped the herbs and prepped the vegetables, his new phone chirped, signalling a text. It was Norma, wondering if they could meet for brunch the next day at her condo. As he responded in the affirmative, regret was wriggling into his mind about his night with Sandra.

It wasn't as if he was married, or even living with anyone, but somehow, what he had done didn't feel right. He had broken some part of his personal moral code, and blaming his actions on an alcohol fuelled relief at being alive was flimsy, at best. A *mea culpa* was going to be needed at some point, but Robert was also king of putting off difficult issues, so he concentrated on dinner. With that pushed to the rear of his mind, he finished his preparations, waiting on the guests.

He decided a whisky wouldn't be out of order while he pondered what he had learned about the good citizens of Bella Kind. Was their behaviour tied to a defence of their lands? It seemed as though there were people on both sides of that argument from what Walter Gray had told him. That Mary Tinlit had shown up at two apparently unrelated protests in Vancouver seemed to shoot a hole in any claim to a moral high ground she might be staking. However it started, the problems seemed to have degenerated into a feud between families. Robert thought he'd go with this line of thinking unless things changed. Mary seemed to display stupidity, no forethought. She was either not very bright, or just possibly, much smarter than she was letting on. Perhaps the swearing and the attitude was all an act, but he doubted if the valley girl talk was a put-on. He had heard too many people expressing themselves in a similar fashion.

# CHAPTER 9

After Robert's return to the office Monday morning, several staff congratulated him on surviving his first floatplane ride. When Thomas heard that he was back, a meeting was called.

After Tony, Robert, and Finn had settled into the guest chairs, Thomas started. "Robert, what did you learn up there? Besides not to get into floatplanes."

"Some bad stuff happened in Bella Kind during the wood protests a few years back, and Archie Hamilton was right in the middle of it. So was Mary Tinlit and her boyfriend at the time, Allo Foot. I would have to say that they are suspects one and two in this mess. And it appears that revenge is the prime motive in all this. And I reiterate this — it appears. We don't know for sure at this juncture what the motives are. If it is revenge, then it was a long time coming. And from what we've seen of Mary, she doesn't appear to be the patient type." Robert looked at Tony. "Any luck on locating them yet?"

"No. Maybe we shouldn't have released Mary."

"Don't think we had any choice. It would have been hard to hold her. A public defender would have pried her out pretty quickly. How was the funeral? Did it take place last Friday?"

Thomas answered, "It was well attended. About sixty officers also came from out of town. A good send-off, I think. We all went. It was at a church on the east side."

There was a rap on the door. It opened and Norma poked her head in. "Sorry to interrupt, but several calls have come in. A body is hanging on a building up Hastings Street. It's drawing a lot of attention, not surprisingly, I guess."

Robert looked at Norma, then at the other three. "Geeez. Let's go. Address?"

"It is a building under construction. East Hastings, past Commercial Street, Tornado House Co-op? What kind of name is that?" Norma asked. Robert shook his head as they left the room to head down to a vehicle.

Robert asked Tony to do the driving for a change of pace. It gave him a chance to see things he normally wouldn't. They drove over to Main and up north to where it intersected with Hastings. Improbably, the impoverished area seemed worse than he remembered. A few people were pushing dented shopping carts, some half full of possessions, either personal effects, or possibly goods heading for the local sidewalk market, which operated daily. One or two carts were filled to overflowing with garbage bags of cans and bottles, ostensibly heading to a re-cycling outlet. What did they do with their carts at night? Several tents sat on the Hastings sidewalk — shelters for people not keen on living in the single room occupancy hotels where vermin and pests had first rights. A couple of citizens were walking at angles on the roadway, not paying attention to much at all. Rain had yet to start, but thick clouds made the mood sullen, any colour in the surroundings dimmed. Things lightened slightly as they made their slow way farther east on Hastings, but not by much.

As the detectives approached the construction site on the north side of Hastings, it appeared as though a circus had arrived in town. They had slowed in front of a couple other building sites on Hastings, but it was plain that this was the correct place. Three news vans were already taking up space on the street, with their crews setting up to do interviews. Some officers had taped off two of the traffic lanes, deploying orange cones everywhere, leaving a single lane heading west. Every vehicle travelling in either direction slowed to view the scene.

Robert looked up through the windshield. Some patrol officers were trying to rig tarps around the body hanging at the top floor, but it wasn't going well. A throng of pedestrians were agog at the spectacle on offer. More VPD cars were pulling up, increasing the congestion.

Robert, Tony, and Finn got out of their car and looked up again. The body was hung by a noose suspended from some kind of beam at the top of the structure, eight floors up. They ducked under the police tape and went through the chain-link gate straight into the construction trailer.

Tony couldn't believe his eyes. He was face to face with the same superintendent that had been on the construction site of his last major case.

Arby Knutson was in a similar state, staring at Tony. "You!" It came out as a yell.

"VPD, how do we get up there?" Robert was all business, no introductions.

"You'll need these hardhats first. I'll show you where the stairs are. But before you go up, I think you should know that it might be the architect for this project. I haven't gone up there yet, but the body looks familiar."

"What?"

"Yeah, I think it's her."

They arrived on the eighth floor after a walk up the concrete exit stairs, with Tony lagging slightly behind, blowing as though he had just finished running a mile. Finn seemed fine.

"You aren't going to expire on me, are you? We already have one body up here."

"Funny Robert." But Tony continued wheezing as he looked over at the three officers who had succeeded in finally erecting some tarpaulins around the body. Robert stood quietly, taking it in. Tony and Finn moved away, knowing Robert liked to have some space while he was viewing the scene.

It was a young woman, fully clothed this time, hung higher up than Archie had been, her feet maybe a metre above the concrete slab. Something was sticking out of her chest approximately where her heart might be. It looked like a pencil or pen of some kind. A useless thought came unbidden to him, something mightier than the sword. Her white blouse had a large reddish brown stain below the projecting weapon. Her hands were taped behind her back. The noose around her neck was similar to the one Archie was wearing on his last day. Something else seemed to be the same, a trickle of blood at the woman's neck. The tape job looked familiar to Robert as well. He would have to compare the pictures. She was minus a coat or jacket. A second thought came to him; he hoped she wasn't cold, up so high in the sky. He shook his head.

"As soon as the scene people get here and do their thing, get her cut down. Put some gloves on and check her pockets for any identifying items." He nodded at Tony. "This is definitely an exhibit for public consumption, a message perhaps?" Robert mused.

"I'd say so, at a guess," Finn answered, while Tony donned his gloves. "Although, what it's trying to say is a mystery to me." While Tony did his examination, Robert went over to edge of the concrete slab, resting his hands on the wood safety railing, looking down at the dispersing crowd. He wasn't comfortable with heights, so he stepped back half a step. With the tarps in place and nothing more to gawk at, the excitement of the morning had dissipated for the passers-by. He looked up and stared south at the long view of East Vancouver. It was not pretty.

Tony finished going through the woman's pockets. There was no wallet, but he had pulled out a business card. They gathered around Tony and examined it. An architect, apparently. Anne Leforet of Hummingbird Architects. The address was in Yaletown.

The crime scene team finally arrived. After they made their way up to the top, using the construction lift to haul their equipment, Robert decided that his group could leave, but not before buttonholing Arby back down in the site trailer.

"So, you think it is the architect up there? What was her name?"

"Anne Leforet."

"What company?"

"Hummingbird Architects."

"Would she be able to get onto your site on her own?"

"No. She'd need a key to unlock the gate."

"And was it locked when you showed up this morning?"

"No. Lock was busted off."

"Anything else disturbed that you can see?"

"Don't think so, but I haven't checked the whole site."

"Okay, thanks. We'll be in touch. Here is my card, if anything comes to mind." Robert concluded. He looked at Tony and Finn. "Let's get back to Cambie." They stepped outside.

"Why did you ask Arby those questions about Anne when we already had her card?"

"Being thorough, Tony. You did pass those detective exams, correct?"

Tony looked sheepish. "Yes. Never assume anything, right?"

Finn smiled as Robert dispensed the lesson.

"Let's go. This is already looking like a long day, and I need caffeine."

Upon their return, Robert looked for Thomas, but his office was empty. It seemed as though the remainder of his Bella Kind update could wait, so he beckoned Tony and Finn for a trip up the street. "We definitely need to locate Mr. Foot and Ms. Tinlit. I have a few more questions for them." They walked into Cafe Paulo and yelled their customary greetings to Gilberto.

"Or, we wait for the next demonstration to take place and nab them there." Tony said.

"Anyone want a pastry?" All the fresh air had given Robert an appetite, despite the gruesome discovery on Hastings.

"Thanks, no." Finn responded.

They sat down by the window, eyeing the people walking by. "When's it going to rain? Robert complained. "It's not natural. If it's cloudy, it's supposed to rain." He sounded childish to himself.

"Is that what you really want, Robert?" Tony asked, "'Cause, once it starts...."

"I agree with Robert, for what it's worth. So, what did you learn up north?" Finn asked.

"Those youngsters seemed to hold Archie responsible for the death of Allo's father several years ago. That is motive squared in my book. Archie tasered Allo's father at a blockade and he eventually died months later. Whether it was connected is uncertain. But those two definitely thought it was."

"Sounds as though you've solved it, Robert."

"Maybe. What we saw this morning looks very similar to Archie's murder, so where would the motive be for that? There was sabotage going on in Bella Kind during the wood protests; arson, and brake lines being cut. I wouldn't be

surprised if my floatplane adventure was more of the same."
Tony's eyes widened at this.

Gilberto brought the Americanos over to their table. "You
have become even more famous, Roberto! I heard you went
swimming up the coast?"

"Unfortunately, yes. I wouldn't recommend it though,
especially at this time of year. Thanks Gilberto." Gilberto
nodded and returned to the command post behind his La
Cimbali machine. He didn't seem to be put out by Robert's
lack of additional gossip.

"So, your crash wasn't an accident?"

"I'd be surprised if that's all it was, I'll put it that way. I
talked with Mary's father the day before. It wasn't a friendly
conversation. I mentioned Mary's inclination to lie. Might
not have gone over so well." They each savoured their coffees.

"Tony, I'd like you to check with the University of Manitoba, their architecture faculty. Mary spent some time there.
See if this Anne Leforet also did. Let's see if we can connect
some more dots." Robert paused. "And we'll see what the
coroner tells us."

"Not easy hauling a body up eight floors."

"No kidding, Tony. It almost killed you going up there,
with no body. Didn't you used to be in some sort of shape?
Don't you have to be, to be let onto the force?"

"You're a riot Robert. Maybe we should get back."

"Sure. I'm wondering why those kids lie so much. Is it a
game?"

"Not normal, that's for sure." Finn responded.

"One more thing, Finn, could you do some research
into Fiona Hamilton, Archie's ex? She might have been at

Archie's funeral last Friday. It's uncertain." Finn nodded as they walked back down Cambie Street.

Once back in his office, Robert considered whether to deliver Rodney's sandwich back to its owner. He decided not to in the end, too lazy to go down a floor. Rodney wasn't worth the effort. He chucked it into the garbage bin.

Robert followed up his theory about the Beaver by sending an e-mail to Walter Gray asking to be kept up to date on any developments with the crash investigation. His thoughts then turned to Anne Leforet and what she had done to get herself murdered in such a public fashion. He wasn't sure what a call to her firm might net, but he'd try.

"Hummingbird Architects, Roy speaking."

"Robert Lui calling from the Vancouver Police. I suppose you know why I am calling by now?"

"Unfortunately, yes. We can't believe what happened. We are in shock here."

"Was Anne in any disputes with others that the firm knew about?"

"We are always in disputes, particularly when a project gets to the construction stage, but they are usually minor. It is just a fact of life in this business. There are many competing agendas, and they usually rotate around money. But they don't result in death, never." There was a pause. "Until now, I guess."

"Was the Tornado project different in any way?"

"Social housing, but otherwise, not to my knowledge. Our client was the City of Vancouver."

"How large is your firm? Will this impact its viability?"

There was silence, Robert suspecting it might be early to be asking questions like this.

"Maybe. I don't know. We are fifteen people, make that fourteen."

"And you are?"

"I am Anne's partner."

"Sole partner?"

"Yes."

"My condolences to you and your firm. Did Anne have family here?"

"Not to my knowledge. She was from Winnipeg."

"I'll let you go then, but I will undoubtably have more questions soon. I'll be in contact." He rang off.

Not much, as he suspected. A visit back to the site would be his next move to talk to that superintendent who seemed to know Tony, but first, there was lunch to consider. As he was pondering his culinary choices, his cell rang with a very annoying sound. He'd need to do some adjustments on his new phone, which seemed to be packed with things he would never use.

"Robert here."

"It's Bernard."

"How are you? Thanks for the protest video, Bernard. Not much there, but I appreciate it. Calling about the architect?"

"The architect?"

Oops, Robert kicked himself. "Yes, it'll come out soon anyway, but the body on East Hastings was the architect for the project where she was found, Anne Leforet. Can't really say any more than that for now."

"Okay. I heard you were involved in a swimming incident up the coast. Any comments on that?"

"Yes, I have. Don't do it, way too cold, and possibly life-ending. I am waiting for any words on the Transportation Safety Board investigation that has been started. Other than that, I'm happy to be alive and back at work."

"Dare I ask why you were up in Bella Kind?"

"Pursuing inquiries Bernard. As you may or may not know, Archie Hamilton, the murdered cop, spent time up there with the RCMP in the past. That's about it. I'll call you about lunch one day soon. We'll have to pick an out of the way place.

"Thanks Robert, talk soon." Bernard was smiling, having learned much more than he had hoped for.

Meanwhile, Tony was having less success trying to piece together Anne Leforet's academic career. There was no one at the school who could answer his questions, save one person not returning for another two days. He returned to the security footage from the scene of Archie's demise on his computer. He was viewing this when a uniformed officer he didn't know stopped at the edge of his partition and looked down at him.

"You guys are real pieces of work you know that? We lose an officer in the line of duty and you detectives are yucking it up in a coffee house while the rest of us are working our asses off. Not impressed." This last came out louder than the rest of the diatribe.

Tony didn't know how to respond, so he kept his mouth shut, but stared up at the officer until he moved on. It seemed as though the Rodney effect had finally taken root. He put his search aside and started looking through one of the social media sites. It didn't take him long to come upon a Rodney Fister site that displayed a picture of Robert and Tony enjoying their coffees at Cafe Paulo. The caption said.

**'This is how seriously your detectives are taking the Archie Hamilton killing.'**

That was it, but it was obviously enough. Now came the tricky part. Tony knew that Robert hated social media, and did not partake in it at all, so he wouldn't know what was being circulated about them, yet. The problem wouldn't be with officers who knew Rodney and his pettiness, but with all the others, which frankly, were most of the VPD. He swore to himself. The whole investigation just became needlessly more complicated. He was starting to appreciate why Robert hated the media so much.

After Robert returned from lunch, Tony beckoned him into a meeting room. Robert looked at Tony with eyebrows raised. Had he found a clue?

"We have a tiny problem, Robert."

Not what he was hoping for. "What kind of problem?"

"A Rod induced problem."

"I can guess. He posted his photos, correct?"

"Yup, and I have already had in-person blowback."

"In person? As in someone came up to you?"

"Yes."

"That is not normal, is it? Doesn't that kind of crap stay online, where it germinates?"

"Usually. Most people are either too lazy or wouldn't have the fortitude to actually take action."

"Well, I'd tell them to stuff it, that we will conduct our investigation as we see fit. They don't like it, take it up with Thomas."

Tony's crumpled eyebrows indicated he wasn't buying what Robert was selling. "Sounds good in theory, but there is a huge swamp out in the blogosphere."

"The what?"

"You know, the interweb."

"Exactly why I stay away from it. My theory is that it's good for a few things, but very bad at many others."

"I don't know Robert."

"We are not in a popularity contest here. We have a job to do. Maybe we shouldn't have baited Rod, but we'll have to live with it for now." He could see the doubt on Tony's face, but it was all part of learning to be a detective. Not all the foes would be external. Some of the hardest obstacles would be right here on the force. "If someone approaches you again, ask him if he knows when the photo was taken. If he doesn't have an answer, then tell him to stuff it and stop wasting your time."

"I think sometimes that kind of information remains embedded with the photo."

"Easily found?"

"Depends on the knowledge of the person viewing it and how it has been forwarded. Fifty-fifty I'd say."

"Well, my comment stands, Tony."

As they left the room, Robert spotted Thomas, so he filled him in on what he had found up in Bella Kind. This accomplished, he added a warning about what Rodney had done to them. He then realized he would be waiting for information on several fronts of both murders, so returned to some of his ongoing assault cases from the east side, which, to be frank, were not exactly retaining his interest.

# Chapter 10

Thursday morning dawned. Robert opened his eyes, but he could only discern darkness outside, no light penetrating the blinds. As he listened for any sign of movement from his children, he heard the light patter of drops on the window. Rain, at last. He lay a while, enjoying a sound not heard in almost two months. Everything was parched in the city. A good portion of the rain wouldn't even make it to the ground. Instead, it would be lapped up by crowns of the trees as the dust slipped away, greens and reds becoming vivid. The traffic officers would be busy this day, sorting out accidents, people not driving any slower until it became painfully obvious that fresh water on well-oiled streets was not a good mix.

Eventually, he pried himself out of bed and readied for his day. After seeing his kids off to school, he saddled up in his old, slow Honda, which he called The Silver Streak, and headed for Cambie Street headquarters, where hopefully some answers might present themselves. He drove slowly, watching less prudent people whizzing by him. He walked into his office and, sure enough, a new envelope lay on his desk that turned out to be the coroner's report for Anne Leforet.

He sat down and started reading the brief notes. As he finished, he stared out the window at the gathering storm, rain picking up in strength, lashing the glass, driven by the usual southeast winds. After monitoring the rain for several minutes, he decided he needed some answers from Tony.

"Tony, you there?" He yelled. Nothing. He rose and looked into Tony's cubicle, discovering that the occupant was on the phone. He leaned against the partition gingerly, knowing it really wasn't good at holding anything up, let alone a detective. Tony eventually ended his call.

"Let's go, bring your coat."

"Not to Cafe Paulo, Robert."

"Don't worry, heading to the Apollo, I'll drive. I'd take you for a False Creek walk, but the weather isn't cooperating." The Apollo Cafe on Main Street had been the scene of a few surreptitious meetings a half year earlier when Robert had been free-lancing as a private investigator, after getting the boot by the VPD.

They entered the cafe, Robert winking at the barista before ordering. After they settled into their seats, Robert looked at Tony expectantly.

"Okay, when you were waiting, I was learning about Anne. The university finally got back to me. Anne Leforet was enrolled there at the same time as Mary, in the same class, a three-year undergrad degree required before you attempt to enter the architecture program proper. There is the link. In addition, Anne didn't stay in Winnipeg after she finished that course, but instead went to Harvard to do her master's degree."

"Expensive school. Ms. Leforet must have had some money behind her." Robert said.

"Mary didn't even finish her undergrad, dropping out in the third year. They didn't tell me anything else."

"Maybe Mary was jealous of Anne?"

The barista called their order out, so Robert went up to fetch the cups, pausing at the counter. "Thanks Adrianne, it's been a while."

She smiled. "Where have you been?"

"My other home, but it seems that I might be coming here more often soon."

"Problems?"

"Nothing I can't sort out." He nodded and returned to their table.

"There is more, Robert. Finn told me that Fiona Hamilton is related to Walter Gray, the RCMP sergeant. His cousin apparently."

Robert's eyes widened. "Really, wow. He didn't mention a connection at all." He shook his head.

"Finn wasn't able to find out much else about Fiona, but I learned something else you probably wouldn't know about."

"Why wouldn't I?"

"Because it's on social media, where you refuse to go. One of the youngsters in the basement asked me if I had seen the chatter about Anne Leforet."

"You mean those cyber-crime folks?"

"Yes. There were some brutal comments posted about her, how the Tornado project was going to be stopped by the city because Anne was putting the project way over budget. Apparently didn't sit well with housing advocates, amongst others. There was a lot of negative feedback. And I am putting that extremely nicely. I think the threats made will get some of those people into trouble now that Anne has been murdered."

Robert was silent, staring outside at the rain bouncing off the pavement. "Motive, possibly, if it is our suspects. What I don't get is how a bunch of homeless people would have a computer to even be online."

Tony shook his head, amazed at Robert's seemingly self-made ignorance. "All you need is a cellphone, Robert, and a cafe with Wi-Fi somewhere, or a library."

"What is Wi-Fi, really? And why do we need it?"

Tony refused to answer, staring at Robert.

"Okay, sorry about that. Any idea where the comments about Anne originated?"

"Whoever did it used a cut out, a burner page, but I told those guys to analyze the text. Ever hear of something called content analysis?"

"No, what is it?"

"The basement dwellers told me that it's an older research tool that allows you to ferret out information that is probably not obvious to the casual reader. You compare how something is written to other examples and hopefully find a link that will identify the author or narrow down the options. That is the extremely short version. It can be pretty powerful according to those geeks."

Robert was impressed with Tony's work. "Coffee's good today. It's nice to get a different perspective."

"One more thing I found out. There is a print on Anne's business card that does not belong to her, but it's not in the system either."

"Mr. Foot's, maybe? We really need to find this guy soonest." Robert finished his coffee and sat looking inside the empty cup. Tony knew the look.

"Be right back." Tony watched as Robert went back to the bar and made some time with the barista. He returned, "Autopsy came back. Not much to relate. Other than the obvious similarities with how Archie was left, Anne had also been conked on the head, again with something circular, like a ball. Not a tennis ball, I'm guessing. No drugs in her system. Died from being stabbed in the heart a few times with a mechanical pencil."

"A what?"

"Exactly. Maybe something an architect might use? You could check that aspect out. Might be another link back to Mary. No prints on the pencil, however. I'm waiting on the crime scene photos to see how they compare to Archie's death, but it sure seems to be the same murderer."

"Maybe we should get back, Robert."

"Okay, you're a jumpy one. You spooked by this internet crap?"

"Maybe."

"Let's go then." He finished his cup, and they walked outside. Robert stood still beside the car, savouring the feel of the rain. His hair slowly glistened, then drops started rolling down his face. His shoulders darkened as he blinked a few times while Tony stood by the car door, waiting for Robert to unlock it.

"It's just rain Robert, I'm pretty sure you are going to be tired of it by tomorrow."

"Possibly, but until then...." He finally relented, letting Tony into the car, and they retreated back to the station, Robert driving slowly and carefully.

As Robert walked by Norma, she signalled him, so he stopped. "They want you upstairs, Robert."

"Who does?"

"Mr. Deputy Chief, David McKnight, that's who."

"Doesn't sound good. Where is Thomas?"

"Unknown, which is strange. He always lets me know where he is."

"I guess I better get up there, then. If I see Thomas, I'll let him know he's offside. I don't suppose you know why I am wanted, do you?"

Norma shook her head, so Robert did as he was requested. Upon arriving on the fifth floor, he walked over to the gatekeeper for the Chiefs, nodding at Ranit. "David is looking for me, I understand."

Ranit turned her hand palm up and silently pointed at David's office door as though she was offering a treat to Robert. She didn't even bother to look at him.

Robert knocked, then entered. Thomas Harrow was already sitting across from David in one of the uncomfortable guest chairs. This didn't look like a 'well done Robert' kind of meeting, not that Robert had ever been the recipient of such largesse in all his time at the VPD.

"Take a seat, Robert." David pointed to the other guest chair. Robert did as he was asked. As he descended into his chair, he looked at Thomas for a clue as to what he was going to be hit with. Thomas did not return the look, instead seemingly focused on David's face.

"How's the Archie Hamilton investigation going, Robert?"

Robert considered his options. Lie, like some of the people he had run into recently, or tell part of the truth. He suspected that the question might have been phrased differently if Thomas hadn't been present.

"I think we are making progress. We have a couple of likely suspects who we are on the hunt for."

"So, progress. Tell me about this cafe that you seem to frequent."

"We sometimes go up the street when I wish to discuss things that others in the office shouldn't hear."

"I thought that was what conference rooms were for."

"Useless."

"Why is that?" David looked truly puzzled.

"Acoustical performance is abysmal. You aren't aware of this?" Robert was treading on dangerous ground, going on the offensive like this.

"No. However, I don't like receiving complaints about my detectives not treating this matter with the utmost seriousness."

"I understand, sir."

"Then you had better do something about it. We are done. Thomas, can you stay a moment?"

Robert stood, and with a nod to both men, he left the room. He was starting to perspire, ever so slightly. With a forced smile for Ranit, he left the floor and headed back down to his office. He suspected that Thomas was going to take some flak for his actions. Not a good feeling, knowing your boss was getting crap for things that you had done, or not done. But he also didn't like being forced to tip-toe around because of that asshole, Rodney Fister. He didn't have any immediate solutions, but he'd keep his options open.

The phone rang as he entered his office. "Robert?"

"Yes, is this Walter?"

"They pulled the Beaver out of the water yesterday. It didn't take too long to figure out why the engine died. There are three fuel tanks in the belly of the Beaver. Each one of them had a hole in it, drilled from the underside. At first glance, it seems like sabotage by someone who knew what they were about. Roger is being interviewed today, so there will likely be more to the story. I thought I'd tell you what I know so far."

"Really. I must say that I am not totally shocked, given the local history you related to me. Don't those planes have fuel gauges?" Robert had a more difficult question to ask. "Walter, why didn't you tell me that Fiona and Gary were related to you?"

"Don't know. Too painful, I think."

Robert didn't know how to respond. Maybe it was painful, but it also wasn't professional in his opinion.

"Okay, Walter, let me know when you find out anything else." He hung up. This was new territory. He had been threatened and come close to losing his life when he had been dealing with local gangs as part of the Taskforce, but all that came with the territory. Having what seemed to be regular working people trying to kill you was a novelty. Added to this were others on the plane who were merely bystanders. Collateral damage, isn't that what they called it in a war? Tony and Finn were going to need warning.

Of course, perhaps he was being hasty here. What if the intended victim was his fellow passenger, or Roger the pilot? He rang Finn and asked him to do some research into his two co-aviators.

Later in the day, Robert figured he'd better go and try to make amends. He stopped outside Thomas's office to check in with Norma.

"How's it going? Boss in?"

"Boss is in and receiving customers. Will we be seeing you tomorrow evening?"

"Yes. What time?"

"Seven is good. Please proceed in."

Robert entered and immediately went to apology mode. "I'm sorry to put you in that position, Thomas. I know you have enough without having to defend me."

"Who says I defended you?" Thomas answered, stone-faced.

This wasn't good. Then Thomas gave a small laugh. "You should see the look on your face. But also, I don't need my job made any more difficult."

Robert sat down and relaxed, but only slightly. "I get it. Just heard from Bella Kind. The floatplane I was on ever so briefly inexplicably had a hole drilled in the bottom of each of its three fuel tanks. Now, I'm no aeronautical engineer, but no fuel equals no engine noise, hence no propeller rotation, ergo, the plane falls into the ocean."

"Ergo?"

"The last word you want to hear on a plane. I do believe someone was trying to kill me. Either that, or Roger the pilot had worn out his welcome in Bella Kind. I'm having Finn check on Roger and the woman passenger."

"Don't those planes have fuel gauges?"

"You'd think. Waiting to hear chapter two in the story. Apparently, they are grilling Roger today."

"Anything else?"

"I am putting my money on Allo Foot as the killer of Archie, with Mary Tinlit as accessory. We have a search on for them. Assuming they are still in town, it shouldn't be too much longer. And the latest murder on Hastings may be by the same duo. There are some connections."

"Well, be careful, is my advice. I understand Archie's gun went missing. Make sure everyone knows this." Then he added. "Archie left a will, from what I hear. I don't know the details."

Robert nodded as he left the room. He returned to his office and stared outside, darkness almost complete, nothing to be seen beyond the tiny rivers of water coursing diagonally across the window. He called the number Gary had given him. It went to message, so he talked briefly about his stepfather leaving a will, but nothing further. His thoughts turned to dinner and what he was going to come up with. He scrolled through his mental recipe book, making a choice, and left to get some provisions, calling it a day.

After manoeuvring through hazardous Vancouver traffic made worse by the rain, he arrived home, tired from the effort and the day. He yelled up at his children, and receiving affirmative answers, he headed for his whisky cabinet. He chose a peaty scotch and then laid out his groceries on the counter — eggs. Sometimes the simplest things were best. Dinner was going to be egg salad beefed up with diced celery and green onions on sourdough toast, garnished with potato chips. Not exactly a traditional dinner, and maybe something more fit for summer, but no one had ever turned it down to date.

His kids eventually came downstairs, peering at the stove, wondering what was being dreamed up.

"Egg salad guys! How was your day?"

Robin spoke first. "Pretty good, Pops."

Robert looked at Sophie. She opened with a couple of questions. "You going over to Norma's tomorrow? When are we going to meet her?"

"Yes, and I wasn't sure if you wanted to after my last dating disaster."

"I wouldn't call it a disaster so much. And yes, we'd like to meet her. You've only been seeing her for what, four months now?"

Robert nodded as he dropped the eggs into the pot of boiled water, flipping the timer on, "Okay, how about next Friday evening, special dinner here? I'll dream up something." After the timer went off, he retrieved the eggs, dipping them into an ice bath to cool.

"Have you looked into the universities we talked about?" This directed at Sophie.

"Doing my research. There are a bunch of schools in Canada that have planning, but they all seem a little different from each other. I think some programs require a degree of some kind before you can get into them."

"Well, there are always the guidance counsellors, or I could ask one of your mother's accomplices to help you. Jean Kwok is still at the City of Vancouver, at least she was five months ago." After fetching himself a glass of wine, his scotch glass unaccountably dry, he peeled the eggs and mashed them, adding mayonnaise and the vegetables. It was nice to have an unconventional dinner.

Sophie wasn't finished. "Could Rose come over next Friday?" This caught Robin's attention.

"Sure. More the merrier."

After dinner was over and the dishes cleaned up, by Sophie for a change, Robert sat on the couch by himself, wine in hand, wondering why the architect had been murdered. Were the protesters really that crazy, and dangerous, more to the point, if they were the ones behind this? Tony indicated that the chatter on the social media sites said yes; but chatter was chatter, while taking concrete action was a major step, especially murder. Perhaps he needed a better grasp on what was being said online. He'd have a word with Tony tomorrow.

# CHAPTER 11

A phone call from Bella Kind started Robert's Friday. He had been in his office speculating about his upcoming date, not paying much attention to anything else.

"It is Walter. I have more information for you. Roger was interviewed yesterday by the safety people. It is questionable whether he will fly again after what he told them. Apparently, the Beaver's fuel gauge hadn't been working for some time. He intended to get the gauge fixed, but somehow hadn't got around to it. Roger compensated by making sure his tanks were full before each flight. His flights were never very far, so it worked for him. He had filled the tanks the evening before your trip, so whoever drilled the holes must have done it that night. The fuel would have dissipated in the water before dawn, so there was no obvious evidence before take-off."

"Don't believe I'll be returning your way anytime soon."

"Who did you talk to when you were here?" Walter asked.

"Other than a couple of the help at the lodge, you, Gary, and Mr. Tinlit. My money is on the latter. He was the one who told me about Roger and his plane. I seem to remember him being on the dock watching as we pulled up in the rescue boats. Didn't look pleased."

"Evidence is going to be hard to find."

"I'm sure you'll find something. It's what law enforcement does best, correct?"

"Right. I'll call if anything else comes up." Walter hung up.

Robert sighed as he replaced the receiver. It was hard to be optimistic about any charges resulting from the Beaver incident. If the past as narrated by Walter Gray was anything to go by, it seemed that sabotage, arson, and attempted murder were all seemingly mere hijinks perpetrated by over-spirited Raven Islanders. He knew this was a rough assessment of the RCMP, but maybe being an officer in one's own community had some negative aspects as well as positive ones.

Robert went looking for Tony, but found his workspace empty. Was he out in hot pursuit of the two suspects? Or was he performing more research? He felt Tony needed some tuning up in the communication area, otherwise, how would their team function efficiently?

He looked at Finn. "Do you know where Tony went?"

"Think he's in the basement visiting those cyber-crime kids."

"Thanks. Let him know I'm looking for him when he gets back."

Robert thought about giving Bernard a call to set up a lunch, then reconsidered it as premature. He didn't have enough questions for Bernard yet. Some fresh air was what he needed, so he went back to his office to grab his jacket. Instead of his usual path along False Creek, he headed in the opposite direction, south, up past City Hall into an older part of Vancouver where enterprising renovators had been restoring and densifying some of Vancouver's original housing stock. The rain had ceased for a short time, but even after a day of rain he found he was walking on mostly dry pavement. Much of the water hadn't even made it below the tree canopy, but he knew this wouldn't last much longer.

As he walked along the avenues, he realized that maybe one in five homes had received the attention and burnishing that made a home stand out. The remaining stock was more modest and some of it needed attention, badly. He marvelled at the colour combinations and extra details evident on some of the refurbished homes, references to an era in Vancouver when life was slower. Most of Vancouver's housing stock didn't exhibit this level of visual extravagance, which served to only enhance this neighbourhood's reputation. He walked by an ultra-modern home that must have somehow slipped past the goalie guarding the traditional standards and by-laws of the neighbourhood. Maybe he would enquire about costs to live in the area. He was still optimistic about owning something in the city. Why? He wasn't sure exactly. Each year, he thought he was making some progress saving money, only to see prices rise markedly higher, while, conversely, his prospects headed lower. Even the shabbier examples in this area were a come-on. He suspected it took millions to even get a real estate agent's attention.

Robert started debating the idea that the same people who had killed Archie would also kill a young architect, with little connection to link the two victims, that he knew of. Mary Tinlit seemed to be the one connection, and her ex-boyfriend so far didn't seem to have murder in his vocabulary. But then, Robert had yet to meet Allo and assess him firsthand. He was basing this on what he had learned up in Bella Kind.

Perhaps Mary had a bit of belief inside her; the kind that would make her treat someone who was sending a social housing project into the ditch as an enemy to be made an example of. Or maybe it was something different, an attempt to get someone's attention, or build up a persona. To what end, he didn't know, but the results were extreme. He needed to talk to someone at the city to find out if the Tornado project was really in trouble, or if it was merely more internet half-truths. He also supposed that low-cost housing was another link between events, although tenuous, at best.

He kept walking, finally encountering wet concrete as the tree canopy became thinner, the trees less numerous the farther east you ventured. He knew that they needed to apprehend Mary and Allo. He shook his head, not seeming to be making anything clearer, then, a vision. He was staring the Apollo Cafe. He had walked all the way to Main Street. As much as he would have liked to partake, he decided to about face and head back to Cambie, not an easy thing to do, given his addiction. More responsible actions, that's what Thomas was expecting of him. As he walked back, he again started ruing his ongoing loss of fitness. It was slowly evaporating, the deeper into this case he found himself. Maybe he should start doing something about it, instead of continually revisiting regret.

At Vancouver City Hall, in the Housing Department, a co-worker of Nancy Brick couldn't avoid witnessing what seemed to be the un-doing of Nancy before her eyes as she raised them from the report she was working on. Nancy had failed to appear at all on Tuesday, and when she did show up Wednesday, it seemed that a good part of the day was spent crying softly off and on. Thursday was a repeat of Tuesday, and today had seemed to start off normally enough, with Nancy at her desk going through her e-mails. Then tears started again.

The co-worker decided some attention was warranted and walked over to her. "Are you okay Nancy?" A common enough question when the answer was obviously not.

"No."

"What's wrong?" Standard question number two.

"I can't tell you."

"Is there anything I can do?" Completing the trifecta of ersatz empathy.

"Not really. I'll be fine soon."

The co-worker had her doubts; but she had tried, even if Nancy wasn't really a friend. She returned to her desk and her report.

After Robert got back, he summoned both Finn and Tony, pointing to one of the leaky conference rooms. After settling in, Robert started the questions. "Any sign of our two suspects?"

"No." Tony answered.

"I'm assuming you're checking the tent cities? If a pretext is needed, come up with one. They have to be somewhere in this city. Or maybe close by."

Finn said. "I have some of my contacts looking as well."

"Thomas reminds me again that Archie's gun went missing, so maximum care should be taken with the search. Make sure everyone knows this. After what happened to me in Bella Kind, I'd say we need to tread carefully. Tony, have you learned anything from the basement?"

"I think they have larger brains than people up here."

"Helpful. Anything else?"

"One of them said that the language in the post is similar to what someone in the construction or design business might use. Or city planning."

"This is the original post, painting Anne as less than a one hundred percent ardent supporter of social housing?"

"Yes."

"Any chance of the field being narrowed?"

"They are working on it. May take a few days, but the main problem is that the post isn't extensive. Not a lot to work with."

"Maybe that site guy needs to be interviewed again. The architect I talked with at Hummingbird said that disputes are a way of life during construction. Tony, you and Finn should get out to the Tornado site and see what you can learn. I'll call the city to find out their perspective on the Tornado project." The meeting concluded with Robert wondering whether it was worth the effort to go to Winnipeg to see what he could learn about the short academic career of Mary Tinlit. The problem would be that the people who knew the most about this would be other students, long since gone from the university. The professors might remember something, but more than a few young people attend the courses, and anything useful would more likely come from a fellow student. Perhaps a review of the student roster from those days would be in order, then track a few down and do some interviews.

After a satisfying lunch at Bountiful Noodles on Broadway, Robert called the architecture department at the University of Manitoba from his office.

"This is Robert Lui, detective with the Vancouver Police Department. I am interested in the third-year class of your undergrad degree from six years ago."

"May I ask why that is?"

"One of the class is a suspect in a murder investigation here. Another woman from the class is a murder victim. They may or may not be connected, hence my questions."

"Oh my."

"Yes, not exactly your normal classmates, I would guess."

There was silence while this was digested, then, "What exactly do you want?"

"A very good question. I suppose I'd like to find out where some of the students from that class ended up so I could ask a few questions of them about these women."

"Both are women, then?"

"I'm sorry, yes, they are. One is named Mary Tinlit, and the other is Anne Leforet."

There was more silence, then, "I remember those two, and let me tell you, with the tons of students that go through here, that is saying something. They were both smart and competitive, similar to most of the people let into the program. You understand that once people graduate, they tend to migrate to cities where construction is booming, with commensurate requirements for architects."

"So, in theory, some of them could be in Vancouver?"

"Quite likely, I would say."

"How many students would be in that course?"

"Up to about one hundred and forty might make it in for the first year. Maybe thirty to forty of those would graduate three years later. But that is just the first step. Some of those would then attempt to get into graduate architectural schools, one of which is here. The course is not for the faint of heart."

"Is there any way to find out who might be out here from that class?"

"The graduates often go on to other schools, so in theory, maybe, but it would be difficult."

"Any help or leads to people would be greatly appreciated."

"Tell you what I can do, I'll send you a list of students from that third-year class and maybe you could contact the architectural association in Vancouver. They could probably tell you who might be in your city. But they would only know about the ones trying to become registered architects."

"Sounds like a plan, thanks." With this resolved, Robert left his case and defaulted into fantasy mode, contemplating his upcoming evening with Norma, which, compared to the previous Friday, was bound to be more predictable.

After a trip home to check on his children and change clothes, he drove over to the Marinaside area of Yaletown. He was off taxis after his near death experience several months earlier in the year. He parked in one of the guest stalls of the condominium and went up to Norma's level and pressed the bell. The door opened and Norma leaped onto Robert, wrapping her legs around his hips, her lips firmly planted on his. He managed to close the door with one hand as they slowly lurched toward the living area before falling onto the settee.

Eventually, they slowed. "Would it be possible to get a drink? Whisky of some sort?"

Norma pulled herself off Robert and looked into his eyes. "A drink? Where do you think you are?"

Robert looked around. "Shangri-La, if I'm not mistaken. You should have seen me last Friday." Then Robert mentally kicked himself when he recalled how that Friday had turned out, especially the evening part. He pushed that memory aside, for now, but realized that he was going to need to deal with it eventually, just not tonight.

"It must have been frightening for you."

"Maybe, a tiny bit, but there really wasn't much time for fear. We were too busy trying to save ourselves. And the water was cold, frigid." Robert reflected, then told Norma a detail he shouldn't have. "It also appears someone conducted some sabotage on the plane."

"Someone was trying to kill you?"

"I think so."

"Who?"

"Someone tied to the Archie Hamilton case, I think. Let's talk about something else, Norma."

"Okay. What?" She rose and went to pour herself some more wine, and some whisky for Robert. Once again, she had neglected to cook any dinner, instead ordering in food.

"How would you like to come to my place next Friday for dinner? The children would like to meet Norma van Kleet. They are intensely curious."

"Really. Not surprising, I suppose, assuming you have told them about me? That would be lovely, Robert. How old are they?"

"Teenagers, Norma. Robin and Sophie. You probably remember Robin from the kidnapping a while back. I'll dream up something scrumptious to dine on. What is on offer here? Do I smell pizza?"

From there, the evening dissolved into pizza and sex, interspersed, so that it was hard to tell one pleasure from the next, not that either were keeping a diary of events. The events of

Bella Kind had momentarily and conveniently disappeared from Robert's mind.

Monday came and Robert tried the Housing Department at City Hall, asking who was running the Tornado project. He was given Nancy Brick's and Ricardo Remuda's names once he had identified as a police detective. Not one for pussyfooting around, he called the one he assumed was in charge, Ricardo. He was quickly advised that Nancy was the project manager and would know everything there was to know about Tornado. Ricardo spoke hastily and sounded nervous to Robert.

Robert then called Nancy. "It is Robert Lui calling from the Vancouver Police Department. I would like to meet with you to discuss your project on East Hastings. It's called Tornado House, I believe."

There was silence. Robert waited.

"Why do you want to meet me?" The reply was tenuous.

"Investigating the murder of the project architect, Anne Leforet."

"Oh."

"So, when would be good for me to come by your place?"

More silence.

"Nancy?"

"Tomorrow?"

Was she crying? It certainly sounded that way to Robert. "Fine. What's your address? Ten okay?"

The address was given, reluctantly, Robert gauged, then the line went dead. He shook his head. Something wasn't right with Ms. Brick. Having someone on your project team murdered would be unsettling, at best, but to Robert, it sounded as though something else was going on.

He put this thought aside and turned to studying the list of students he had received from the University of Manitoba. He quickly realized that the class had been winnowed down, just as the person he had been talking to the previous week had indicated. There were about fifty names on the roster. Anne's as well as Mary Tinlit's names were included. His next step would be to contact the local architectural association.

Tony took Finn along for the trip back to the Tornado construction site. He had tired of the bluster affected by the site super, Arby Knutson. Finn was larger than Arby and despite his friendly looking face, could be quite intimidating. After parking on Hastings, they knocked on the trailer door and entered Arby's domain, not waiting for a reply. After Arby told the only other occupant to get lost, the conversation started.

"What can you tell us about Anne Leforet?"

"Prima donna is about the size of it. Although, for an architect, this is not unusual."

"Not impressed, were we?"

"No."

"How was the project going?"

"Normally enough. A lot of changes came through. Never good for a project, financially speaking."

"Were there disputes?"

Arby started to laugh, as though it was the best joke he had heard in a long while. "You don't know much about construction, do you?"

Tony stared at Arby, quiet. "Please, enlighten us."

"I have never heard of a project without disputes. We have weekly site meetings, and usually we are going at it with the architects, or the client rep is. And if it's not them, then we are fighting with our sub-trades."

"Who is the client rep?"

"A Nancy Brick - City of Vancouver. She didn't much like Anne I believe. Thinks Anne was sending the project into the ditch, money-wise."

"Why would she do that? And how?"

"Not on purpose, but she kept making changes, and that always means extra money after the contract is signed. It is one of the reasons projects always cost more than the advertised value. It's just a fact of life. Owners usually have contingency funds, but I suspect in this case, they were getting thin."

"Anyone else have it in for Anne?"

"Not really, at least to my knowledge."

Tony and Finn sat, silent for a moment, then stood. "If you think of anything else, call us." They walked out, not even offering a goodbye.

"I am starting to understand why there are disputes on building sites. No one seems to have respect for anyone else," Tony offered. They headed back to report to Robert.

Later that afternoon, Robert suddenly remembered that he had promised something to his daughter. He called Jean Kwok at the city to see if a meeting could be arranged for some guidance counselling. A Friday was eventually selected for Sophie to come in, a professional development day. A couple of Fridays a semester were allocated as time for teachers to upgrade their skills, in the process, giving the students another day without instruction. That accomplished, he left for the day.

# CHAPTER 12

R obert woke up early, donned his running gear, and finally did something concrete about his fitness. After a strenuous run and back home, he took his time after showering, drinking juice and eating toast, as his first meeting was to be with the City.

He parked at the station and took the short walk up Cambie to the City Housing offices, steeling himself as he walked right past Cafe Paulo. After presenting himself at reception and telling them about his meeting with Nancy Brick, the admin person consulted his phone. It was not a short call.

After several minutes, the young man turned back to him. "I am sorry, sir, but Nancy Brick is not at work today. Are you sure about your meeting date?"

"Yes." Robert took a piece of paper out of his jacket and studied it. "Mr. Remuda, then. I would like to meet with him."

"Do you have an appointment?"

Robert's smile vanished as he took out his business card and slid it across the counter. "It is a murder investigation. Call him."

"Oh, okay."

After Mr. Remuda had fetched Robert and taken him back up to his office, he sat, staring at Robert from across his oversized desk. "How can I help you?" He had black spiky hair atop a dented face straight off a wanted poster.

"Where is Ms. Brick? You gave me her name, didn't you? She was supposed to meet with me this morning. This was arranged only yesterday. But then, Nancy didn't sound totally stable when I was talking with her."

"I believe she is ill today."

"So I have been told. How was her relationship with Anne Leforet on the Tornado project?"

"I don't know."

"You sure about that? She reports to you, correct?"

Ricardo was silent, considering his options, then, "Okay, it wasn't the best. She thought that Anne was putting the project's viability in jeopardy."

"And would Nancy try to do something about that?"

"I don't know. What do you mean?"

"Do you follow social media?" Robert waited for the lie he thought would follow.

"Not much, no. Hardly ever."

As Robert watched, Ricardo started shifting in his chair every few seconds while he talked, its comfort suddenly vanished.

"Someone tarred Anne with a pretty vicious online post. A few days later, she was killed, in a very public fashion. I am wondering if your Ms. Brick would have done the posting?"

Ricardo stayed silent, obviously assessing how much he should say.

"Mr. Remuda?"

Ricardo's hand twitched, knocking over his coffee cup. Coffee ran across his desk, some of it sopped up by a few papers on the surface. Robert couldn't tell if it had been done on purpose or by accident. Either way, he had a strong feeling as to the answer to his question. He pushed his chair back to avoid the streams dropping over the desk edge near his knees.

"Okay. Here is what I'm going to do. I want Nancy Brick's home address and contact information. I will be returning here Friday. If Nancy is present, I'll meet with her. You may sit in if you wish. If she doesn't show, I'll visit her residence and question her there. Sound like a plan?"

"I guess."

"The other option is that she comes down to the station to give her statement. Address?"

Mr. Remuda went onto his computer and copied down the information for Robert, handing it to him, not saying a word. Robert grabbed it and stood up. "I'll let myself out."

As he descended in the elevator, Robert was breathing deeply, trying to calm himself. He wondered if everyone who had to deal with City Hall ran into people like Ricardo Remuda, whose real job, it seemed, was ass-covering, not housing. It was head-shaking stuff. He walked back down Cambie, this time entering Cafe Paulo.

He could only be a saint for so long, especially after his ordeal at Housing. He didn't even experience the joys that he imagined came with sainthood — he could only ponder what it must feel like, to be that worthy. On the other hand, sainthood was usually only confirmed much later in time, and by a particular institution after one's passing, as far as he knew. Maybe sainthood was being overly dramatic. Perhaps he had merely stiffened his resolve for a few moments before it melted away, like it had so many times before. Robert did not tarry, however; drinking his espresso standing up, at the bar, passing a few words with Carmelita, Gilberto being absent.

Back in his office, Robert considered his next steps. He couldn't understand why the two prime suspects in the investigation had yet to be apprehended. They probably knew they were being searched for and were keeping their heads down. But Finn's contacts should be turning up something, a rumour, anything.

He called the local architectural institute to check out the names on his list from the university. After some back and forth, they were able to give him three names who were in the registration process locally. He tried the first name. The phone number looked familiar to him, but he couldn't figure out why until his call was answered.

"Hummingbird Architects, how can I help you?"

"Interesting, I am looking for a Sally Pivonka."

"I'll transfer you."

"Sally speaking."

"My name is Robert Lui, a detective with the Vancouver Police. I am interested in learning what I can about your recently lost principal, Anne, as well as a Mary Tinlit. Could we meet somewhere to discuss this?"

There was silence for several seconds. "I guess so. When?"

"This afternoon?"

"We are kind of busy today."

"It's important. I can come to your office if that makes it easier. This shouldn't take very long. Do you have a room we can use?"

"Okay, yes."

"See you around three o'clock then."

Sally hung up, while Robert thought about the chances of one of his contacts working for the murder victim. Something seemed weird. He also wondered how objective Sally's viewpoint was going to be given that Anne was one of her bosses. He stood up and looked out onto the floor, but couldn't see either Tony or Finn. Pursuing enquiries, he supposed. It was well past lunch, so he'd head downtown and grab something before his meeting with Sally on Homer Street.

After wrangling his way past the receptionist at Hummingbird by showing his card, he was led to a very smartly outfitted meeting room, totally unlike anything existing in his office building. He was in awe. A long, curved wood table of indeterminate species centred a collection of chairs that appeared to be a product of NASA. A large video screen on the wall indicated possible connection with anybody and everybody. Photos of sharp-looking buildings laddered down a side wall beside a glazed partition. After a few minutes, a well-dressed young woman, with short blond hair combed to one side, entered.

He stood up. "Sally, I assume? I am Robert Lui." He extended his hand.

"Yes, pleased to meet you." She asked Robert to take a chair and sat across from him, extending her business card. "What do you wish to know?"

Robert appreciated the directness, so rare. He also appreciated the chair. Why didn't they have some like these in his office?

"You were in a class at the University of Manitoba with both Mary Tinlit and Anne several years ago. I'd like to know what went on between those two, if possible. And I am also curious as to how you came to be working for Anne, given that you were in the same class at some point."

"I'll answer the second one first, if you don't mind. Anne was driven. She wanted her own firm from the beginning, which is fairly audacious, in this field. You probably already know that she went to Harvard for her Masters' degree after Manitoba."

"Yes, I do. And I know it is very expensive." He raised his eyebrows.

"Family money, I think."

"Why didn't she go straight there then?"

"You need a degree first. It is a graduate design school, and she was from Winnipeg, so Manitoba it was, for the undergrad. It has a good rep."

Robert shook his head at the complexities of higher education. Hopefully, he would learn something to help his daughter. "They have Planning at Manitoba?"

"Yes, they do. Again, it's a graduate school." Sally continued. "Once Anne had her Masters, she came out here and met up with her partner, both working their first jobs at a small local design firm. She tore through the courses and exams to become registered, which you must be to have your own firm. It isn't easy, and many graduates decide not to pursue it after they realize what it entails. Or they quit halfway through the process."

"Is this what happened to you?"

"I took my time, considering my options, but I am now enrolled in the registration program. It is frankly difficult, and for what we get paid, I am finding out that the liability is onerous."

"How did you come to be working in this office?"

"Word of mouth is how this profession works, like most professions, I would imagine. The University of Manitoba has a good reputation, as I said, and I knew Anne from school. When people hire, they go with what they know. I did my master's at Manitoba."

"And working for a former classmate? That didn't put you off?"

"No."

"Mary Tinlit. What can you tell me?"

There was silence for several moments. Maybe Sally was figuring out what to keep close. It was difficult to read her.

"Anne and Mary seemed to be friendly at first, but by third year, it was open warfare. I don't know what caused the change, or where they got the extra energy to spend on pranks. Frankly, we spent all our time and effort working on design projects."

"What kind of pranks?"

"Oh, you know, regular stuff. Except it wasn't well received by either of the two girls. Anne got hold of some official stationery from the faculty, and wrote a letter to Mary saying that she had won a scholarship, something to do with being native, I think. Mary was ecstatic, and told her family about it, then started spending the remainder of what little money she had, confident that all her financial woes were history. After a month, she found out that not only did she not get the scholarship, but that no such honour even existed. It didn't take her long to figure out who was behind it."

"How did she react?"

"She pulled her own trick. She withdrew Anne from the course."

"She what?"

"Yeah. Mary pulled her out of university. It took a couple of weeks for Anne to find out, but she was not amused. Then things got physical. Mary suffered a broken arm in a ditchball game, courtesy of Anne, who said it was an accident. No one was buying that, of course."

"Ditchball?"

Sally smiled. "You can look it up online. It's an annual event put on by architecture students in the middle of winter, and it is physical, even dangerous. Someone usually gets hurt every year. The odd thing is that they were on the same team. Anyway, Mary pulled out of the course at that point and scurried back to BC. Never did graduate to my knowledge. Which was odd, because most of the dropping out happened in the first two years. By the third year the professors were actually helping the students and one could reasonably expect to graduate."

Robert shook his head, then looked through the glass partition at other people, all studying their computer screens. "Nice office you have here."

"There are some perks in this business. We need to present a good face for the clients."

"I think I have the general drift of the girl's relationship, so I'll let you get on with your day. Wait, one other question for you. What can you tell me about mechanical pencils?"

Sally's eyebrows wrinkled. "I can tell you that no one uses them anymore. It is all computers, all the time. The pencils are archaic, from a time when drawings were done by hand. Those days weren't all that long ago either, but it is almost like a distant era, now."

"Were the pencils used in school?"

"Yes, when I was there, but only peripherally, in one or two of the courses. Why do you ask?"

"Can't say. Thanks for your time, Sally." He slid his card over to her. "In case you remember anything else. I'll let myself out."

Ditchball? This case was getting stranger by the minute. Robert chose to walk the Cambie Bridge over False Creek back to the office, wanting some extra time alone. It was not a short walk. When he finally returned to the floor, Norma beckoned to him.

"Yes, Norma, what may I do for you?" He smiled.

"A certain Robert Lui is overdue for his yearly firearms proficiency test. One has been booked for you this Thursday over at the Training Centre."

"Craps." The smile evaporated.

"How eloquent."

"Might be slightly rusty, is all. Could you book me some practice time tomorrow?"

"I suppose. What will be on the menu this Friday, Robert?"

He smiled again. "Great food, and sparkling conversation, Norma." He realized that he better start preparing for the upcoming dinner. It had slipped his mind. "Any sign of Tony, or Finn?"

"No, I haven't seen them all day."

"Okay, I'm heading home then. See you when I see you." He had some menu planning to do.

Robert didn't show his face on Cambie Street, Wednesday. He spent the morning at home, going through the cleaning and safety operations for his service pistol. After he was satisfied with his maintenance procedures, he headed over to the Tactical Training Centre for some practice.

A year ago, he wouldn't have worried about the test, but things slipped when your mind was on cases, and women, not in that order. He didn't need a failure on his record. It already contained enough notations to write a short story. He had two other firearms at home, but he had not disclosed either of them to the VPD, so he wouldn't be firing them on Thursday.

He showed up at the Training Centre in the early afternoon and proceeded to set up for some target practice in the range. He was about to put on his ear protection, his gun on the ledge in front of him, when an older officer came over to him.

"You're Robert Lui, correct?"

"That's right, and you are?"

"Doesn't matter. How's Archie's investigation going? You are one of those guys in that cafe photo, aren't you?"

"Investigation is going fine, thanks for your concern." Robert turned away, donned his gear, and picked us his gun. He was about to start firing when he noticed that the officer hadn't moved, still staring at him. Robert slid his earmuffs back down around his neck.

"Something else?"

"You guys are real pieces of work. Archie was one of us, and you're treating the whole thing like it's a carnival."

"Tell me Mr. Doesn't Matter, do you know when that picture was taken? Because, if you don't, then why don't you go screw yourself?" He then re-adjusted his muffs and started to fire. After a few seconds, he noticed that the man bothering him had turned and left. Robert was so angry that most of his shots didn't even hit the paper target, let alone the head profile he was aiming at. After expending a few more clips, his accuracy not improving, he called it a day.

When he returned home, he realized that he couldn't afford the same thing happening the next day. He needed to calm down. Elevated blood pressure wasn't helping things. He suspected that the people running the qualification would not be cutting him any slack, probably the opposite. Not that he was worried about his skills, but he realized that he was going to need to shut the world out at the range until he passed.

Robert normally wouldn't keep ledgers, life being too short for such pettiness, but he was making an exception for Mr. Rodney Fister.

The next morning, Robert ate a full breakfast, and made a pot of coffee, all to put him at ease before he drove over to the Training Centre. Despite his trepidation, and the obvious frostiness by some of the range personnel conducting the tests, he passed everything on the first attempt. He smiled at the range master as he departed, happy to have this ordeal behind him. The smile was not returned, but that wasn't Robert's problem.

He headed over to Cambie Street, where he hoped to find out the search progress for the two suspects from Tony or Finn. As he walked onto the floor and by Norma, he grinned.

"Pass?"

He stopped. "They have never seen more accurate shooting. They were calling me Billie the Kid."

"Right."

"I've also firmed up the menu for tomorrow. Seven okay? Earlier if you wish."

Norma returned the smile, then studied her desk.

Robert looked at the work pods in the middle of the floor. Still no detectives, so he went to his office and called Tony's cell. Rain had started up again. He watched the veins of water coursing across his window as the phone rang several times before going to message. Concern was growing, but he supposed that Tony would appear when he was good and ready. Perhaps he was feeling somewhat cocky, his status as a detective enlarging his head one or two sizes. Wouldn't be the first time it happened with a newly promoted officer.

He looked at the other case files on his desk. Time to pay some attention to his other work if his murder cases weren't cooperating. He spent the remainder of the afternoon finalizing some case reports, then left, satisfied that he had put a dent in the backlog. But the concern about Tony was not fading away.

# Chapter 13

Friday morning saw Robert at his desk early. Around nine, he called up Nancy Brick and confirmed that she was in her office. Robert told her to stay put, he'd be over directly. He walked up Cambie, and after dealing with the main floor reception, he was required to wait for Nancy to come down to escort him back up to her work area. Robert was getting used to this security precaution at City Hall offices, but still didn't like it. He didn't know the reasoning behind it, but perhaps an enraged developer had tried to throttle a planner in the past. He could easily imagine this happening.

Nancy led Robert up to a meeting room on her floor and took a seat across from Robert. Her eyes darted around, unfocussed.

"Thanks for seeing me." He did not mention her failure to appear earlier in the week. "Will Mr. Remuda be joining us?"

"Uh, no. What do you wish to know?" Nancy led off.

"The Tornado housing project. Odd name. How did that come about?" Robert tried some deflection to start.

"When a tornado hits, it rips your life apart, as well as your home, sometimes. We chose the name as a way of standing up to such a disaster, saying that the people who will call this building home are tougher than any disaster, and will put their lives back in order," Nancy finished triumphantly.

Robert stared at Nancy, baffled by her attempt at logic, then shook his head ever so slightly. "How was your relationship with Anne Leforet?"

"What do you mean?"

"You hired her firm for the Tornado project. Is that correct?"

"Yes."

"And the project was going well?"

"Not really."

Robert stared at her, waiting for more. When nothing further was added, he tired of the charade. "We believe that you were the one who posted the unflattering message about Anne, just before she was killed."

Reaction was immediate. Nancy burst into tears. Not one to get in the way of a confession, Robert waited, playing the hard-boiled cop.

"I didn't mean for it to turn out like it did." Her sobbing continued, but softened.

"What did you mean, then, exactly?"

"The project was developing problems, and I thought people should know why."

"So, Anne Leforet was to blame? Is this correct?"

"I believed so."

"Apparently, someone else believed what you posted." He stood up.

"Am I in trouble?"

"What do you think?"

Tears were rolling down her face. "I think maybe I am."

"Yes, maybe you are." He turned, rose, and left the room, heading for the elevator, no sympathy on offer this day. He didn't have much of a handle on whether Nancy was legally responsible or not. He would let her stew over it. Maybe it would put her off posting entirely, but Robert wasn't confident in this kind of miracle occurring in the social media world.

He left the City Hall and made tracks for Cafe Paulo. On his way, he tried Tony again. This time, the call was answered. "Tony, you okay? I'm heading to our cafe. Meet me if you can."

"Sure, see you shortly."

Robert entered the cafe and waved at Gilberto, who was busy with a young customer. He looked down the bar at what should have been Carmelita, but it wasn't. It seemed that she had been transformed into a barista with a distinctly Asian background.

When Gilberto finished, Robert went over to him. "Where is Carmelita?" He felt it was his duty to keep apprised of any and all changes at Cafe Paulo.

"Travelling in South America for a few weeks. Yuko is filling in."

Robert remained silent, staring at Yuko, then ordered two Americanos. "Tony is joining me." He explained when

Gilberto gave him a questioning look. "Carmelita is coming back, right?"

"Of course." Gilberto wasn't used to being questioned about his staffing decisions, his brow slightly wrinkled.

Robert went to his favourite table, waiting for Tony and the coffee, not in that order.

A few minutes later, Tony walked in, followed by Finn.

Robert waved at them, then his order was called. He went to the bar and returned with the two coffees, which he placed gently in front of his co-workers. He signalled over to Yuko for another one, then turned his attention to the previously missing pair of detectives.

"Where have you been? Thought maybe you had both quit or something," Robert asked.

"Pursuing enquiries. We have visited every tent camp and rooming house we can find. No luck," Finn started.

"Keeping their heads down, or left town." Robert looked at the others' cups.

"The boys downstairs have been monitoring an online site that is connected to the housing protests. Seems to be the starting point for organizing things. Something is percolating, so we may get lucky shortly," Tony added.

"You mean another protest?"

"It seems so."

"We'll need to be careful. If it is this Allo Foot, he may be armed."

Tony smiled. "Nothing we can't handle, Robert."

"Anything from your contacts in the community?" Robert looked at Finn.

He shook his head. "It is very odd."

"I wonder how they get their money. They can't operate without it. Maybe you should look into social services, see how cheques are distributed. How are you guys otherwise?"

"Still getting some flak from that Rodney post," Tony replied.

"Yes, me also. I was qualifying at the range the last couple of days. Reception was frosty. I told one guy what he could do with himself. Probably didn't help things, but there you go. I've always said, our worst enemies are within the force."

Tony looked outside. "Happy now?"

"What? The rain? Yes, I am happy. It makes things grow."

"I agree. The land needs it." Finn added, "This is good coffee today."

"Now you know why I spend time here. I visited the city project manager today for the Tornado job. She was the one who posted the rant about Anne."

"She admitted it?"

"Pretty much. There is no doubt she was the one."

"Guess I can tell the people in the basement to work on something else," Tony responded.

Robert stared down at his coffee, then spilled some gossip. "I'm having Norma over tonight for dinner. The kids are curious."

Tony and Finn smiled at each other. "Well, hope it goes well, Robert." Tony said.

With that nugget of information out in the open, Robert decided it was time to finish up and head back.

The rest of the day passed quietly, except for one call, from Bella Kind.

"Robert, Walter here. I believe that Roger's flying career is finished. Not only was his maintenance work less than stellar, but he also seemed to miss his pre-flight plane inspections. Three holes in the under carriage would be the kind of thing you might find if you were the least bit diligent."

"I don't think Roger would be the only pilot in the world to miss that task. I was in a boarding lounge at YVR a while back and, looking out at the plane, saw a man in uniform on the tarmac, walking around the jet just before we were to board. It looked odd, then I realized it was the pilot, doing his due diligence. But, in all my flying career, only saw it the one time. Guess the other pilots rely on faith."

"That is about all I have to report."

"Any progress on the culprit?"

"Not really."

Robert wasn't surprised at the answer, "Okay, take care." He hung up and left the office early to provision up and get things ready for the big night.

After arriving home, he asked his children to help with clean up while he arranged the food, laying vegetables on the counter and the fish in the fridge. He poured some wine and prepped the vegetables. Dinner was going to be light tonight: Arctic Char on the grille, with rice, and a wilted cucumber salad. The starters would consist of smoked salmon, a couple of cheeses, and baguettes. Three teens came over and stood around, watching Robert work. He prepared a marinade of soy sauce and maple syrup to slide over the fish.

"Okay, if all you do is set the table, that would be a great help." With that, they sprang into action, seemingly let off the hook as far as cleaning things went. He opened up a bag of chips for them, knowing how voracious they could be.

When the food was prepped and ready, Robert went up to change. His phone bleeped with a text. Norma was just leaving Yaletown.

"Norma will be here in less than twenty minutes." He yelled. Was he feeling slightly nervous? He supposed it was only natural. There was a bit riding on this dinner.

Twenty minutes later, the doorbell rang. Robert opened the door to Norma.

She smiled. "We are in the neighbourhood. Wondered if you need your lawn aerated?"

Robert looked past Norma. "I don't own any lawn, but you look hungry. Care to come in for a bite?" He was laughing. She moved forward, grabbed his head, and kissed Robert, knowing that would be it for the evening as far as physical pleasures went.

"I'd be delighted, thank you. Could my crew come in as well?"

"Don't think so."

Robert took Norma's coat and entered the family part of the home. "This is Norma." The three teens got off the couch and turned.

"Hi, I'm Sophie. This is Robin and Rose. Pleased to meet you." Sophie came forward to shake hands.

Norma was confused. "Robert, you told me you had two children, now I am seeing three."

"Oops, guess I'm getting forgetful. Rose is a fast friend of Sophie's. They are inseparable most times."

"Okay, I am also pleased to finally meet you. Robert has told me a few things about you." Norma smiled as she said this. "All good, by the way."

Sophie immediately started with the questions, "Are you a policewoman?"

"No, Sophie. I am what is called a civilian administrative assistant. I help out Robert's boss, and try to control all people working under him, including your father. It isn't easy, let me tell you."

"I completely understand, Norma."

"Hey, who wants some wine?" Robert was not a fan of how the conversation was going. "Here are a couple of whites, which hopefully go with the fish tonight. I'll prep a sauce for the smoked salmon, then join you. Robin, can you lay out the cheeses? Thanks."

Robert had prepared Norma by mentioning Sophie's ideas about studying city planning after finishing high school. As the evening progressed, he realized that Norma was deft in her questioning of the three teenagers, teasing out some aspirations that even he had not known about. One of those was Rose's dream to become a doctor. Robert announced that he was lighting the grill and starting the rice maker. No one seemed to be paying attention, which was just fine. He was grateful that the kids were engaged with Norma. Most teenagers would have preferred to be anywhere else on Friday evening, possibly looking for trouble.

"And how are you doing Robin? You are still quite famous around the station." Norma was referring to his kidnapping a year earlier when Robert had been chasing gang members around the Lower Mainland.

Robin smiled, loving the attention in front of Rose. "I am fine. No nightmares. It was mostly boring, with bad food. I think I got off easy."

"He is being modest. Gets it from me," Robert said. "Trying to escape from kidnappers is not something most people would have the courage to do." He was only trying to make Robin look good in front of Rose. An escape attempt is not something he would have counselled Robin to attempt. He would rather talk about almost anything else. "I enrolled them in a self-defence course offered by the Justice Institute a couple of months ago, so if there is a next time..." He changed topics. "Can you cut up the baguette please, Robin?"

"No problem, Pops."

From there, the food came out and the evening went smoothly. Robert had even remembered to get a tart for dessert, a rare move for him. His tooth was not sweet, so he rarely ate dessert.

"Sophie, how old are you? Are you driving yet?" Norma wasn't finished as she tipped her empty wine glass in Robert's direction. Robert re-filled her glass as he glared at Norma. He only had one car, not the most recent vintage, but he valued it.

"I'm eighteen. I've been thinking about it, but not many of my friends are driving yet."

"I guess it's different these days. When I was younger, everyone couldn't wait to get their licence, usually by sixteen."

"Driving doesn't seem to be all that great here in Vancouver. None of my friends are keen about it, so far." Sophie looked sideways at Rose, knowing she felt the same way.

Norma glanced at Robert, noting the less than friendly eyes. "Well, there are lots of options to get around these days, aren't there" Robert's face softened. "Any dessert tonight, Robert?"

"It is a miracle, I will grant you, but yes, we have a lemon tart. Would you like to do the honours, Sophie?"

After dessert was finished, and the remainder of the wine bottles emptied, Norma thought it time to get back to Yaletown. "It was a great pleasure meeting all of you, but I must get back home before all the ride hailing company's vehicles turn into pumpkins."

"It was nice to finally meet you as well, Norma." Sophie spoke for the two others.

"Think you could get the driver to drop Rose off as well, on your way?" Robert asked. He was still nervous about the kids walking around in the dark after the events of a year ago.

"It's okay, Pops. We can walk Rose home later." Robin came to life. Sophie looked over at him, but nodded her assent.

The evening ended for Robert as he kissed Norma goodbye — at least the fun part did. He surveyed the mess in the dining area and kitchen, thankful the next day was Saturday.

# CHAPTER 14

Monday morning, back in his office, Robert called Bella Kind. "Hi, it's Robert. Think you could do us a favour, Walter?"

"Sure thing."

"We'd like a fingerprint from young Allo Foot, if we may. We want to check a few things."

"Let me puzzle as to how to get this. As I think I told you, his family aren't on the island anymore and he kept his nose clean while growing up here. I'll send it on if I find something."

This didn't sound very likely to Robert. "Thanks Walter."

"One other thing. The chef from across the water was over here asking after you."

"Oh. What did you say?"

"Nothing. I don't know much about you, do I?"

"Guess not," said Robert. "Let's keep it that way for a while, okay?"

"Sure. I'll get on that task for you."

It sounded as though Sandra was not finished with Robert. He sighed, then went over to the bullpen area to collect Finn and Tony to make their way down to where the police cyber-operations were conducted. Finn had visited several times, but this was a first for Robert.

There were four younger officers in the room, all staring at screens, two apiece. Two of the officers were female, which puzzled Robert. He assumed that any cyber expert would be male. Just another prejudice, he supposed. Some posters advertising music groups that Robert had never heard of adorned the pale green walls. All four officers appeared not to have seen daylight in years, their skin a paler shade of white, perhaps a result of the fluorescent lighting.

"Ladies and gentlemen. How are you? You already know me and Tony, but this is Detective Lui." Finn made the introductions. Curiosity was evident on the faces as they turned towards the detectives. Robert had a certain reputation, or several reputations, to be accurate.

"I suppose you have heard what has happened the last several weeks. We'd like to find out about coming attractions, aka, any upcoming protests. And I'll tell you straight out, that I am not a follower of social media, at all," Robert said.

What appeared to be the youngest of the crew spoke. "I'm Rory. We've been following a chat group that seems to be composed of some Marxist-Leninists mixed up with a native group. I don't know what they have in common, but they are planning another housing protest, in two days, we think."

"You know where?"

"Might be up the street outside the city's housing offices, but we are not certain. The other possibility is the social housing project where that architect was found out Hastings Street, Tornado."

"How did you get into the chat room?" Finn asked. "Aren't those places secure?"

"Well, yes, they can be, but in this case, the group seems to be encouraging new participants, the more, the better. They don't seem to be overly concerned with security, so far, anyway."

"Do you have any names for us?" Robert asked.

"They use pseudonyms. There are about fifteen regular participants."

"Are they chatting now?"

"Yup. You want to watch?"

"Please."

"Let's get these guys chairs, and some coffee." Rory thrilled at the sudden interest in his group's work.

"I'll take the chair, but forget the coffee, thanks." Robert sat down. Office coffee was strictly a non-starter for Robert. Both Finn and Tony preferred to remain standing, to one side.

"So, as a participant, who are you? What is your story?" Finn asked.

"I am Red Hammer, from the Upper Nicola Band. I got beat up by a cop in Merritt, so I have a large chip on my shoulder," Rory answered.

Finn nodded. Robert read as the conversation rolled up the screen, much of it moronic. "Do you record this stuff?"

"Yes, we have tons of crap in our archives."

"I'll bet you do. Wait a minute...." Robert studied the screen. "Who is Bigfoot?"

"Haven't a clue. We don't know who any of these people are."

"My money would be on our Allo Foot."

"I don't know, people rarely use any part of their real name in their online names."

"Well, frankly, these people don't seem too bright, so, is it possible?"

"Suppose." The young officer looked at the others. They all shrugged. Robert watched more of the scrolling conversations, some of it profanity laced.

"So, how do you know that some of these people are Marxist, or native for that matter?"

"Content analysis. Some of the participants spend enough time on their messaging that we can get a fix on probable affiliations."

"Content analysis, this is the second time the subject has come up. How do you know about it? I reviewed the topic, and it seems to be something from over fifty years ago."

"Doesn't make it any less valid as a tool. We picked it up as part of our training. Very little on the internet is as advertised, as you probably already know, so we need to be devious in our analysis."

Robert looked up at Finn, his eyebrow raised. Finn shrugged. Robert tired of watching after a few moments and stood up. "Please let us know about the protest, as soon as you find out anything, thanks." He nodded to Finn and Tony, pointing up. Then he thought of something, turning back to the group. "Have any of you done time for cyber-crime?"

Four heads shook slowly from side to side, no audible answer on offer.

"How about charged?"

Rory answered for them. "We went through all this when we were hired."

"So, that is a maybe?"

"Possibly."

"Good. Just checking to see if you guys are any good. Thanks." He grabbed Finn's arm, and they returned up to their floor, thankful for the luxury of having a view to the outside world.

"How did you know to ask about that?" said Tony.

"Would you trust the hiring practices around here? Excluding us, of course."

"Good point. So, they might be halfway decent?"

"Hopefully. We'll soon find out."

Robert came in Wednesday morning, but couldn't sit in his office. He was antsy, expecting a demonstration somewhere in the city. He paced around the floor, then headed to the basement to check on his new friends. They all looked over at him. "Any word on the protest?"

"A minute ago. Looks like East Hastings, near that Tornado project. It is slated for eleven this morning." Rory responded.

Robert looked at his watch. "Okay, thanks. I'll notify upstairs. Let me know if you learn anything else. Text or call me."

He returned to his floor and motioned for Finn and Tony to follow him into Thomas's office. "Another protest, out Hastings. We're going to attend and take a few more plainclothes officers if we may. One or both of our suspects may be there."

"Fine by me. You better have uniforms ready to go in after you do your recon work. Things may get nasty if you arrest someone before they really get going," Thomas said.

"We'll see you later, then." Robert signalled Finn and Tony to follow him as he went into the bullpen to round up a few junior detectives. "Protest on East Hastings. Who is interested?"

Robert smiled as every officer present raised a hand. "We are heading to the Tornado housing project." He filled them in on the details, warned Norma about the upcoming traffic disturbance, then headed to the parkade for some transport. Once again, Robert declined to drive, wanting to be able to concentrate on the surroundings, so Finn gladly volunteered. One other officer made a fourth in their car. The remainder were in a second car.

"Everyone armed?" Robert asked, being the mother to the junior officer.

"We got the memo about the suspects." The fourth officer replied from the rear seat.

Finn drove slowly east along Hastings, the traffic growing heavier as the protest shut down the flow of vehicles. He turned off Hastings, parking on a side street, a block short of where the protesters had set up camp. It wasn't raining yet, but the dark skies were threatening to unleash something special. The four detectives moved back to Hastings and made their way slowly along the sidewalks, splitting up as they moved, blending in with the crowd that had gathered. More patrol cars pulled up, ostensibly to provide some traffic management. Two of the uniformed officers went over to what seemed to be the core of the protesters to have a word and find out their intentions. Robert hung back, eyeing every person in the crowd, looking for any sign of Allo or Mary.

The protest group was setting up for a fire in the traffic lane closest to the Tornado construction site. The construction trailer was only a couple of metres from the sidewalk. Robert watched as a small metal cauldron was loaded with wood and set alight. The youngsters stepped back as flames exploded, obviously having been juiced up by something extremely inflammable. Robert felt a couple of raindrops hit his face.

He looked over at another small group of young people, standing on the opposite side of the street, probably protesters, but it was uncertain, as they had no signs with them. One of them was staring back at Robert, even though they were some thirty metres away. Robert kept his eyes on the young man, who didn't look away. He sported crewcut black hair, and even at thirty metres, his dark eyes were as intense as any Robert had seen. Robert tried to put an ethnicity to the man, but failed. He could have been South Asian, Indigenous, or Oriental. Maybe all three, it was impossible to tell.

He was about to pull his phone out to nab a picture of the man when the door to the construction trailer banged open. Robert looked back. Three burly men came out, led by the superintendent, Arby. They walked out to the street, heading straight for the cauldron, and kicked it over. Flaming wood and sparks spewed all over the road. The protesters started screaming and yelling at Arby and his men, something about defiling a sacred fire. The only thing keeping violence from breaking out were the uniformed officers standing close by.

Arby replied with his own rant. "How are we supposed to make any progress on building social housing with all you morons blocking access to our site?"

Robert supposed he had a point. The uniforms were waiting to see how the scene would play out, interested that someone had done something they were forbidden to do. Robert returned his gaze to the group where the staring man was, but he had vanished. However, bingo! In the man's place stood Allo Foot. Robert looked over at Finn and waved briefly, pointing at their prey. Allo was talking calmly to another protester, seemingly oblivious to what was about to happen to him.

Finn barely nodded at the two other detectives, and they spread out, moving slowly over to the group. Robert touched an officer's arm, warning him of what was about to happen. The officer communicated with the others spread out along Hastings, preparing in case the arrest went off kilter. Robert stayed put, searching the crowds for any sign of Mary. The rain was thickening, the pavement starting to darken, then glistening with the dancing lights of the police vehicles. Officers came for Allo from the front and his rear. As he finally realized his peril, he turned and walked right into Tony's arms. Tony hadn't drawn his weapon but its safety was off, just in case.

Allo started to yell. "You have no right to arrest me. We haven't done anything." Other protesters moved closer, yelling at the detectives, uncertain as to what was happening. A tight group formed around the two detectives and one uniform that had a grip on Allo. As other officers moved closer, Tony loudly informed the group that Allo was being arrested for a murder investigation. This caused them to loosen and step back, momentarily confused. It was enough for a couple of uniformed officers to break through, grab Allo and head to a car.

Robert watched the action at a distance, his head swivelling, still on the lookout for Mary. He looked east, down Hastings, and thought he saw the young man who had stared at him earlier, but the rain was coming down so hard that it was impossible to tell. A yelling confrontation was still playing out in front of the construction trailer, some officers trying to mediate. The fire was truly extinguished by this point and the entire affair was losing its lustre, as the heavens finally opened up. Robert concluded that getting Allo was all they were going to accomplish, so he headed back to the car, got in, and waited for the other three sodden detectives.

"Well done, gentlemen. We now have suspect number one in Archie's killing." The other three had piled in, and grinned as Finn started the engine for the return trip to Cambie. "Maybe that social bullshit thing has a use after all." Robert added.

"We'll have you signed up for Facebook before you know it, Robert." Tony replied.

"Not likely, Tony. I'm going to need some time getting Archie's file in order before I go see the prosecutor. Don't want Allo slipping away, do we?" The rest of the officers murmured their assent. The air was thick with the smell of wet overcoats, so Robert lowered his window, ignoring the water flying into the car as they speeded back west.

"Were there any news people at the event?" Robert asked.

"I saw a van pulling up as we left." Finn said. "One of the private stations, I think."

"Okay. Think I'll call Bernard, for services rendered to date." The junior detective sitting next to Robert in the rear seat looked puzzled.

Finn caught the look in the mirror, so he explained. "Things have prices, which need to be paid." This really didn't clarify anything to the detective, but he supposed it was all part of learning the ropes.

# Chapter 15

Upon their return to the station, Robert retreated to his office, but not before letting Thomas know about their success on East Hastings.

"Well done, Robert."

"Still need to track down that Mary character, but at least we have the killer locked up." He was revelling in the partial success. "Maybe those wankers will cut us some slack now. I have to organize myself before seeing the prosecutor." Thomas nodded as Robert departed.

Robert settled into his office chair and rang Bernard. "Bernard, you may or may not have heard about the disturbance up Hastings Street this morning."

"Another demonstration, correct? A different crew is covering it today for us."

"Hope they are wearing their waterproof scarves out there. It is miserable. Not why I'm calling, however. We have a suspect in custody for the Archie Hamilton murder. That's all I can say for now, but thought you could be the first to know."

"From the demonstration?"

"Yes."

"Wow, thanks Robert."

"Don't mention it. I'll be in contact." He rang off, and sat there, feeling pleased with himself as he gazed out the window at rain lashing the glass.

After several moments of woolgathering, he shook his head. He needed to compose a list of evidence tying Allo to the Archie murder. After a couple of hours at this, he realized he was short on hard evidence. Most of his case was circumstantial. He felt in his bones that Allo was the culprit, but how to convince a prosecutor? He went out to the bullpen area to see if the others could help fill in the missing pieces. A couple of bravos rang out from the younger officers, obviously pleased that Archie's killer had been caught.

Tony hung up his phone. "Hey Robert, guess whose fingerprint was on that business card I pulled from Anne Leforet?"

"Let me think.... Allo's?"

"Bingo. Matches his prints from being processed."

"Guiltier and guiltier by the minute." Forgotten was Robert's evidence problem for the moment. "We'll interview Allo tomorrow morning, then lay charges. I want to get a feel for this bastard. Do we have anything else linking Allo to Anne's murder as yet?" Robert asked.

"No prints were pulled off anything else found at the site," Finn responded.

"Anyone figure out where this guy was living recently? It'd be good to turn the place over, see if there is any rope around matching what was used at the scenes."

"He hasn't revealed much so far." Tony said. "And there was nothing on him at the time of arrest that ties him to either scene. No weapon either."

"Hmm. We need him to fess up as to where Mary is. Once we have her, I'd say we would be ninety percent done." Robert looked around. "I think I'm going to head home. Need to think. I'd go for a walk, but...." He nodded at the storm outside, which wasn't letting up. He returned to his office, grabbed his briefcase, and left.

As he drove home, he pondered how his team were going to fill in the evidence holes in the murder cases. If charges weren't filed, Allo would be walking free. Nothing revealed itself on the wet drive home, so he parked his thoughts and concentrated on dinner and his children.

Next morning, still elated with how things were going on his case, Robert arrived at his office and asked Tony when the Allo interview had been set up for.

"Half-past nine. He'll have a court-appointed lawyer present." Tony's eyebrows were raised.

Robert shook his head, knowing what Tony was assuming. "We'll go for coffee after the interview." He needed to arrange his thoughts before grilling Allo. "I believe I will take Finn with me for this one. Sorry, Tony."

"I get it, no worries."

At half-past nine, Robert beckoned Finn and they made their way down to the interview room. Allo was sitting beside his publicly funded defence lawyer. Allo looked up at the detectives, a puzzled look pasted on his face.

Robert dropped his manila file on the table and didn't waste any time, speaking as he took a seat. "Do you know why you are here?"

"No."

"A policeman by the name of Archie Hamilton was murdered a few weeks back. And in a most gruesome way. You are here being questioned because of that. Charges of first degree murder are being contemplated, which is what happens when you kill a cop." He looked directly into Allo's eyes.

"I didn't do that."

"But you know who Archie is, right?"

"Never heard of the name."

"Not going to fly, Allo. I've visited Bella Kind. I know your back story. Want to rethink your answer?"

Now it was the lawyer's turn to look puzzled. Allo cupped his hand as he leaned over to whisper to his lawyer. Robert smiled to himself. He knew the audio taping system would pick up anything said in the room, no matter how careful suspects thought they were being. The lawyer said something back to Allo.

"Okay, I knew Archie, but I did not kill him."

"So, you lie, then not? You were there the night he died. Your girlfriend was leading Archie to his doom. We have video."

"I don't have a girlfriend."

Robert looked over at the lawyer. "I don't suppose Mr. Foot will tell you, so I will. He enjoys lying. Much like his friend from Bella Kind, Mary Tinlit. If you are going to represent this character, your work will definitely be cut out for you." The lawyer didn't respond, so Robert continued, looking at Allo. "I've heard you and Mary are not an item anymore, but things change, and revenge is a powerful motivator."

The lawyer shifted in his chair. "Do you have any actual evidence that my client did this?"

Robert ignored him. "Where is Mary?"

"Don't know."

"We also have your fingerprint at a second crime scene — Anne Leforet's murder. You've had quite the busy few weeks, Allo."

Both detectives watched Allo's eyebrows scrunch together, as though he had been asked a most mind-bending question.

"Who?"

"Anne Leforet, the architect for the Tornado project, where we picked you up yesterday." Finn said.

"I don't know her."

"Why was your fingerprint on the business card in her pocket, then?"

The lawyer was staring at Allo, head slightly tilted.

"I don't know."

Robert countered. "We know you blamed Archie for the death of your father."

Allo looked down at the table, as if divination could emanate from it. "That was Mary. She was the one pushing all along."

This correlated with what Robert had learned up on Raven Island.

"So, you were fine with it all? That's a bit rich. Is Mary the murderer?"

Allo continued staring at the table. Robert and Finn waited silently.

"Maybe, I don't know."

Robert had had enough. "Interview is suspended for now."

The lawyer came to life. "Are you releasing my client?"

As Robert and Finn walked out the door, Robert answered without looking back. "To remand." Then they were gone. The detectives walked the stairs up to their floor where Robert beckoned Tony to join them for the journey up Cambie.

The trio settled into their chairs at Cafe Paulo and Robert looked at Finn. "What did you make of that?"

"Hiding something. What it is, I don't know." Finn lifted his cup, taking a sip.

"There was a young man staring at me yesterday, at the protest. As if he knew me, or knew about me."

"Get a photo?" Tony asked.

"Unfortunately, not. I wonder if the contractor has video coverage of the street. Can you check, Tony?" He nodded.

"The public defender seemed slightly clueless."

"Maybe they just met?" Finn said.

"Probably." Robert stared at the sidewalk traffic. "Not sure if this guy is the murderer or not. Usually, I have a good feeling about a suspect. Not so sure about Allo. And I'm coming up short on hard evidence. Think a prosecutor may tell me to take a hike if I present what I've got to date."

"I'm unsure about Allo as well." Finn added.

"So, we might not have the murderer?" Tony asked.

Robert shrugged. "Hard to tell. We need Mary. They seem to be two peas in a pod."

As Robert sipped at his coffee, he found Tony staring at him. "Yes, Tony? You have something you want to say?"

"Well, I don't exactly want to say this, as it is slightly off topic, but I heard an ugly rumour this morning. You know how we haven't seen our buddy, Rod, around the last few days? Apparently, he quit."

"That is excellent news. Why the long face?"

"He has enlisted with the Independent Investigations Office, that's why."

Robert considered this for a moment. "Craps. This is in no way good. Do either of you know whether they can re-open investigations after they've been concluded?"

"You talking about last spring? Manny's death?"

"Maybe."

"Not sure. It seems unlikely, but...." Finn responded.

The gloss had suddenly gone off the day for Robert. Having someone with a dislike for you working for the civilian oversight committee investigating police involved deaths didn't seem fair. He wasn't even sure why Rodney had it in for him. "If I had to guess, good old Rod will give it the college try. He'd like nothing better than to screw me over."

Robert waved his hand aimlessly. "Let's forget Rod and concentrate on our case. I need to pile up some evidence, or Allo may be taking a walk on us." The more Robert considered it, the larger the problem seemed to be. The prosecutor wasn't up in Bella Kind, and would be relying solely on the facts in Vancouver, which, Robert was realizing, didn't add up to much. "Let's get out of here. I've got work to do."

# CHAPTER 16

The next day, Friday, Robert took his Archie file into Thomas Harrow's office to lay out his best case for charging Allo.

Thomas quietly perused the evidence, or lack thereof. "Seems thin. I think you should take this over to prosecutions today. They'll let you know pretty quickly what their opinion is."

"I suppose. He won't fully understand the Bella Kind back story though."

"Neither will a jury, Robert, if it comes to that." With that sobering assessment, Robert gathered his file and went to make an appointment to see the prosecution office. As he walked by Norma's desk, he slowed.

"Want to eat out tonight?"

Norma's eyes sparkled. "Good idea. Regular time? We can mosey around Yaletown, see what strikes our fancy."

"Sounds great." He kept moving, needing to get his meeting organized.

Just past two that afternoon, Robert exited his meeting, feeling flustered. It hadn't taken the prosecutor very long to ascertain that Robert's case was built on air and excitement, nothing more. "You better release that Allo character pronto. Don't need a complaint brought before us, do we?" The voice echoed behind Robert's back as he left the short meeting.

Robert returned to his office, closed the door, and stared out the window. He couldn't come up with anything further that might hold Allo in custody, so he picked up his phone. As far as he knew, Allo had not been sent to the Surrey Remand Centre as yet.

"It is Robert Lui speaking. I'd like you to release Allo Foot. I think he may be guilty, but we have to let him go. The case is a bit thin."

There was silence on the other end. "You still there?" Robert asked.

"Yes. Okay, if you are sure about this."

"We don't have a choice."

"There's always a choice." The line went dead. Robert stared at the receiver. For a Friday, this was turning into bad day. He gently put the phone down, got up and left, heading for home. As he drove east, he tried to relax, feeling sure his date with Norma would offer a more pleasant end to the week.

After changing clothes and meeting up with Norma downtown, they walked the streets, looking for a suitable dinner spot, eventually ending up at the sole hotel in Yale-town. Its restaurant was quieter, both of them wanting to avoid the more boisterous offerings along the loading docks. These eating spots were filled with youngsters with a seemingly endless capacity for spending large on cocktails and letting everyone in the neighbourhood know about it.

The hotel's restaurant offered largely Italian fare. After some starters of olives and a salad, Norma could not turn down a dish with her name on it — *Rigatoni Alla Norma*. Robert went with the *Ragu of the Day* and was not disappointed. The meal made up somewhat for the bad news that had filled the working day, and turned into a very pleasant interlude. Then Robert learned something.

"That was a very nice dinner you presented last Friday. Thanks for having me over."

"I'm glad you enjoyed yourself. You seemed to be a hit with the kids. You have a certain gift, I believe." Robert was smiling at Norma.

Norma wasn't one hundred percent certain if this was the time to tell Robert something he obviously hadn't a clue about, but he would find out eventually, so....

"Your son seems attracted to Rose."

"I know. I doubt he has a chance, due to the age difference, but it keeps him going."

"Are you aware that your daughter is also very attracted to Rose?"

"Of course, they are best friends." Robert looked into Norma's eyes. She didn't reply, staring back at him, waiting for the penny to drop. Which it finally did, with a mild thump. "Wait, you mean?"

"Yes, Robert."

Robert considered this for a full minute, staring at his wine glass." Well, I have to admit, I didn't see that coming."

"It's a modern world, Robert."

Then guilt about what happened in Bella Kind re-surfaced and finally got the better of him. It had gnawed at him for too long.

He stared at Norma. "I have been putting off telling you something. I was offside the last night in Bella Kind with the only staff member at the lodge I was staying at. Alcohol and relief at being alive may have contributed, but I regret it bitterly." Norma pulled back in her chair, eyeing Robert with a look that was a cross between hurt and confused.

"Let me get this correct. You slept with a chambermaid at the lodge?"

"Yeah. Norma, I am really sorry. She was also the chef and manager." As if her resume somehow made the whole affair more appealing.

"I think you should leave, now, Robert."

He knew it was useless to try to mitigate his sin, at least for now, so he didn't try. He got up; straightened his jacket, went over to the bar, paid, and walked out of the restaurant without saying another word. He returned to his car. As he drove back over the bridge to head home, he seemed to remember something about office romances.

He laughed out loud very briefly, "What a yutz you are, Robert." He had learned something however, and this was how Norma thought about him. After meeting Sandra, he wasn't sure his feelings for Norma were reciprocal anymore. He was getting very confused. His transgression up in Bella

Kind was something to consider carefully. He wasn't sure if he could fix things with Norma, or if he wanted to.

It was a quiet Saturday afternoon. The kids were out, and Robert settled on the couch to read the local weekend paper, including the Life features he normally ignored.

He was bobbing around in the Salish Sea, dressed in a bright red life preserver, when he heard a bell. Was it a light-house signal? A buoy? He looked around, over at the shore, and couldn't see anything. The sound was persistent.

He realized he'd fallen asleep, and his cellphone was ringing. He grabbed it off the coffee table and sat up, rubbing his head.

"Yes?"

"Is this Robert Lui?"

"Yes, who is this?"

There was a long pause, the voice hesitant when it started again. "This is Angelo, with the VPD. I am sorry to be the one to call you with this, but Tony Bortolo has been found, dead."

"Excuse me, what?"

"Your partner has been found, murdered, apparently. Out at Crab Park by the port."

"But...." Robert was stunned. "When?"

"He was found an hour ago, so he is still at the park. Crime scene is there."

"I will head over there right now. Shit." He ended the call, shaking his head. He scribbled a message for his kids on a piece of paper, left it on the kitchen counter, then went up to his room to grab his gun.

He sat in his car, warming the engine as he tried unsuccessfully to calm himself. He called Finn, asking him to meet at Crab Park after explaining what had befallen Tony. He then lit out of his carport, not wasting any time on his drive north to the waterfront. He rounded the last curve of the overpass at speed, his tires screeching over the train tracks below. He lurched to a stop and abandoned his car behind the jumble of VPD vehicles, their lights flashing relentlessly. He ran over to the group gathered beside a few tents.

"Where is he?"

One of the cops recognized Robert and signalled him to draw closer. "He's over here, behind the tent. I don't know whether you want to see him. His head has been bashed in."

"I want to see him." His inside voice countered, indicating that maybe he didn't want to see Tony, but it was too late. The officer raised the sheet covering Tony. Robert leaned over, then turned his head and almost retched. He looked up. The coroner had also arrived and came over to join the group.

"Robert. Is it really Tony?"

"Someone has split his head open. This can't be happening." He looked over at the cranes in the port, silhouetted, dark orange against a slate sky. A moment later, Finn Black walked up behind him.

"What happened?" Finn asked.

"I don't know. Who found him?" Robert looked at the officer who had shown him Tony.

"One of the homeless people here."

"Where is he? Or her?"

"It was a guy. He is over there, giving a statement." He pointed to another group standing in front of a small blue tent. Bicycle pieces were strewn beside it.

Robert grabbed Finn by the coat and dragged him over to the interrogation. They stood to one side and listened, but the man wasn't talking in complete sentences. It was hard to discern any logic at all in the conversation.

After a moment, Robert turned and walked away with Finn. "His head was bashed in."

"Is there a weapon?" Finn asked.

"Beside the body. Looks like a mace, or club. It has a ball on the end of it."

Robert reluctantly asked the officer to raise the sheet again.

Finn sucked in his breath. "That looks like a war club. Perhaps from up the coast." He was leaning over, peering at it. "Looks native, but not from around here. I would have to study the markings once we get it back to the office. This is disgusting."

Robert stooped down, rocking slightly on the balls of his feet. "I can't believe this. Why Tony? I wonder if he was armed? How could someone get the best of him?"

"Let me go see if he has his holster." Finn walked back and looked again, lifting Tony's jacket open.

"Holster is there. No gun. If it's the same person, then they have two guns now."

"But why Tony? He has nothing to do with any of that Raven Island nonsense."

"Well, we were looking for Mary. Maybe that is what brought him down here."

"Check his cell as well, if he still has it." Robert stood up, looking over at the group beside the tents. "I am going to head home. There is nothing more we can do here. I need a drink. Let's meet tomorrow. We need a plan." Then he slowly turned back to Finn. "I had that guy released yesterday, Allo Foot. I can't believe this."

Finn nodded, then watched as Robert slowly wandered back to his car. He turned and joined the rest of the officers processing the scene. A news van pulled up, people piling out, not helping the situation in the least. Robert watched from his car as the reporters tried to finger someone into speaking, knowing that Tony wouldn't have wanted the publicity. But he supposed Tony was past wanting anything now.

As Robert drove back south on Main Street, recrimination growing, his cheeks dampened. He was astounded. He hadn't really cried since his wife had passed. As he drove, he realized that Tony's parents would need telling, and he should be the one doing it, but there was no way he wanted to. He pulled into his carport, sat silently for several moments, then rang the station. After some back and forth, he told the duty officer that he would drive over to Burnaby to give the bad news. The officer was naturally grateful that someone else would be attending to a task no one wanted in the least to do.

After receiving the address, Robert left again to make the slow drive east. He had never met Tony's parents, and his visit went about how he thought it would go: crying, offering of tea, which Robert declined, and his promise to the parents to find out who had done this horrible thing to their son. And these weren't mere words. Robert vowed to himself that he would find this person and exact some token of revenge for a young life taken. What did they call it? A tragedy. That fit perfectly. Tony had so much more to give in his life and to the force.

Robert left after a half hour, not at all equipped to be the consoling presence. Tony's mother wouldn't stop crying. Perhaps their priest could provide the solace that Robert wasn't able to. Robert suggested contacting him, then headed home.

When he walked through the back door, both his daughter and son were in the kitchen, studying his scrawled message on the counter.

"Hi."

They looked up at him, eyebrows raised. He hadn't written the reason for his absence.

"You know Tony? My partner? He's been found, murdered. I was just out to Burnaby, letting his parents know." He sat down, staring at the floor.

Their eyes widened. They knew what dangers their father encountered at work. This was just more confirmation, which they didn't want. They both moved over to hug their father.

After a moment, Robert moved. "I need a drink. Can you guys root around the freezer to see what we have for later? I don't feel like cooking tonight."

He then poured himself a healthy shot of his favourite whisky and sat down on the couch, contemplating the immediate future.

Sophie hauled something out of the freezer and looked over at her father, "Dumplings, Dad?"

"That's fine — I'll do them up in a while."

What was Tony thinking? Was a race war breaking out in Vancouver? Or was it simply angry people venting their frustrations with the system? Or, a crazy person, someone very unstable? He and Finn were going to need some serious thinking to sort this out. Tony must have been on the trail of Mary, taking some initiative. Why couldn't he have waited? Robert sipped his drink, feeling the familiar relaxation slowly take hold as he started to think about Tony and all the adventures they had been through.

Sunday morning arrived. Robert not rested in the least after his nightmare ridden sleep. He had returned to the Salish Sea, but this time Tony was bobbing alongside; life preserver on, but unconscious, or dead, it was difficult to tell. But he was smiling at Robert, eyes closed as if at peace. It was deathly cold. They were surrounded by fish, curious about the humans. There was no reprieve from the water.

He showered after he woke, drank some juice, and started the coffee. He texted Finn to meet at noon. Then he arranged some eggs to make omelettes when his kids decided to open their eyes. He texted Thomas to let him know what he and Finn were up to.

He took his coffee mug and sat down at the table, trying to puzzle out the murderer's motives. It had certainly started during the wood protests on Raven Island as a family-to-family vendetta of sorts. Then things quickly became murky. Perhaps Mary was some sort of puppet-master, directing people to her bidding. What was her hold over Allo? Love? Sex? Everyone had said they were through as couple, but there was the lying aspect to consider. Perhaps Mary and Allo had reconciled, cementing their bond by committing these murders. He had heard of stranger things.

Someone came down the stairs. Robin entered the kitchen, surveying what might be on offer. "Morning Pops. You okay?"

"I'll be fine Robin. But I have some work to do. I'll be going into the office at noon. Omelettes first though. See if your sister is stirring, please." While his son retreated back up the stairs, Robert chopped some green onions and pulled cheese and fruit out of the fridge. He peered out at the herb pots on the patio, but the chives seemed dead. Chives never seemed to do well after mid-summer, and it was long past that.

After breakfast was over, his children seemingly full, Robert went up to his room and retrieved his Beretta with its ankle holster. Until they had a better handle on this case, he'd be wearing his back up. He bid his children goodbye and headed west to Cambie Street.

Finn was already at his desk, so they convened in Robert's office to plot their next moves.

"The weapon we saw yesterday next to Tony looks to be a match for the wounds on the other two victims. I guess the coroner will shed light on that," Robert said.

"It is odd that it was left there," Finn said.

"Perhaps because it was the murder weapon this time? The weapon of death was left at the other two murders, if I may put it like that."

"You may, and you are correct. Don't know what it means, though."

"Any witnesses from the scene?"

"None apparently. The local residents may not be paying attention to much of anything."

"I think it's time to alert all the other police forces about our two suspects. Perhaps those two are close, but in a different city." Robert lapsed into silence.

"Actually, Robert, it's not two suspects, only one."

"What are you talking about?"

"Just before you came in, I found out that Allo Foot is in the hospital. He never made it out of custody. Properly, anyway."

"What?"

"Some sort of incident late Friday in the lock-up. He has head trauma, not in great shape actually."

Robert looked at Finn. "So, he couldn't have killed Tony?"

"No." Finn stared out the window. "Wonder if Tony was asked to Crab Park. We need to go through his messages tomorrow. And if he was lured, how would they get his number?"

"Maybe he instigated the contact. I am out of my depth with all this social media business."

"We'll both go talk to the basement dwellers then, tomorrow. I'm slightly more with it, if I may put it like that."

"You may," Robert responded. "I would suggest carrying your gun from now on. I have two on me. Not taking any chances."

Finn nodded. "Not sure what else we can do until the scene items are released to us and we get the coroner's report."

"I'm going to look at all the information from the first two murders again. Maybe I missed something. We'll meet with Thomas first thing tomorrow. Maybe we need more people on this."

"Never heard of you asking for more people. Usually, it is the opposite, you are trying to shed people."

"Things change. Who could we ask for? Give it some thought, Finn. Then we'll get Thomas to help us." Finn nodded and went back out to his desk, while Robert fruitlessly looked through all the information gathered to date. After an hour, and not any wiser, he headed home to be with his children. While he drove, he came to the realization that perhaps he was the one responsible for Allo's injuries. And if Allo indeed was not the culprit Robert imagined him to be, then.... he required a drink, badly.

Robert and Finn met with Thomas in his office first thing on Monday.

"This is pretty shocking," said Thomas. Two police officers murdered within a few weeks. We are the talk of North America. I would appreciate any ideas you two may have to moving this case forward. I don't need to tell you about the pressure building from above. And I am really sorry, Robert, I know you were close to Tony. You are going to need to put your feelings aside for this one, if you can."

Robert didn't reply, staring out the window at some unknown entity.

Finn spoke. "All three murders seem to be connected. We'll be sure after we go through some items from Tony's scene. The weapon left beside Tony looks to be one of the common links. The coroner will likely tell us."

Robert came to life. "We need to find Mary. Priority number one. She may have a different boyfriend. Someone much more dangerous than young Allo."

Thomas shook his head. "Why do you always attract this kind of lethal attention?"

"'Cause I get results?"

"Not sure about that, Robert. Maybe you are unlucky."

Robert considered this. Luck was not a subject spoken about at all in the station. Robert's father had certain superstitions from his life in Hong Kong that he had passed onto his son, perhaps not in a direct way, but Robert had picked them up, nevertheless. Good luck, and the things one did to make sure you had it, were not to be trifled with.

"No. If I was unlucky, I'd be dead by now." He smiled thinly, then considered Tony. He looked down at the floor. "I am going to call Walter Gray, then let's go downstairs, Finn."

Robert entered his office, noting a plastic bag on his desk. Tony's cellphone, he guessed. He yelled out the door. "Finn, can you find out where that club is? I'm assuming the coroner has it."

He sat in his office, eyeing Tony's phone. He called Norma to get its password, taking it out of the evidence bag after he had gloved up. Robert gauged that the password had been given grudgingly. Once in, he checked Tony's phone calls, in and out. He wrote down couple of reoccurring numbers for Norma to check. There weren't many other calls. His own number was there, a couple of times. He went to the messages. There were several with his girlfriend, Chiara. He wondered how she was doing. Not well, he guessed.

The last group of messages were between Red Hammer and Tender Girl. Robert was puzzled. Wasn't this what the youngster in the basement was calling himself? He got up, went to his door and called for Finn.

"Didn't that guy downstairs say his alias was Red Hammer?"

"Yup."

"Well, Tony seems to have been using the same name in his last messages before he got clubbed. Maybe it was his way to get into the inner circle." Robert went through the messages. "Whoever Tender Girl is was inviting Tony over to Crab Park to meet up Saturday morning. Bigfoot was also supposed to be there. Seems to be a clear case of a setup. What do you think?"

Finn nodded. "Tony probably assumed the same thing you did, that Allo Foot was this Bigfoot character. And Allo was supposed to have been released Friday afternoon. So, a murder, planned, and pre-meditated."

"How would they know that Red Hammer wasn't who he appeared to be?" Robert asked.

"Perhaps the fact that he was interested in Bigfoot was enough to make Tender Girl suspicious."

"Well, they would have known that we had Allo. Anyway, I think the secret is out. That chat group would now know that Red Hammer is with the police, even if Tony wasn't who they thought he was. You should let the youngsters downstairs know that. They need a new alias, or they won't be finding out anything of use. But they should keep on using Red Hammer as well, act stupid."

"I like it. You are devious."

"We need to find out who Tender Girl is, somehow. My money will be on Mary Tinlit. Meanwhile, are those tent city people being grilled? Someone must have seen something."

"I'll check. Meanwhile, I am going to chase the coroner down for that club."

Robert sat, thinking, as he studied the clouds over East Vancouver, then decided he needed food.

After lunch was well past, Finn knocked on Robert's doorframe. "Got the club. The coroner says that it matches the indents made on the other two victim' skulls. And it was definitely the cause of Tony's death. He got bashed twice by it. No prints, however."

"You will figure out where it's from?"

"Yes. But it looks familiar to me."

Norma came to the doorway. "Tony's funeral is being planned for this Friday. They are wondering if you want to speak, Robert." Robert looked over at Norma. She studied the floor while waiting for his reply.

Robert was silent, studying the wall. "I hate public speaking, but I will. I owe it to Tony and his family." He stood up. "I'm going to head home. The last two days have been draining." He grabbed his jacket and walked past Norma. "See you both tomorrow."

Norma and Finn looked at each other, shaking their heads in unison.

Later the next morning, Robert arrived on the floor, looked over at Finn, and signed the coffee ask. Finn nodded, so they proceeded up the street to the cafe. Naturally, Gilberto was sympathetic as they stood at the bar, recounting what little they could tell him.

"Tony was a great fan of this place, you should know." Robert said.

Gilberto leaned forward with both hands splayed on the marble, shaking his head. "He was so young, that man. It isn't right. What animals would do such a thing?"

"No, it isn't right, Gilberto, and we will be doing something about it, make no mistake." Robert summed it up for both of the detectives. They ordered their coffees and went to sit at the back of the cafe, a young couple inexplicably taking up space at Robert's favourite window-side table.

"So, Finn. How are you doing?"

"Fine. How are you and Norma doing?"

"Don't ask me that."

"Okay...." The response drawn-out. "Haida."

"What?"

"The club. Its design is based on a Haida war club. Same markings, but it was made recently. It's not a relic from the past. As you may or may not know, the Haida were somewhat warrior-like. Slavery was also part of their business."

Robert's eyes opened a tad wider. "Really?"

"Yup. Something maybe not many people are aware of. Raids up and down the coast would sometimes lead to people being captured if they weren't killed, then either bartered away, or kept as slaves. The Haida weren't the only ones doing it, but they have a certain reputation. They were very good at it."

"So, not exactly peaceniks." He took a sip of coffee. "But Allo Foot is not Haida. According to the people up on Raven Island, he was raised there."

Finn shrugged. "I think we've already figured out that Allo isn't the murderer."

Robert thought about this. "Almost everything pointed to him."

"Almost being the key word."

Robert shook his head. "I think we are being played with."

They finished their drinks, staring at nothing, each thinking about Tony, and his killer, somewhere out there, loose and unaccounted for.

# CHAPTER 17

Wednesday morning, Robert went down to see the youngsters in the basement, intent on figuring out a way to set up a meeting with Tender Girl. He entered the room, where nothing appeared to have changed. Four sets of eyes turned to focus on Robert.

"That demonstration you led us to last week was everything we had hoped for, and less."

Rory answered. "What do you mean, and less?" Did he look hurt?

"You must have heard, we made an arrest, but it turns out the guy is probably not the killer." He continued, "And now that my partner has been murdered, it has become extremely personal. I want to get hold of this Tender Girl, and I'd like some ideas of how to go about it." He looked at Rory. "And Red Hammer is a compromised name, if you hadn't heard. I think you should keep using it however, pretend stupidity."

Rory nodded.

"Tony used Red Hammer to possibly set up a meeting, where he was killed. Someone knew he was coming."

"They may not have known he was an officer."

"Well, they do now. They took his pistol. And he had his badge on him, which was left."

"Oh."

"Is the security on that chat room still open?"

"Yes. They still seem to be encouraging new participants." Rory answered.

"Anything being planned?"

"No, but they seem hopped up about Bigfoot."

"I assume he isn't taking part."

"Correct."

"'Cause he's in the hospital, in a coma. He was supposed to have been released from custody last Friday. Something went wrong."

"Oh. That might explain some of the cop-hating posts." Rory said.

It didn't seem as though the basement dwellers kept up with the news, even when it concerned them. Robert shook his head slowly. "Let me know if you come up with a brainwave." With that, Robert left.

When he arrived back at his office, Finn waved him over. "I asked Vito to be added to our team."

Robert barely smiled. "Good. We'll turn this thing around. Having someone from Naples on their ass won't be very comfortable for these killers. Fill him in on what we have to date."

Robert stood still, tapping the top of Finn's cubicle divider, looking down at Finn. "Maybe we could provoke these people."

"How?"

"Two ways. Bad-mouthing Allo Foot, for one. Or inventing something further about the Tornado project. A reaction is what I'm after, so they do something stupid."

"Feels kind of low, bad-mouthing someone who's in a coma."

"Yeah, maybe. But I don't think he'd care right now, and there is Tony."

Finn nodded, "Yes, there is Tony."

Meanwhile, ex-VPD detective Rodney Fister was being introduced to staff at the Independent Investigations Office, in their headquarters at the Surrey Centre Tower. It was a substantial change from the VPD Cambie Street headquarters — like a different world, which he supposed it was, after all. As an investigator, he would be one of those chasing after bad cops, putting them in their proper place. While he listened to the blathering of his new boss, who was giving his welcoming speech to Rodney and another new face, he was considering how he could get Robert Lui's last case re-opened. Rodney had some suspicions about how it had all turned out, with the death of a notorious gangster in Robert's presence. He wanted nothing better than to pin that hot shot to the board and watch him flail around helplessly, like a mortally wounded butterfly. He was still fuming about the kidnapping case where Robert had done an end-around to rescue his son, leaving Rodney looking like the incompetent detective he really was.

"Rodney, are you paying attention?"

"Sure. What did you say?"

"Your first case is up in Prince George."

"Oh."

"You can get the file and the particulars from my assistant. Good luck."

Did this mean he would need to spend time up-country in the middle of nowhere? As if his boss could read his mind, he then added, "She'll also give the travel protocols you need to follow when you go up there."

Shit. How was he going to nail Robert when he had to spend time in British Columbia's hinterland?

"You should aim to get up there this week. Good to have you aboard." He shook Rodney's hand. "We may get called in on a new case in Vancouver. Someone got seriously injured in custody while being released. We should have the particulars by the time you are back."

This sounded more promising. Rodney had heard something on the news, but hadn't paid much attention at the time. Another assistant showed him to his new office. He walked in and immediately knew he had made the correct career decision. The office was large, the furnishings recent, and the view to the south was endless. If he squinted, maybe he could see Seattle, or more likely Blaine, just over the international border. He started whistling a tuneless song to himself as he settled in to test his new springy work chair.

Back at Cambie Street, Robert wasn't having any success divining a method to find Tony's murderer. He changed gears and started to write notes for his oration at Tony's funeral. It wasn't difficult to recount the hilarious episodes in Tony's career, but Robert wanted to talk about Tony's dedication to his chosen craft, and the effort he had given to become a detective. While he mused about his wording, a knock sounded on the doorframe. Vito Cotoni's head appeared. Robert waved him in.

"How are you doing, Vito?"

"I'd be better if Tony wasn't dead, but otherwise, okay."

"I am working on my funeral oration for Friday."

"Ah, something like that speech by Pericles?"

"I wish. Just some thoughts about the goodness of the man." He peered at Vito. "You are obviously well educated."

"The Jesuits did a fine job on me in Montreal."

"Montreal?"

"My family emigrated from Naples when I was a teen. I entered high school, then did Loyola College, where I received my real education. I'm not sure how we came to be in Montreal to start, but I'm betting family had something to do with it."

"The Black Robes. I've heard about them. How did you end up in Vancouver after all that?"

"A slight disagreement with my parents. So, I headed west."

"Disagreement?"

"They thought I should be a priest."

"Oh."

"Exactly. I wanted more. And hailing from Naples, I had some baggage to overcome, so I figured law enforcement might be my calling. Not that there is anything wrong with Naples."

Robert smiled at the optimism. "No, of course not. Well, I am happy you are on the team, Vito."

Finn came over to them. "I've heard that officers are coming in for the service from all over British Columbia and Alberta, even a few up from Washington State and Oregon."

"Hope the church can handle it all. I'll talk to Thomas."

Robert went over and rapped on Thomas's doorframe. He peeked around the jamb and went in. "Do you have the particulars for Tony's service?"

"Well, as you probably know, the force wanted a large show made of the funeral. Tony's parents disagreed, so it has been toned down significantly. It will be at Our Lady of Grace Church in Burnaby — service starts at eleven. Then, internment at Memorial Lawn. The cemetery isn't that far from the church. I believe there is a dinner planned at one of those Italian supper clubs on Commercial Drive later on, for close friends and family. You and I are on the list, Robert. I don't know how I rated, but...."

"He worked for you, Thomas. And respected you greatly. Maybe that's why."

"Hmmm. Any progress on the hunt?"

"Still trying to figure out how to arrange a meeting. This Mary is pretty intelligent, I believe, so we need to be devious."

"I heard she is kind of crazy."

"That too. I'm sure we'll come up with something as bait."

"I understand you are going to talk at the service. Well done, Robert."

"Don't 'well done' me yet, Thomas. I haven't spoken. Gonna spend tomorrow at home, going over what I'll say."

"Good idea."

Robert went up the street for a late lunch, and it was while he was walking that the idea came to him. A tethered goat. Bait. This always worked, didn't it? The twist to it would be that he would be the goat. Mary Tinlit knew him, and if he had to guess, the young man staring at him at the demonstration might also be interested. All he had to figure out was how to do it, without getting himself killed. He didn't know if Mary communicated with her parents or not, but he had talked with her father, so it was possible that she knew about that. He was uncertain if he could make use of this.

After another successful noodle lunch, temporarily sated, he returned to his office, considering how to flesh out his plan. Then he remembered he had a call to make.

"Walter? It's Robert."

"Yes. What can I do for you?"

"A few things have happened down here, as you may have heard. Was there another young man in Mary's life when she was on Raven Island?"

"I'm quite sure there were a few. Why?"

"Because someone is murdering people down here, and it doesn't appear that it is Allo. And Mary seems to be the connecting factor. I assume you heard about my partner?"

"Yes, unfortunately. My sincere condolences Robert. I can't get down there for the funeral, but one of my men is attending."

"Did you also hear about Allo? I don't know what happened yet, but it doesn't reflect very well on us."

"Heard he got hurt. Yes?"

"If you can put any names to who Mary hung with, I'd appreciate it. Thanks Walter." He ended the call, again, not optimistic about receiving anything useful from Walter. He returned to the notes for his speech, but, after another hour at this, and not getting any closer to something half good, he left for home.

Thursday was spent at home, finally drafting something on his laptop that would be useful in the church. No one from Cambie Street bothered him. After lunch, he went out to the local grocery store to get the ingredients for an easy to make Thai chicken dish. Stressful times were on the horizon, so this day was to be enjoyed — in a sad way.

When his son and daughter got home from school, he told them what was on the menu.

"I know that usually I am on a date with Norma, being as how tomorrow is Friday, but instead, it is Tony's funeral. I have been invited to a dinner on Commercial after, so if you are here, it will have to be leftovers. He declined to mention the frost that had developed in his relationship with Norma.

"We'll be thinking of you tomorrow, Pops." Robin said. Robert nodded and wondered where this adult concern came from as he laid out the ingredients. "Can I help?" Robin added. Robert shook his head, staggered by the very idea of unsolicited help from his son. He spoke quickly, before the offer was withdrawn.

"Sure, you can chop up the lemongrass. Finely, please!" He smiled at his son. He headed over to where his whisky bottles were kept and chose a Japanese offering. After pouring a couple of fingers, he got the rice prepped and laid out the chicken thighs, patting them dry.

"We could use some veg with this. Do we have anything in the fridge, Robin?"

After some rustling, Robin came out with half a bag of asparagus.

"It'll have to do. Maybe you could shave their ends, as well." Robert opened a can of coconut milk, turned the rice maker on, and prepared to start cooking. As he sipped his whisky, he replayed the goofier moments with Tony. He started to chuckle to himself.

Robin looked over. "Cracking up, Pops?"

"Remembering some of the funnier things Tony did on our cases."

"He was also there when you guys rescued me."

"Yes. He was always ready to go the extra mile, especially for me. That's why I appreciated him so much. I still find it hard to believe that...." He looked down and finished chopping the cilantro, then started searing the chicken thighs in his deepest frying pan, all to take his mind elsewhere.

As dinner wound down, Robert looked over at his children and knew he'd need to have a word with them, maybe Sophie first, after what he had learned from Norma. He wasn't sure how equipped he was to deal with the subject of sexuality, not well, he figured, but he'd try. Maybe he needed to talk with his late wife. Perhaps she could help him. But that was for another day. He had the service tomorrow, then, a killer to trace. His list of things he had put off was growing and was starting to agitate him.

Friday dawned, but Robert lolled in his bed for a time, listening to his children make their preparations for school. After they hollered their goodbyes, Robert rose and looked out the window. A sky the colour of old concrete spread as far as he could see. No rain, so far, but definitely a day for a funeral. He slowly made a healthy sized breakfast, knowing he wouldn't be eating until the dinner much later. After enjoying a pot of coffee while he checked on the news, he dressed in his only decent suit, snugging his tie, then sat down to strap the Beretta to his ankle. Even at an event surrounded by police officers, he was taking no chances. He checked the location of the church again and was preparing to leave when his phone made its annoying sound signifying an arriving text.

He pulled it out to check. The message was from Basement Rory.

**'Chatter from the group says they are planning to demonstrate at the funeral today.'** Great. How appropriate. He forwarded the message on to Thomas, asking for some constables to attend just in case. He doubted Mary would attend, but he'd be keeping his eyes wide open. He got into his car and headed east to the church.

After arriving, Robert greeted Tony's parents inside, then he spotted Chiara, Tony's girlfriend. He didn't know her very well, having only met twice, but he went over to have a word.

"Chiara, how are you holding up?"

She blinked twice, then answered. "Okay, I think. I'm not used to any of this." She looked back at the entry as more and more officers in full dress uniform entered the church.

"None of us are. Nor should we be." Robert laid a hand lightly on her shoulder. "I need to talk to the priest. I will be speaking today."

She dipped her head, giving the barest of nods, and went to take a seat. As Robert turned, he noticed some top brass from Vancouver in full dress enter the nave, led by the Chief Constable, Caleb Woo. Nothing less than what Tony deserved.

After the service ended, Robert gathered with Thomas, Finn, and Vito. They waited as the church slowly emptied. It had been full, with many officers having to watch from the entry foyer. Robert even recognized a couple of people from the firing range — the ones who had attempted to give him a hard time. He had nodded at them, which was returned in kind. Reconciliation seemed like an apt thing to be doing at a funeral for a fallen officer.

"Good turnout," Thomas said. "Even better than for Archie's, I believe."

"Well, here's hoping that this is the end of it. We don't need any more funerals," Robert responded.

"That is kind of what David McKnight indicated earlier today."

"I bet he did. I didn't notice Rodney Fister in the crowd. Did anyone see him?"

"Don't believe so," Vito offered. "It figures."

"We should get along to the cemetery." Robert turned to leave, but not before going over to the priest, who was talking with Tony's parents. "Thanks for the opportunity to speak on Tony's behalf. He meant a great deal to me."

The three nodded, with the priest offering the slimmest of smiles. "Yes, we could tell."

Robert touched his brow with his fingers in a salute and turned to leave. Just then, shouts were heard from outside the church.

"Wonder if it's our friends, the demonstrators?" Robert asked himself, as he headed for the door. Outside, constables had indeed surrounded a group of eight or nine young people yelling at the police. Robert joined the other three detectives outside, watching and listening as insults were hurled.

"They seem worked up about Bigfoot. Hope someone is getting photos of all this. They may be that chat room — in person." Finn observed.

"Well, I suppose I can understand their anger about Allo, but doing it at the funeral of a fallen officer is beyond the pale — in my opinion." Robert said. "Who taught them manners?"

After the internment, Robert drove the three other officers over to Commercial Drive to find a bar where they could toast Tony's journey across the river Styx before the dinner started. Oddly, they had trouble finding one, so they ended up in the dinner venue, where the hostess led them to its lounge.

"I seem to recall more places to drink along the Drive. Guess things change. Maybe it's better this way. No confusion about which way to go once we are soused." Finn said. "Vito and I can stay here while you two are at the dinner. I'm sure we can survive on lounge food, and more booze."

Robert nodded as they sat, then looked down as he texted Sophie to let her know that the service went well, and he'd see them later. She replied promptly with a few emojis, which Robert didn't understand.

After the first round arrived, the Tony stories started. As they laughed and laughed, Robert noticed a few other uniformed officers showing up, as well as people in civilian dress he didn't know. Probably family, but he wasn't sure. The uncertainty was cleared up when one of them got up slowly and came over to thank him for his talk.

Robert nodded. "He should be here. I know Tony hated missing a party."

"Yes. He'd be ticked at not joining us." With that, the older man turned and retreated to his table. Perhaps an uncle, or family friend.

The detectives returned to the Tony stories, when a large platter full of *antipasti* arrived at the table. Marinated olives, bruschetta and some cheeses were surrounded by several types of sliced salamis. Robert looked over at the man who had just visited their table, who was grinning back at him. Robert tipped his head and smiled his thanks. He knew part of the generosity was based on the tradition of keeping police officers happy, particularly the ones seeking vengeance for a fallen comrade. Whatever, the gesture was appreciated.

Over an hour later, everyone feeling well-lubricated, some of the crowd in the lounge started to head into the main hall. As Robert and Thomas stood to follow, Tony's father came over to them.

"I've arranged some seats for your friends as well. You can all proceed in." He smiled.

"You don't have to do this," Robert responded.

"Tony would have wanted it." He extended his arm, pointing the way. Robert nodded. Finn and Vito looked up in surprise, but were pleased to be invited into the inner sanctum. The detectives were led inside to one of several long tables where the man who had sent the *antipasti* to their table sat, along with a woman and several younger people. Cousins, Robert guessed.

The man stood up. "Anthony, one of Tony's uncles. This is my wife, Vonda." Vonda rose and offered her hand in greeting.

"Robert. This is Thomas, Finn, and Vito — all detectives. Thomas is in charge of us. Pleased to meet you."

Anthony and Vonda ignored the other two and studied Vito intently, trying to divine where in Italy he hailed from.

Vito obviously felt the pressure. He relented, slightly. "I'm from Montreal." This piece of useless information did nothing to stop the staring, so he cracked. "Family is from Naples."

"Ah. Welcome Vito." They returned to their seats, semi-satisfied. Robert knew that the Bortolo family hailed from Modena, so he expected some suspicions would be flowing Vito's way, no matter how virtuous Vito might appear to be.

Anthony stood again, and poured red wine into everyone's glass from the large carafe that was the centrepiece to all the tables. From the head table, Tony's father rose to thank everyone for attending, and the priest gave a brief homily as a follow up to his readings at the service. Then the first course arrived, ushered out by a small army of servers. It was a spaghetti carbonara — not a large helping, but apparently one of Tony's favourite dishes. One of many, Robert suspected. A green salad with a generous helping of dressing accompanied. As the food was delivered to each table, it was as if a signal had been tripped, and Anthony started in on the questions.

"Do you guys know who did this terrible deed?" Anthony asked. Vonda appeared semi-annoyed at her husband's attempt to spoil the dinner, grabbing her husband's arm.

Robert turned to Thomas, offering him the chance to say as much or as little as prudence dictated.

"This looks very good," Thomas said, as he looked down at the pasta starter. But Anthony wasn't going to be diverted by a small compliment. He kept staring at Thomas, who eventually looked up. Robert knew exactly what he had been doing, gathering his thoughts, playing for time. Robert had been somewhat leery of attending this meal, fearing exactly what seemed to be playing out. Of course, not attending wasn't really an option either. It was a classic lose/lose situation. Robert stared at Anthony, willing him to back off a bit.

"We have an idea about the players involved, thanks to Robert and Tony's work on the case."

"You mean Tony was investigating his own death before it happened?" Anthony appeared incredulous.

"A related murder enquiry," said Thomas. Don't think we should be talking about this tonight. The case is in hand, I'll put it that way for now. We have our best people on it, and they all happen to be sitting at this table."

This was a first, Robert had to admit. Being complimented on their efforts was a very rare occurrence. He couldn't recall it happening to him. He looked down at his pasta starter to avoid any more questions, and started eating.

Anthony wasn't done, however. "You're gonna nail him, right?" This was aimed at Robert.

"If it's a guy, yeah. Tony was special to me, so...." This finally seemed to mollify Anthony somewhat. Vonda was somewhere between embarrassed and curious about the exchange, but also seemed satisfied with Robert's stand. Their three sons were studying the detectives, and appeared somewhat younger than Tony, maybe in their early twenties.

Robert was also curious, so he tried to change the subject. "And what are you young men up to?"

"I'm taking my MBA out at UBC," the first said, perhaps the eldest.

"I'm a plumber. Just got my ticket this year, working on my Red Seal certification," the second one said.

"I'm thinking about going into your line of work," the youngest said. "After what happened, more than ever."

Robert studied the third son. "Name?"

"Sergio."

"Come down to Cambie Street next week, Sergio, and we'll have a talk, okay?"

"*Si.*" Sergio smiled. Thomas looked over at Robert and gave a thankful nod.

The next plates delivered featured *Osso Bucco*. Robert had never tasted this before, so he anticipated something special. He was not disappointed. It was so refined that he vowed to give it a try at home. A whole library of cookbooks adorned one wall of his family room. Surely, somewhere in there was the appropriate recipe. After Tony's relatives started concentrating on the food and drinks, instead of the detectives, the remainder of the evening played out much as Robert expected. Contented stomachs, and heads full of wine.

Then the grappa came out.

# Chapter 18

Saturday was a hazy blur for Robert. He couldn't recall being this hung over, ever. He mentally saluted Tony as he gingerly approached the kitchen. After some juice, and while waiting for the coffee to drip out, he looked out the rear window at an empty carport. His car must be somewhere out on Commercial Drive, probably sporting a ticket. Maybe he cabbed it home, he was uncertain. Later, he'd pull on his runners and trot back over to the Drive to retrieve his vehicle, but that was for later. He had to recover some of his senses first. He seemed to recall talking to a Sergio, what about, he was unsure, but hoped he hadn't made an ass of himself.

As Robert prepared some toast, his mind went back to the problem at hand. How to get Ms. Tinlit to expose herself — not literally, of course, but his mind drifted in that direction anyway. He shook his head. One avenue might be to arrange the arrest of her father on suspicion of having tried to murder some aviators up in Bella Kind. This strategy was dubious at best, considering how little evidence Walter had probably amassed. He also doubted that Mary kept in any kind of regular contact with her parents if his conversation with her father was anything to go by. So, whether her father was in custody or not was probably of little consequence to Mary. However, he wasn't ruling it out. The other route was the social media option — try to aggravate someone into making a mistake. Gone for now was the tethered goat option. Time for a meeting of the minds at Cambie Street on Monday. Till then, he'd work on recovering his senses, and his car.

He grabbed his coffee cup and headed for the sofa, where he proceeded to ruminate about Norma and whether it was possible to patch things up. If he was a guessing man, then no would be the answer. He sipped his coffee while he pondered how little he had done to try to make amends. The case superseded all at times, but he also knew his penchant for avoiding difficult situations.

Promptly at eight on Monday morning, Robert asked Finn and Vito into his office for a strategy session.

"You two recovered okay?" Robert started once they had settled into the guest chairs.

"I was slightly bent, but I'm good now," Finn said, looking at Vito.

Vito looked back at the other two with a puzzled expression. "What was the problem? Just another very good Italian dinner."

"Obviously you can handle your grappa with ease." Finn responded.

"Naturally. Comes with the heritage. It's the homemade crap you have to be careful with. It could burn holes in things, like your stomach. Many of the people at that dinner probably make their own after they have made their wine each fall. The grappa they were serving Friday was great stuff — not homemade."

"I agree. I'm just impressed with your capabilities, Vito, that's all I'm saying," Robert said.

Vito shrugged. "We have a killer to find. How we going to do it?"

Robert then explained what he had come up with on the weekend.

"Yes. Let's do it. All of it." Vito said.

"All of it?"

"Yeah. Think so. What are we pussyfooting it for? Let's go all in."

"Mary's father might be the biggest problem. I don't know what Walter and his crew are doing up there, but it doesn't seem like much. Shouldn't be too difficult to go and see if Mary's father has a drill on his property. I bet he still has it. Probably not worried at all, given who he's dealing with." Robert looked out the window, then, "Finn, what if you went up there and did a reconnaissance? All we need is some evidence, enough to arrest him for a few days. I suppose you'll need a search warrant to do it properly. Unless we don't care about whether he stays in custody or not." Robert added, "I'd go myself, but I vowed to stay away from water for a long time. And I plan to keep that vow."

Finn grinned. "Sure, I'll go. It'll be nice to get back up the coast. Haven't been in a while."

"Talk to Thomas first, then Norma. She can make the arrangements for you. And here is a tip — take a real plane, both ways."

Robert stared at Vito. He had an idea.

"Maybe we could create our own protest group, using the guys downstairs. Cast aspersions on the group they are following and intimate that we are taking it up a couple of notches. What do you think?"

"You mean organize something and see who shows up?"

"Yes, then tail a few after to see where they hide."

"Assuming someone comes out, that is," Vito responded.

"We'll need some youngsters to go undercover."

"Shouldn't be difficult. Officers love getting out of uniform."

"Yes. Tony was definitely one of those before he passed his exams." Robert shook his head gently as he stared east at the jumble of commercial buildings stretching into the distance. "Okay, let's make this happen. Vito and I will visit the basement, while Finn gets permission to go on his jaunt north."

After giving Basement Rory his marching orders, Robert left the office and went up to Cafe Paulo, alone. As he entered, from behind the bar, Gilberto looked over at him, eyebrows raised.

"Wheels are in motion, Gilberto, wheels are in motion."

Gilberto nodded approvingly as he set up to pull a double espresso for Robert. Robert paused by the bar, watching the expert movements of one of his favourite people. He smiled as the cup was proffered, steam drifting up from the *crema* covering the black gold. Taking it to the rear of the cafe, he sat and mulled over how he was going to talk with his daughter. He wasn't even sure if he should raise the subject, but, he considered, some reassurance might go a ways to making Sophie feel more at ease. He suspected his wife would have known what to say. Well, she wasn't here, so it was up to him. This coming Friday was the meeting he had arranged for Sophie with his late wife's planning partner up at City Hall. Thursday night was a game night for his son, so maybe that would be a good time to talk to Sophie. He wasn't looking forward to it.

Thursday morning came and Vito reported that the new chat group was performing famously. New players were already signing on to join the rants, and Rory was watching to see if any of the names from the older chat room were joining in. Finn was due to return to the office in the afternoon from his odyssey. Robert was eager to hear how he made out on Raven Island. He offered a small prayer, hoping Finn would return in one piece.

His phone rang. "Robert Lui speaking."

"Hi. This Sergio Bortolo, from last Friday?"

"Yes, of course, Sergio. Good to hear from you."

"You said I should come by this week?"

"I did?" His mind was blank. Then it came back to him. "Yes, how about tomorrow morning then — say nine?"

"Great. I'll see you then."

Looked like tomorrow was going to be career day, what with Sophie's meeting with Jean Kwok as well.

At the IIO headquarters, Rodney Fister had returned from his first case up in Prince George. It had felt like purgatory to him. Perhaps he had erred somewhere, and this was penance required of him before he could get back to his number one concern, nailing Robert Lui.

He gathered the few files together on his desktop screen and slid them onto a thumb drive, then walked out of his office and over to his boss's assistant. He hadn't been able to build much of a case against the constable who had discharged his weapon at a suspect, wounding him, during a bank robbery in Prince George. The heist was weird enough. He couldn't remember the last time someone had tried to rob a bank at gunpoint. Perhaps the northern reaches of the province operated in a past era. It was difficult to figure out. He had spent a few days up there and found no one who was eager to discuss much of anything with him. Rodney hadn't thoroughly thought through his new job before taking it. He was only now starting to appreciate the difficulties he would be facing every day as he investigated law enforcement personnel.

He was about to return to his office. Instead, twirling around, he asked the assistant, "Do you know how I can access the Robert Lui files from that case last spring?"

"What for?"

"I have some information that may have a bearing on the case." He smiled.

She wasn't having any of it. "The case has been concluded. Cases are rarely re-opened around here. We have enough to do with the current caseload." She returned his smile, devoid of any warmth, then shifted her eyes back to the screens on her desk. Rodney stood, motionless for a moment, then thought better of getting into an argument with a gatekeeper he didn't know, and left.

He returned to his office, sat down, and admired the view all over again. His thoughts slowly returned to Robert Lui. Perhaps he would hold his powder for a while. Figure out how cases were dealt with at the IIO, and what happened to them once they were complete. Then he'd be in a better position to attempt entry into the file and find out some case details. He smiled to himself, starting tuneless whistling. His phone rang.

"Rodney?"

"Yes?" He couldn't identify his boss's voice yet.

"Good. You're back. Next case up is a Vancouver Police Department matter. Should be right up your alley given your resume. A young man ended up in a coma after something happened during his release from custody."

"That doesn't sound very good."

"No, it doesn't. The officer in charge of the case is a Detective Robert Lui."

"You don't say."

"I do say. Why? Did you work with him?"

"Certainly. He used to work under me." Rodney could hardly believe his luck. "Very happy to take the case. Thank you. I really appreciate this. Can't wait to get going on it." Suddenly, he loved his new job. The item about Robert working for Rodney wasn't exactly accurate, but it sounded good to Rod.

His boss hung up his phone, looking down at it. Something seemed weird. He hadn't ever encountered this kind of enthusiasm by any of his investigators. He suspected the only thing keeping most of them on his payroll were largish salaries. He put it down to Rodney being new to the job, not familiar yet with the immense difficulties involved in going after your own kind. Well, he'd learn pretty quickly.

Finn arrived back at Cambie Street just after four. He had a huge grin on his face as he headed to his desk. "Made it back alive, Robert," he yelled out.

"Good news, Finn. I knew you could do it. I'll get Vito up here." Robert responded from his office. He texted Vito, who was down in the basement, fomenting rebellion or something similar. Finn dumped his bag and laptop on his desk, then sauntered into Robert's office.

Norma had given Finn the thumbs up. "You are obviously a superior traveller to Robert, Finn."

Finn started grinning again. "Not hard to be, Norma." He sat down in a heap, seemingly exhausted.

"So. How'd it go in God's country?"

"Pretty nice up there, Robert." He rose to close the door, not waiting for Vito. "I stayed at the Arnott Bay Lodge." Finn stopped, waiting for a reaction.

"Oh." Robert hadn't thought this escapade through, obviously. Now he was going to be reaping things he maybe didn't need.

"Sandra says a big hi." Finn was grinning again.

"Hmmm." Finn wasn't stupid. "How did the case work go, Finn?"

"Fine, Robert. She says she might make a trip down to Vancouver." The discomfort apparent on Robert's face, increased after this latest revelation. "I told her it's beautiful this time of year, and that she would really enjoy herself."

"Oh, great. And Mary's father?"

"She is really good looking, Robert. I'm impressed." He paused before returning to Robert's question. "Arrested on suspicion of drilling holes in the undercarriage of a Beaver floatplane," Finn said triumphantly.

"Charge?"

"Mischief." Don't know how long they will hold him."

"Not long, I'd guess."

"I did some nighttime reconnaissance and found tools. I went back to Walter the next morning and expressed my belief that a search of George's property would net a drill worth examining."

"Who is George?"

"Mary's father. You did visit Bella Kind, didn't you?"

"Sloppy. I'm getting sloppy. Not good." Robert shook his head. "You were able to get a court order that fast, up there?"

"Any other questions, Robert?"

"I suppose not."

"I was also able to get in to look at the Beaver. They have it in a warehouse while they do their investigations. It is a bit of a mess, at least the front is. You are one lucky man, Robert."

There was a knock on the door, then Vito's head appeared. "May I enter?"

"You may. What is the report from below?"

"The boys and girls have organized a demonstration against the latest City Hall master plan to build huge condos along a subway line. They are saying that all the cheap rental housing will be razed so that the developers can make windfall profits building whomping great towers."

"Sounds like these guys have a new career — fomenting insurrection against the city. Better not let the senior staff around here know what we're doing." Robert said. The other two grinned like mischievous imps. "I'm serious. Don't think City Hall will take kindly to what we're doing, either."

"You are probably right, Robert."

"Where is it planned for? And when?"

Vito answered. "City Hall, naturally, and next Tuesday, ten in the morning. They gave a few extra days to get some anger building. And they kept it close by, for your convenience. And some of the usernames from the older chat room have shown up. Looks like this might work out."

"Is Tender Girl one of the names?"

"Yup, once anyway."

"I'm sure something will screw-up, but great work, you two. Think I'm calling it a day. See you tomorrow." Robert evicted the detectives from his office while he considered dinner. After discarding a couple of ideas, he called the pizza place he used when he wasn't making his own. He couldn't help thinking about Sandra as he drove home. He had been halfway hoping she'd make an appearance in Vancouver. Just not now, however, too much going on.

Forty-five minutes later he arrived home, just before Robin was picked up for his game. He had purchased three pizzas this time, knowing how hungry a teen-aged hockey player would be. Robin smiled as he left through the front door to catch his ride, his stomach already anticipating his post-game meal.

"Hey Sophie, guess it's just you and me tonight," he said nervously.

"Thanks for the pizza, Dad." She smiled as she hauled out two plates and some cutlery. Robert pulled a small glass of white wine, knowing he needed to be careful until his talk with Sophie was over.

"Are you ready for tomorrow's meeting? You can come in with me if you wish, but it is set for half past ten."

"I could do that. I can check out Cambie Street until then."

"What did you think of Norma, and the dinner, two weeks ago?" He hadn't gotten the debrief from his kids, too pre-occupied with his case. He slipped two of the pizzas into the oven to keep warm, while he tipped some peas for a simple salad.

"I really liked Norma. She didn't have an edge to her, like...." She stopped.

Robert looked up and smiled. "Yup. I know what you're saying. I think it's partly because her work is different."

It was now or never. "She told me something afterwards, that I think I should talk to you about. She said that you are very attracted to Rose."

"Dad!" She put both hands over her face.

"I know, I know, just hear me out. I can't advise you on what to do about it, but I just want you to know that I am totally fine with it. Okay?"

Sophie dropped her hands. Her eyes were darting around the table, seemingly confused at having her innermost thoughts revealed to her father, then she eventually calmed, partially. She looked back at Robert. "Really?"

"Yes. I have no idea what Rose thinks, but if I had to guess, her parents may not be as keen as me on the matter."

"I haven't talked to Rose about this. I'm kind of scared to, and yes, her parents are very conservative."

"I know that you'd really rather not talk to me about this sort of thing, but you have my full support. You should know this, okay?" Sophie nodded. Robert could see the wheels turning behind his daughter's eyes. He knew his daughter was going to be in turmoil, but he had done what he could. Other than reassurance, he didn't know what else he could do. He was fairly certain that if this was another family, the daughter would have run, screaming from the room, distraught at having her innermost thoughts revealed to her father.

"Let's eat, Sophie. I'm hungry." With that, he pulled one of the pies from the oven and served a couple of slices onto each plate. They sat together, and after Robert re-filled his wine glass, they ate and discussed things that hitherto, they had never talked about. It turned into a relaxing evening, for Robert, at any rate. They had finished, and Sophie had retreated up to her bedroom, when Robin came through the back door, hauling his equipment bag and hockey sticks.

"Scored tonight, Pops, twice." He laughed.

"Darn, sorry I missed it. Take a shower, and I'll warm up the pizza for you." He took his wine glass into the family area and sat, considering what he would say to Sergio tomorrow. He didn't wish to be the cause of a second tragedy for the Bartolo family, but he'd gauge Sergio's enthusiasm for what he would be undertaking and hopefully give some sage advice. As for other portion of career day, he trusted that Jean could direct Sophie onto the correct path. He grabbed the remote and flipped the television on to help his mind flip off.

Promptly at nine the next morning, Sergio showed up on the floor and was directed by Norma to Robert's office. He gently tapped the door frame, peering around the edge. Robert waved him in.

"Welcome Sergio, please have a seat." Sergio seemed to be blessed with a normally sized nose, but his hair was every bit as thick and black as Tony's was. "So, you are interested in following Tony's lead?"

Sergio settled into a chair, his eyes darting around the sparsely furnished room. "Yes, more than ever, now."

Robert found it tough to tell if it was ambition, or revenge that was at the root of Sergio's career choice. "Okay, however, revenge is not a good motivation for what you are about to embark on. As long as you realize that, you should be fine. I'm assuming that you wish to apply to the VPD?"

"Yes. And I want to be a detective."

Robert laughed. "Okay, okay. One thing at a time. You realize you have to become a constable first, before learning the ropes, then taking the courses and exams to become a detective. It takes time and perseverance. Have you been online, studying the application process?"

"Yes."

"And do you have some college or university courses completed?"

"I took a year at the college in New Westminster, and I've taken some courses at the Justice Institute. I think I have all the necessary credits."

"I don't think there is anything else I can tell you. I assume you are of sound moral character and will write you a reference, Sergio. And if I don't get myself killed, I'll be here to help guide you as needed. You can call me any time." He would complete the reference only after talking with Sergio's father, but didn't let Sergio know this. He didn't want another Bortolo signing on without some kind of family approval first.

Robert shook Sergio's hand and led him out and over to the elevators. He was about to bid Sergio goodbye when the elevator door opened and Rodney Fister stepped out. He had an unpleasant smirk pasted onto his face. Sergio stepped around him to get into the elevator, waving at Robert.

"Just the man I want," Rodney said.

"Can't say the same, Rod." Robert turned to walk away.

"Hey. Come back here. You are being investigated by the IIO." By now, several people in the area were staring at the pair of officers, listening, and wondering what this was about.

"Should have made an appointment, Rod. I have a meeting to attend." He moved towards his office.

"Hey, how'd you like to be arrested?" Rodney yelled at his back, fishing, with no licence.

Robert stopped, turned, and started laughing. "Have you lost your mind, Rod?" He wasn't worried in the least. "Why don't you go over to Norma and make an appointment if you want to talk with me so badly? And why weren't you at Tony's funeral?" This stopped Rodney cold. He stood still, while the admin staff and officers listening all stared at him, waiting. He mumbled something no one could understand, then made his way over to Norma's desk. Robert went to his office, grabbed his coat, and left for Cafe Paulo before the meeting at Planning with his daughter.

"And what is the meeting about?" Norma looked up at Rod. She wanted details.

"IIO have opened an investigation into the severe injury suffered by an Allo Foot while in custody here. Robert's case."

"Oh. He could see you Monday morning, I think." She studied her computer screen intently, trying her best to wish Rodney away.

"Fine. I'll be here Monday then. Robert had better play ball with me."

"Don't think Robert plays ball, Rod. See you Monday." With that, she picked up her phone. She didn't have a call to make, she just wanted Rodney gone. He finally got the message and reluctantly left the floor, angry with the disrespect he felt flooding his way.

After a successful meeting with Jean Kwok at City Planning, Robert treated his daughter to lunch at his favourite noodle haunt. Lunch was an animated affair as Sophie considered herself one step closer to fulfilling a dream. She had gained some tips from Jean on the profession and which universities were up and coming. They talked about some of the options available to her as she would likely need to apply to several institutions.

"I'm going to do some online research and get going on applications." Sophie was animated. To Robert, it seemed she could barely contain herself.

He smiled as he bid Sophie goodbye at the bus stop, and he took his time walking back, looking into some of the smaller shops along Cambie, before returning to his floor. He went over to Norma to find out what Rodney was after.

"Thanks for that, Robert. You owe me something. I don't know what, but it had better be good." She wasn't smiling. "He is after you for that Allo Foot injury in custody. He's coming back Monday morning."

"Hmm. And it is because I am in charge of the case, correct?"

"Seems so."

"Just what I need. Thanks, Norma. I had to take a meeting with a city planner and Sophie, regarding her desire to become a planner, like her mother."

"Go well?"

"Yes. Now I have to go plan for next Tuesday."

"Tuesday?"

He kicked himself, mentally. Why couldn't he keep his mouth shut? "Yes. Something might happen."

"Mysterious."

"Yes. That's one way of putting it." With that, he returned to his office and his hopes about the upcoming demonstration.

# CHAPTER 19

Monday morning came, the week starting off in a most unpleasant way for Robert. Rodney Fister was sitting on a plastic waiting area chair, looking impatient, when Robert made his appearance shortly after nine. He walked by Rod, barely acknowledging his presence, deposited his briefcase in his office, then returned, beckoned him with a finger and led Rodney to a conference room. He sat across the table from Rod, next to the door, which he left open, and folded his hands.

"So. Why are you here?"

"You know why I'm here. Someone in your care suffered a horrendous injury."

"My care?" Robert knew he shouldn't say anything, but he couldn't help himself.

"As the officer in charge of the case, yes, your care."

Robert stiffened his resolve, not replying. He didn't know the details of what had happened to Allo, but wasn't about to let Rodney know this.

"And?"

"I'm here to investigate and hold you accountable."

"Well, investigate away, Rod. If there is nothing else, I have things to do. Great seeing you again." Robert got up, turned, and left the room. Rodney sat, staring at the open doorway, mouth open, totally flummoxed by the disrespect shown him.

As Robert walked by the bullpen area, he signalled for Finn and Vito to join him in his office. The guests followed and settled in, staring at Robert with raised eyebrows.

Robert closed the door gently. "Our friend Rod is investigating Allo Foot's unfortunate situation for the IIO."

"What did you tell him?" Finn asked, leaning forward.

"Nothing. Partly because I don't know what really happened down there, and partly because it really is none of his business. I am not going to say anything to that schmuck." Robert was flustered, and he knew why. Being the subject of an investigation was no longer a new experience, but it was still unsettling, and he had no desire to be part of another one.

"Let's get down to business. Did you guys line up some undercover social disturbers?"

Vito answered. "You bet we did. Working on their signs as we speak. We also have a few others who will join in after things rev up. They will do some tailing after the show is over."

"I'm thinking we should watch from a distance, maybe inside City Hall. Mary knows us, well, me, anyway." Robert said.

"She hasn't seen us. We'll wander by the protest after it gets going, pretend to be interested citizens."

"Maybe I should call the news people — make sure they know to show up. Nothing like the press and cameras to bring out the nutters." Robert said. "Everyone have a photo of Mary?"

"Yes. We are ready to go tomorrow."

"And make sure everyone is armed."

"Yes, mother." Finn smiled. The meeting adjourned. Robert stayed behind to call the CBC.

"Bernard?"

"Yes. Robert? Good to hear from you."

"Nice. I have a tip for you. Demonstration tomorrow. Ten, I believe. At City Hall."

"Great. Can I ask how you know this? I know sometimes organizations will warn the police about what they are planning."

"We monitor chat rooms. That's all I can say. Let's have lunch later this week. How about Thursday?"

"Usual place?"

"Yes. See you then." He hung up. He stayed in his office, looking at some other case files, not wanting to bump into Rodney if he was still lurking around. It wasn't until later, after lunch, that he found out what Rodney had been up to after harassing Robert.

An officer knocked on his door jamb, peeking around the edge. "May I have a word?"

Robert pointed to one of his guest chairs with an upraised palm. The constable was young, seemingly too young to be permitted to carry a firearm.

"I'm Marcus. I work in the basement, usually. Handle the prisoners, mostly. This guy showed up today, asking questions. I think he used to work up here with you lot."

"Rodney Fister."

"Yes. You know him?"

"Unfortunately. What did you tell him?"

"Nothing. He tried to throw his weight around, but our sergeant warned us ahead of time to keep our mouths shut. Eventually, he gave up and left."

Robert nodded but said nothing, knowing there would also be an internal investigation underway by the VPD. How thorough it would be, impossible to know.

He considered carefully before asking his final question. "What did happen down there with Allo?"

"I don't know. I wasn't on duty at the time in question."

Robert suspected this would be the answer from everyone who had ever come close to working in the holding cells, but he relented. "Thanks for the heads up, Marcus." Sounded like the wagons had been circled.

It was time to visit Thomas. He waited for Marcus to leave before making his way over to Norma. "Boss in?"

"I believe so. Please proceed." The invitation wasn't cold, but neutral, Robert gauged.

Robert stuck his head around the door jamb. "Can I have a moment, Thomas?"

"Of course." Robert entered and closed the door behind him.

"Thought I should let you know what we are up to regarding Mary Tinlit." He told Thomas about the event happening the next morning. Thomas nodded. "But wait, there's more. We may have had something to do with organizing it."

"May?"

"Okay. The boys in the basement started a chat group as a way to ferret out the protesters. No one else knows about this. We have undercover officers attending, and if Miss Mary does not attend, we'll trail some people after the thing winds up and hope to find her that way."

"So let me understand. The guys in the basement organized a demonstration at City Hall tomorrow?"

"Maybe. I might have suggested it to them." Concern started to develop.

"Brilliant. As long as you keep that part close." Thomas smiled at the audacity.

"It will eventually get out. But hopefully, by that point, we'll have our suspect in custody. I doubt City Hall will be thrilled."

"No, there will be repercussions, I expect. Maybe I'll get another meeting with Mr. McKnight out of it."

"Another topic, Thomas. Do you know what happened with the Allo Foot release?"

"No. I have asked, but haven't heard as yet."

"I only ask because I feel some guilt. He may not have been the murderer we were after. After we interviewed him, I felt that maybe he wasn't our guy. But it wasn't definitive. And he obviously didn't kill Tony."

Thomas nodded, studying something outside the window.

"But there is more. Rodney Fister showed up this morning trying to pin the blame for Allo on me. You heard he is with the IIO now?"

"Yes, I heard. What did you say to him?"

"Nothing. And that is the way it is going to be, going forward. Last item. Finn arrived back successfully from Bella Kind. He was able to find a drill that may have been used on the Beaver that I was on, ever so briefly. Arrested the owner of said drill — Mary's father. Don't know how long he'll remain in custody, but at least Finn tried. We are hoping to put some additional pressure on Mary, if she even cares about her father. Which is doubtful."

"Anything else?"

"That is plenty. Thanks for the ear, Thomas." He waved as he left. Robert wandered back to his office, reviewing the conversation with Thomas. He couldn't discern any real interest from Thomas in the Allo Foot incident. The more he considered this, the more it troubled him. He didn't know who was running the internal investigation, but he'd find out, and get a clue as to what had happened, maybe. In the meantime, there was tomorrow to consider. He prayed that Mary would show herself. He didn't have much else to hope for in a case that now seemed to revolve around a single suspect. After several more moments of useless woolgathering, he called it a day and left to get some rest, anticipating action tomorrow.

In Surrey, Rodney had returned to his office. He was puzzled as to how he was to make any progress at all in the Allo Foot affair. His natural instincts were not to trust anyone, so he didn't bother to ask any of his fellow investigators how he might move things along. Instead, he was developing knots of fury as he replayed the responses given to him at Cambie Street. He stared out at the view of South Surrey for a while and, not finding an easy way forward, he re-focused. Perhaps he could get into the case files involving Robert last spring. He looked at his computer screen, clicked his mouse, and started a careful search of the file structure in his new world.

Robert arrived early on Tuesday and met again with Finn and Vito to confirm details. This done, he headed up to City Hall. Amazingly, his path took him right by the entry to Cafe Paulo. He would need to thank those basement dwellers on the canny demonstration locale. Of course, he entered and, waving at Gilberto, went to the bar and took his espresso standing. He stared out the window at the rain sprinkling down, willing the day to be a success.

"You're a doing well, Roberto?" No mention of Tony.

"Fine, fine. About to attend a demonstration up the street. I'll fill you in tomorrow. We are still on the hunt for Tony's killer."

Gilberto smiled, confident that Robert had everything under control. Robert slid his empty cup across the marble bar, turned, and walked out into the rain.

As he headed south, he looked down at his watch. Half-past nine. City Hall had a couple of entries. The south side faced 12th Avenue and was the formal address point for City Hall. The north entry fronted a small plaza of sorts through which an internal traffic lane passed, with some parking and a large green area farther below it. Wide stairs connecting several levels were the major feature, common enough for older public buildings when grand statements were the order of the day, not ease of access for wheelchairs or strollers. Unsure which side of the building the demonstration would take place, he entered the north side. After talking to the man guarding the reception desk, he was let into secure stairs up to the third floor, which was occupied mostly by the mayoral suite of offices. He went up to the first administrative person he came upon and pulled his badge out. He was certain that only a few years earlier, one could walk wherever one wanted in the building. He suspected a few nutcases with civic gripes had probably caused the city staff to rethink their security options.

"I'd like to get out to the windows on this floor. A demonstration is about to take place, and I need to monitor it."

"Oh, my."

"Yes." Robert waited for something further. Then he remembered where he was, City Hall. He raised his hands, palms up in a silent plea for action.

The lady rose. "You can follow me. Where is it? Which side?"

"Don't know, yet. If you can show me some spots, I'll soon figure it out. North side would be the best guess." He followed the woman as she went down a corridor behind the curtains of power. Everything seemed old and from another era, as if he had stepped back decades in time. The walls were wainscoted with dark wood and boasted all the trims. The framed pictures hanging on yellowish plaster above the wood depicted scenes of bygone eras. This wasn't surprising, but the general feeling was not of this century, odd for a city known for proclaiming its place amongst the leading modern places to live in this world.

Looking down the hall, beyond the lady guiding him, he spotted a wispy figure clad in a dark pin-striped suit from another time. The man sported mutton-chop whiskers and carried a large envelope under his arm. Robert looked at the woman leading him into a room, then looked back at the man, but he had disappeared. Robert shrugged, then entered the meeting room that had a delightful view, looking north at the mountains beyond the downtown towers. On this day of rain, they were only partly available for viewing. Grouse was there, but the rest of the mountains were shrouded. The room's decor was similar to the halls he had just left. Uncomfortable look-ing chairs surrounded a long, dark and scarred wooden table.

"If you need anything else, let me know." With that, the lady left. Robert went over to the window and spotted a few people below, gathering together. A couple were carrying signs, proclaiming the city's inability to protect its most vulnerable citizens. He wondered if these were officers, or real protesters. Some of the spelling didn't look to be on point, so maybe officers trying to fit in? Or were they merely illustrating the results of a poor education? He would ask later, after the day was done. The light rain wasn't treating some of the signs very well, letters starting to run. He waited patiently as the area slowly filled with people, some starting to make noise, the ruckus easily heard through the single glazed windows. Everyone seemed on the young side, dressed in rough looking out-door gear. He grabbed a chair and settled in, elbows on the windowsill, scanning with small, opera-like binoculars, searching for his prey as more people joined the group.

On the pavement below, a bald man dressed in army fa-tigues, with a bullhorn, started exhorting the crowd to do something about bad decision making by the city. Robert spotted Finn and Vito, both now dressed in some of their rattier attire, ranging around the periphery of the crowd, watching everyone. Robert knew they had previously met some of the undercover officers attending the demonstra-tion, but not everyone, so it was probably hard for them to tell who was sincere with their diatribe and who was acting.

The light rain didn't seem to be an impediment to attending, so the crowd slowly grew in size and intensity. Clumps grew into groups. Several uniformed police officers in rain gear stood off to the side, watching the proceedings. So far, everything was calm and under control.

Then, Mr. Bullhorn ramped it up a few notches, starting to scream. It had the desired effect. The crowd roared back, all the rants aimed at City Hall. The demonstration rapidly became ugly. A few rocks were thrown, not at the police this time, but at the building. Their aim was pathetic, but it didn't take long for a couple of rocks to strike and break windows. The heritage building wasn't built to handle demonstrations. Once this happened, the police swung into action, literally. Batons were arcing as the police tried to drive the crowd away from the building. More officers were arriving, tumbling out of vans, dressed in riot gear and running after the demonstrators who dispersed in all directions.

Because of the rain, Robert was having trouble seeing faces. However, he had no problem identifying a camera crew from the CBC. A few protesters had umbrellas, but most had hoods over their heads. Robert was intent on his task, so he didn't hear the door open. Several city employees entered the room, intent on viewing the ruckus outside the building instead of doing whatever they were supposed to be doing. They ignored the man at the window with binoculars.

A rock flew and shattered a pane of glass next to the one Robert was looking through. He sucked in a breath and stood up, trying to see who had thrown the rock. It was of no use. Chaos reigned. He was focusing on female protesters, but the difficulty was getting a look at faces. He could only hope that officers on the ground were having better luck.

He suddenly tired of being the eye in the sky. It was a stupid idea from the outset. He dashed from the room, intent on joining the action outside. Robert descended the stairs, exited City Hall, and spotted Vito over by a rock wall. He joined him, but Vito shook his head at Robert. No luck on this day.

A couple of arrests had been made, but, other than four broken windows, no further damage had been inflicted on the building. Robert felt slightly sheepish about the whole affair, seemingly a complete waste of time and effort. He beckoned to Finn and the three made their way back down Cambie, all of them sodden. It was Finn this time who suggested they stop at Cafe Paulo. Robert wanted to head back to the office, but it didn't take much for him to relent, realizing how little it took to change his mind. The three settled in at a table, water dripping onto the table from their heads. Whiffs of steam rose from their coats as the cafe's heat slowly did its work.

"Well, we tried, didn't we?" Robert said.

"Yeah, pretty exciting when the rocks started to fly," Vito responded.

"You didn't spot Mary?" Finn asked.

"No. It wasn't the best idea, made worse by the rain. I couldn't recognize anyone from my perch. They did manage to break a window right bedside where I was sitting. That was something, I suppose." Yuko made her way over to their table balancing three Americanos on a tray. Robert looked over at Gilberto, and with a smile, nodded.

"So, you guys rent?" Finn asked. The other two nodded, considering what had brought the protesters together at City Hall. "You think they have a point?"

"Remember, it was us who made this whole thing up," Robert said.

"Yes, but it obviously hit a nerve, correct? We weren't arresting officers out there, so...." Finn lapsed into silence.

"From what I've seen on the news, the councillors and mayor say that no one will be forced out of their low-cost rentals by pillaging developers. Safeguards are in place." Robert smiled at how serene the future was to be.

Vito started laughing. "Good one, Robert."

Robert felt the need to point out the obvious. "People hate change, but last time I checked, every single person in this city, even the mayor, lives in something developed by someone. God knows, there are some bad developers out there, but there are also very good ones. I think those protesters see life through very selective lenses."

"Selective is one word for it, but killing off the architect for a social housing project just because of some media crap about her seems way out of bounds." Vito said.

"Yes, I agree. Something else is going on. Let's finish and get back." Robert drained his cup, stood up and grabbed his still wet coat from the chair back.

It was not a detective this day, but one of the uniformed riot officers who became golden. He had attended the protest on Clark and Hastings weeks earlier, so when he spotted the familiar face of a rioter from that melee, he grabbed one of the plainclothes officers and pointed the man out just as the protest exploded. Words were spoken and a tail was started after the excitement had abated, with participants running in all directions. Two officers dressed in shabby street clothes followed the young man as he headed west, taking turns, occasionally overlapping as they exchanged positions. West was the last direction they had expected to be taking, but they stuck to their routine, careful not to be spotted. Their prey weaved his way through the streets, first of modest homes, then of some of the oldest and most expensive mansions in the city, working his way south before heading up a back lane. The streets were empty. No residents in the area walked anywhere, so the two officers had a difficult time of it.

One of the officers entered the lane, moving quietly from garage to garage, staying to the side in case the man looked behind him, but he never did, confident in his actions. The officer stopped as he watched the man about thirty metres ahead suddenly disappear. He waited, then slowly made his way up to the point at which he'd lost sight of his quarry. Blue metal construction fencing ran along the lane for a ways. An old mansion slated for demolition, it seemed, or renovation. Likely a squat. He signalled back to his partner, pointing to the house. The partner reversed course and made for the street side to get an address. All that was needed was to set up a surveillance operation. He smiled as he got on his cell to call it in.

Robert was in his office, ruminating on the lack of progress, when Norma peeked her head in.

"They were successful. At least they found a squat."

"Who did? Where?"

"Someone recognized a protester from the Clark Street fiasco and he was followed."

"Great news. Where is it?"

"West side. Shaughnessy. A mansion slated for demolition or a reno. I think there are more than a few of those over there these days."

"Right where we wouldn't look for them. Brilliant. Has a watch been set?"

"As we speak. I have to get back to my desk." Norma turned and disappeared, nothing extra on offer.

Not a total waste of effort. Robert smiled to himself. He dialled Norma's number and got the address of the house, thinking he'd slip by on his way home. He started to consider how to hang on to Mary, if she was indeed finally captured. A prosecutor wasn't going to buy Robert's long and drawn-out tale about her, that was certain. Trespassing by being in a squat wouldn't pass muster, either. If he couldn't come up with any further incriminating evidence on the murder files, perhaps resisting arrest could be used, or break and enter. He was certain that she would not be detained quietly, based on past performance. He'd check with Finn and Vito tomorrow — see what suggestions they might have.

Robert couldn't wait, he wanted to see this mansion for himself, so he went down to get his car, then headed south and west into the heart of old Shaughnessy. He was on the correct street, so he slowed and looked over to check the address again from the paper scrap he had placed on the passenger seat. He passed a panel van with a construction logo on its side - probably a watcher already in place. He slowed to a crawl, looking through the blue fencing at a ruin of a house. It was large, maybe from the thirties or forties. He wasn't current with the styles of each era, but there didn't seem to be anything modern in the entire neighbourhood. No one was evident on the grounds. He wondered how long it had been occupied, but didn't tarry. He trusted that the watchers would have things in hand. He headed home, satisfied that a good start had been made.

# CHAPTER 20

The watch in Shaughnessy was layered, the VPD taking no chances. A few static posts were maintained in vehicles posing as trade vans, a common sight anywhere in construction crazy Vancouver. As well, roaming undercover officers covered the surrounding streets and lanes, by walking, riding bikes, and on the occasional scooter. Two murdered officers tended to focus minds and concentrate efforts. An ant wasn't going to enter or leave the property without being photographed.

Robert showed up early Wednesday morning at the office, eager to hear if anyone had been spotted.

He waved at Finn, stopping at his desk. "Any sign yet?"

"Not of Mary. But there have been a few people in and out. I'm getting hourly updates. I also have some photos already." Robert beckoned Vito over as Finn pulled them up on his screen and started a short scroll. The only person Robert recognized was the last one. The photo was grainy and the light dim, but Robert had no trouble with the identification.

"That is the guy who was staring at me when we nabbed Allo out on Hastings. I'd like to speak with him. Can you run him through our system, see if we know him somehow?"

"The facial recognition software? Don't think it's working too well just yet."

"Try anyway, please. He may be the new Allo. And any ideas about how to hold on to Mary, if we get lucky, would be welcome."

Robert returned to his office, where he proceeded to get nothing accomplished. He stared out the window, willing Mary to show her face, as he re-visited everything that had happened in the case to date. His thoughts drifted to Mr. Foot. He called Thomas on his internal line.

"Thomas. Do you know who is running the Allo Foot internal investigation?"

"No. I can find out if you wish."

"I wish, thanks." He hung up. Again, not thrilled with the less than enthusiastic response from his superior. He came to a decision and called Vancouver General Hospital.

"I'm Detective Robert Lui with the VPD and I'm calling about an Allo Foot, who, I understand, is in your care." He waited while the person on the other end shunted the call either up the line or down it.

After a full two minutes, someone else came onto the line. "Renata here. You wish to know about Allo Foot?"

"Yes."

"And you're with the police? Nothing has changed. He is still in an induced coma — prognosis is uncertain."

A thought came to him. "Has anyone visited him, to your knowledge?"

"I was here when a woman visited. That is all I know about. No one else has come by, I think, but then, I don't work every shift, despite what many people think."

Robert ignored the bitterness. "A woman?" Could you describe her? Young, or older? If I send you a picture, could you look and let me know?" Could it be Mary surfacing? He was kicking himself. How could he be so incompetent as to not have a watch at the hospital?

"I suppose. She wasn't old." She didn't sound totally convinced, so Robert reluctantly upped the pressure.

"This is a murder investigation. Two police officers were killed." He wasn't sure what the response would be to this. Everyone had their own opinions of the police, so it could go either way.

"Okay." She didn't sound totally sold, but gave him an e-mail address and hung up.

Robert didn't waste any time, grabbing Mary's picture from the file and sending it onto VGH. He yelled, "Hey Finn, get in here."

Finn peered around the door frame. "What?"

"I screwed up. Not paying attention, I suppose. That Rod is messing up my concentration. No one put a watch on at the hospital, did they?"

"Not sure, Robert. Why?"

"I think Mary may have visited Allo, that's why."

"Shit."

"Exactly. I've sent a picture over there. We should know soon enough. Allo has no family in Vancouver, as far as I know, so it might make sense that Mary went to see him, given their history, although pretty risky, I have to say."

Finn nodded. "I'm going to check on the spotters at the mansion. Let me know."

"If Mary shows her face, they know to go in and arrest the lot of them, correct?"

"Yes, chief." Finn smiled. "Don't worry, Robert. We know what we're about." Robert nodded and sat back down, at a loss as to what to do next.

He drummed his fingers on the desk, Tony's goofy smile coming back to him as he stared out the window, willing something positive to happen. His mind turned to a moment when Tony had shown up to help free Robert's son, using the 'going for lunch' gambit. This, despite Robert having advised him not to risk his career by aiding him. He sat like this for ten or fifteen minutes, then his computer made the annoying ping that accompanied an arriving e-mail.

He studied the screen for a second.

**'The photo you sent matches the woman I saw visiting Allo Foot.'**

That was it, but it was enough. It also didn't mean much, other than to reinforce how lax he had been. He hoped that Tony wasn't keeping a ledger on him as he oversaw the investigation, from wherever he was.

He yelled. "Finn, it was Mary at the hospital." Finn muttered something in return, unintelligible to Robert. He stood and, walking by Finn, pointed to the stairs. "I'm going down to see if there has been any blowback from yesterday's commotion."

Finn nodded, head down.

Robert descended and entered the youngsters' domain. Two of the four officers were missing, but Rory and a woman were in place, ruining their eyes as they studied their screens.

"How are you two?" Robert tried to be sociable. "Any blowback from yesterday's action?"

"Hi, Robert. Think some of them might be getting suspicious, but it's indefinite, so far at least," Rory responded.

"Well, Rory, no matter what they think, yesterday was a success for us. Thought you should know."

Rory looked up at Robert, eyebrows furrowed.

"We found a squat after the demonstration, where some of our targets are spending their idle hours. So, well done, I would say."

Rory looked over at his partner, smiling at the unexpected praise. Robert imagined they didn't receive much of this in their work life. He was pretty certain the majority of the force didn't know who they were. "Let me know if you learn anything more." He headed back upstairs and out for a quick bite in case the squat was raided. He didn't want to miss it.

Down south, in Surrey, Rodney Fister arrived at his office Wednesday morning and promptly went back down the filing rabbit hole on his computer. After several attempts, he found that he couldn't get into the final files for completed cases. A password was required, that he didn't know how to obtain. After another hour at this, he grew irritable. Then he discovered a folder labelled 'Case Drafts'. He entered this easily and discovered early versions of recent case investigations.

It was a motherlode of information, seemingly organized under the name of the victim in each case. Rod's grasp of the basic facts in Robert's previous case, however, didn't even run to the gang member's full name. A quick online review of events the previous spring from news clips cleared this up. Manny Dhillon was who he was after. His phone rang, but he ignored it, concentrating instead on copying as much of the file as he could onto his hard drive.

Some moments later, a rap sounded on his door, and it opened without his invitation. His boss's assistant peered in. "Good, you're alive. Thought maybe you had expired when you didn't answer your phone. Didn't you hear it?" she asked rhetorically. "The boss is waiting for your report on the Prince George case, *tout suite*, as they say in Quebec." She treated Rodney to her humourless grin and left, leaving the door ajar.

Rod's irritability increased three-fold. How was he to screw Robert Lui when he had to perform common work tasks? He stared at his clunky workstation, the computer of choice the world over for working drones. If he had a laptop, he could take the files home with him. He looked for something on his desk that he could throw at the wall. It was empty. Screw it, he thought, I'm going for coffee. The report could wait.

Robert returned from lunch, watching as Finn and Vito stood at Finn's desk, grinning back at him. His eyebrows raised in question.

"Yeah, bingo. We got her!" Vito said. "We nabbed seven of them. They are being brought in as we speak."

Robert smiled, silently savouring the moment. "We should head over there, look around while they are being processed here. Could you call down and impress upon them that we don't want another Allo Foot incident happening to any of them?" Robert was looking at Finn.

"I'll do that. Let's meet at the car."

Vito drove so Robert could admire the older neighbourhood he usually never visited. Shaughnessy wasn't far from their station, and boasted large older houses with expansive gardens, mature trees, and winding streets. He didn't know much about the area, other than it was where the tycoons and industrialists of the day in the early part of the twentieth century made their homes.

Many of these old mansions no longer fit the needs of the nouveau riche who were flocking to Vancouver. If a home wasn't protected by heritage rules, it was inevitably demolished and re-developed into something more appropriate to modern luxe living. Robert supposed it was progress of a sort. Many older Vancouverites thought differently. He regularly read articles in the local press ruing the loss of what little built history Vancouver had acquired. Robert supposed that the city didn't want to see a repeat of what had gone on across the water in West Vancouver a while back, where the upper slopes of the North Shore mountains presented one bad idea after another, all cheek by jowl, as the wealthy tried to outdo each other. It was frightening to behold, and was available for all to see after the native vegetation had been stripped out. No wealthy person in the District of West Vancouver wanted trees impeding their views south, of downtown Vancouver and points beyond.

As Vito slowed to a stop, the detectives witnessed what could be a chase in progress. A dog handler with his puppy was in hot pursuit of someone down the street in the opposite direction. Robert supposed it could be a late arrival to the party, not realizing that the squat had been rousted. The three got out of their vehicle, nodded to a couple of uniforms keeping watch outside the blue construction fencing, and made their way through a gap onto the grounds.

They studied the three-storey house, long past being a home, until recently, apparently. It was large enough to house several families if needed. English Ivy tendrils grew up one side of the front stucco wall, trying to devour the house whole. Some windows were intact, but an equal number were shattered or completely missing. Squares of ancient plaster enclosed by rectangles of dark beams made the whole thing look like some kind of Tudor disaster, if that was a style on offer.

Whoever the owner was obviously thought little about keeping the grounds tidy. Perhaps they weren't even in the country. Weeds abounded and litter of all description covered the lot. Large trees had started shedding their foliage because of the recent dry weather.

The front door was ajar, so they each squeezed through and stood in a two-storey entry hall admiring the garbage cluttered on the floor. A uniformed officer stood to the side by another wide opening. He pointed behind him. "Their main living area, it seems."

Robert briefly considered calling in the crime scene team, but, as no real crime had taken place, he thought better of it. Vito and Finn followed him into the next room. Filtered light came in through windows covered in dirt and dust. There was some garbage near the walls, but the room was several shades tidier than the outside grounds. Protest signs lay against a wall, in pieces, likely assembled on the site of wherever the next demonstration was to be. He was looking at rolls of heavy construction paper and piles of felt pens. Knapsacks and sleeping bags sat in a jumbled heap. Scattered beer cans lay amongst the mess, most of them empty. He spied what looked like one of those mechanical pencils that had ended up in Ann Leforet's chest. Robert quickly changed his mind and called the station to request a crew be sent out to process the scene. "Looks like some users in the crowd." He pointed to a couple of spent needles by the wall.

"I'm checking upstairs. You guys look in the other rooms down here." Robert paused, assessing the curved stairway before trying it out. It seemed stable. He kept to the wall side as he ascended slowly, praying that the creaking didn't signal some kind of impending failure. As he reached the top, he looked to his right. A dark hall extended several metres. He could just make out something moving, a shadow, maybe a small child walking away from him carrying a toy animal. Robert looked back down the stairs, then at the hall again. There was nothing. He put some gloves on and walked down the hallway, trying doors as he went, no sign of the child he thought he had seen.

The third door opened onto what was obviously another living quarters for the squatters, perhaps the ringleaders. The window was intact, but grimy. Light was mottled. A couple of sleeping bags lay on the dark wooden floor. Dust was everywhere, drifts and motes floating in front of the window. By a wall wainscoted in more dark wood, a police officer's service belt lay. Robert came closer but didn't touch it. Archie's, if he had to guess. The pistol was missing. Farther down the room, some rope was coiled, perhaps waiting for its next victim. The squat seemed to be ground zero for evidence of the recent murders.

He stood quietly, looking around, then went back to the hall, checking on the remaining rooms, which were all empty, sort of, if you didn't count bird's nests and evidence of vermin. He returned to the main floor hall, looking for his partners.

They wandered in from the rear of the house. "The kitchen is back there. It'd be surprising if they all didn't have cholera or something similar." Vito said. "It's disgusting in there."

"I think I found the room upstairs where Mary and whoever her new beau is kept house. Found rope, and a service belt — probably Archie's. No gun, though. Think we'll leave the rest for the photographers. Let's get out of here." His skin was crawling. It was hard to fathom people willingly living in this filth. Maybe the protesters considered it an adventure of a temporary nature, willing to put up with anything in order to further their cause. As the three of them squeezed back through the perimeter fencing, they witnessed officers patting a young man down against a cruiser. His cargo pants appeared torn, as though the German Shepherd had detected a tasty morsel inside them. They walked over to get a closer look, but no one recognized him, so Robert signalled a return to their car.

Robert sat in the rear again, admiring the homes as Vito retraced their route back to Cambie Street. "I'm going down to cells when we get back. I want to see if the staring guy was part of the round-up."

Finn looked back at Robert. "I'll make a list of the items found on site that we think relate to the murders. Don't want anybody released until the site team has done their work." Robert nodded as he contemplated how they were going to interrogate Mary. One thing was certain: he would be in no rush to question her this time.

After arriving back at Cambie Street, Robert visited Thomas to make certain that Mary was not to be released, no matter what any lawyer may be contending. In any other case, that assumption would be tenuous, at best, but murdered officers made things different. Thomas agreed and made a call to the prosecutor. Robert left and went down to see who had been rounded up. He checked the cells, but they were all strangers, except Mary, so he left and made his way up the street.

Gilberto noticed Robert as he made his way into the cafe. His raised eyebrows were met with a smile. "Things are in hand, Gilberto." Robert stayed by the bar, rubbing the marble as he waited for his espresso, watching the other patrons.

Gilberto nodded to Robert, beckoning him closer. As he bent his head, Gilberto leaned forward, hands on the bar. "Someone was in here a day ago, asking about you. A young guy. He didn't feel right. I said nothing to him. Asked him to leave."

Robert nodded, now worried. How could someone know he frequented Cafe Paulo unless he was being tailed? He also didn't want his friends put in danger. He had no illusions about what his unknown foe was capable of.

"Gilberto, I have a picture. Could I bring it by and see if you recognize him?"

"Of course, Roberto." He finished pulling the shot and slid the demitasse over to Robert. Robert could sense some excitement in Gilberto at the prospect of helping out in a police investigation. All he could feel was fear, and it wasn't for himself. He finished the espresso, smiled at Gilberto in spite of his trepidations, and said he'd return in a few moments.

Robert went back to the station and up to Finn's cubicle, rapping on the frame to get his attention. "That guy who was eyeballing me may have been in the cafe asking about me. Print that picture and I'll take it back to Gilberto to see."

"Pretty bold, if you ask me."

"Let's see if it's him first." Robert went over to the printer and waited for the paper to be ejected, grabbed it, and returned to Cafe Paulo.

He signalled Gilberto, who asked him to step behind the bar. Robert felt privileged to enter the domain of the master. He pulled out the paper from his jacket and unfolded it, presenting it to Gilberto.

"That is the guy. No question, Roberto."

"Okay, here is my card. You see him in here again, call me. This man could be extremely dangerous."

Gilberto took the card, shrugged, but didn't look troubled in the least by Robert's news. Robert nodded and left the cafe, realizing that he didn't know much about Gilberto's past. Perhaps he could take care of himself. He looked fit and was not a small man. As Robert walked the few steps back to the station, his eyes were taking everything in, checking off everyone he saw. The paranoia had returned. He wondered if his children were, once again, in danger. Back on his floor, he waved at Vito and Finn and went over to them.

"I think we should mount a watch at the cafe. Maybe not continuous, but get a couple of the young guys to lounge around the cafe, drink some coffee in a tag team. Shouldn't be especially difficult for them, should it?"

"Wouldn't be the worst duty they ever pulled."

"Remind them that he may be armed."

"Yes, mother." Vito shook his head. "I do believe that you worry too much."

"For very good reason, Vito." As he turned, he said. "I need some thinking time before the interview." Instead of his office, he headed for the elevator. As he descended, he texted his two children, asking them to be extra aware. He didn't know where they were, but assumed they had left school. His foes seemed penniless, therefore carless, he assumed, so being followed by someone as he drove The Silver Streak seemed outside the realm of reality. He headed home.

# CHAPTER 21

Showers dropped relentlessly from a jumbled, dark ceiling that gave no hope of anything different happening this Thursday. Robert roused himself, taking his time. His daughter and son said their goodbyes from the main floor as they headed out the door. He had had a word with them the previous evening about being vigilant for the next few days, showing them the picture of the man Robert considered to be the threat. They weren't happy, but understood. He still wasn't certain the young man was dangerous, but the malevolent stare that day at the demonstration hinted at something unpleasant.

He descended to the kitchen and opened the freezer, looking for something to make toast out of. After pouring juice and readying his coffee paraphernalia, he sat at the counter, thinking about Mary. Her intelligence was not to be underestimated, but she had also exhibited a very short fuse. If all else failed, as he expected, then he would light that fuse. He slathered some marmalade onto his toast, then poured boiling water into the filter, the resulting aroma relaxing him as he watched water slowly sink through the grounds.

His thoughts then wandered back to Norma and making amends. That is, if she would accept any. How to do it was the question. He sipped his coffee as he looked at his rear garden, watching the rain bounce off the few plants that still boasted leaves. He shook his head, drained the cup and made ready for his day, making sure both of his guns were loaded and secure in their holsters.

Robert arrived on his floor later than his usual start time. He went over to Vito before going to his office.

"Has a time been set for the interview?"

"One o'clock. A lawyer may be present, not certain."

"Fine. I'll take Finn in with me this time. No disrespect, Vito."

"No worries, Roberto. I get it." With that, Robert went to his office and started jotting down the thoughts he had come up with about possible angles of attack for Mary. After an hour of little progress, his internal line rang. It was the admin person manning the main floor public entry.

"Robert?"

"Yes."

"There is a young woman here wanting to see you?"

He had a feeling about the answer before he asked. "Name?" He waited a moment while she asked.

"Sandra Kour."

"You can tell Ms. Kour that I'll be down in about half an hour." Not what he needed on this day. On reflection, he also didn't need a half hour, so he left his office and took the elevator down to the ground floor. He went into the lobby and there she was, staring out the window at the wet pavement. She hadn't noticed him, so he walked over slowly and stood to one side.

"Sandra." She turned her head, looking up at him, uncertain.

A small smile broke out. "Robert."

"What are you doing here? Visiting?"

"Yes. I had some time off and thought I'd see some friends in Vancouver."

"Nice. I appreciate you coming by, but I am really jammed up here, in the middle of an investigation. I have to conduct an interview shortly." He looked down at Sandra, willing her to get the message, then he inexplicably relented. "Tell you what, can you come back around three? We can take a walk."

Sandra nodded, the uncertain smile returning as she rose. "See you then, Robert." She turned and went out into the cold rain.

Robert took the stairs slowly back up to his floor while he considered this complication. He shook his head, needing to focus on what was important this day. He walked by the pod area and signalled Finn to join him. As they settled in, Robert's phone rang.

"Yes?"

"Hey, Robert. It's Bernard, lunch today?"

"Oh, craps. I forgot. Can we do it next week? I'll get back to you on a day that works for me."

Bernard acquiesced, so Robert turned back to Finn and together, they plotted lines of questioning, and fallbacks if Mary was as obstinate as they assumed. They wearied of this after a half hour. Robert suggested heading up to his noodle restaurant for a plate of luck.

They settled in and studied the menu Robert already knew by heart. Of all the various noodle dishes on offer, Robert chose the House Special *Chou Mein*. It brought the most auspicious luck in his experience. Junior *Gai Lan* and some dumplings completed the order. He watched the other customers as he flicked his chopsticks around, waiting. "Guess who showed up this morning?" he said, knowing Finn would take great delight upon hearing the gossip.

"That girl? From the resort?"

"Bingo. Her name is Sandra, Sandra Kour. Not sure how she spells her last name."

Finn started laughing. "You are so screwed, Robert. Norma know about her?"

"Sort of. She knows what happened up there because I told her."

Finn shook his head. "Don't know if I would have done that, Robert."

"Well, it's done. It's the way I am wired, I suppose." The dumplings arrived first with the dipping sauce, followed by the remaining dishes. The conversation stopped while the detectives made quick work of their food.

Robert leaned back. "That was good. This place has always helped when I run into case problems, which is quite often, oddly."

"That's good, Robert, because with what little we have, we are going to need a boatload of luck."

Robert asked the server for the cheque, which came quickly. He took it up to the front, paying for both of them before Finn could object. "Battle time, Finn." They walked back down Cambie, squinting through the light drizzle, thinking about what lay ahead, and what lay behind.

When they returned to their floor, Robert went over to Norma. "Is Mary ready?"

Norma replied succinctly. "She is in the room."

"Lawyer present?"

"I believe so."

"Thank you, Norma." Robert put his best manners on offer, as if it would make any difference.

He waved at Finn and went into his office to collect some paper. After descending to the cell level, they entered the adjacent room to look at Mary through the mirrored glass. She was sitting calmly, looking slightly mussed compared to the last time she had been a guest of the VPD. But then, the accommodation where she had been found wasn't the Four Seasons. She seemed to be ignoring her public defender, who was unfamiliar to Robert.

Robert led Finn into the room, his eyes never leaving Mary's eyes. She looked at Finn as the detectives took their seats. "What happened to your last friend? Found out he was like, too stupid?"

Robert didn't respond to this jibe at Tony, instead looking down at his sheaf of papers, which contained mostly old reports. He shuffled through a few, hoping to build some tension.

"Is this how you talk of the dead?" He shuffled papers again. "Your friend is dead." Robert said, referring to Anne as he looked up. He couldn't believe the change that came over Mary's face as this registered. It was a look of pure shock.

"What!" She screamed. "What did you do to him?"

Finn exhibited just the slimmest of smirks.

"Nothing." Robert not elaborating, seeing how far Mary would dig her own hole. He watched the lawyer stare sideways at Mary.

"Your father is under arrest as well." At this, Mary stood up. The sheriff standing by the wall took a step forward, fixing her eyes on Mary with menace. Mary had lost what little control she imagined she had of the interview. The only act left to her was defiance.

Her lawyer, of course, had a different view. "What exactly are the charges against my client?" Mary reluctantly sat down.

Finn responded. "You must already know, if you are here defending Mary. Maybe you should take notes; breaking and entering, mansion on the west side." As if the location made the charge twice as serious.

"What proof do you have that my client did the breaking and entering?"

Both detectives ignored this. "We think of it as a placeholder." Robert said, then he fixed a stare at Mary. "Why would you be in possession of the same rope that was used in two recent murders, one of a police officer, and the other, your university friend, Anne Leforet?"

Mary's eyes darted around as her brain engaged. "Like, it's not my rope."

"Oh, I'm sure it's not. Not what I asked you, however." He continued to stare.

Mary remained silent, digesting the situation. Her eyes were darting everywhere except Robert's face. The lawyer was staring at Mary.

"Why are your fingerprints on the mechanical pencil that was used to kill Anne?" This statement wasn't exactly accurate, but Mary's prints had been found on a matching pencil recovered at the squat. Robert wanted to see the reaction. The lawyer continued to look at Mary, perhaps re-assessing her new client. She had probably heard about the murders but was likely unaware of the connection to Mary until now. And also likely wondering why murder charges had not been filed.

"Like, that pencil was clean. You are making stuff up. I want out of here." Finn smiled again. Another mistake. This was turning into an excellent afternoon.

Now the lawyer appeared confused. "I'd like a private word with my client."

Robert and Finn stood, stopping the interview. "We'll be outside when you feel like resuming." Finn had no sooner closed the door, when Robert spoke. "We need the ID on this boyfriend. Tell the guys working with that software." Finn nodded, pulling out his phone.

The detectives sat down on a couch. "I suppose that's it for the interview, Robert."

"Yes. The lawyer will tell her to clam up, now that she knows murder is involved. Only have one card left." Finn looked over at Robert, wondering what he was going to do.

The sheriff came into their room after several more minutes. "They are ready to resume." The detectives stood and followed her back into the interview room. Mary looked slightly calmer. She glared up at both men, who sat down, but switching chairs. Robert could sense this bothered Mary. He waited, looking down at his pile of paper to prolong the tension.

"Why do you think the pencil was clean, Mary? Did you try to wipe it? Or use gloves? How would you think that it was clean?"

Mary remained silent. Robert had to admire the effort it took. Obviously, the lawyer had laid the law down for her new client.

"Heard you visited Allo. How's he doing?" He affected a nonchalance he in no way felt.

Mary screamed again. "You bastards! Andy will have your head."

"Why the excitement, Mary? Last time you were in here, you said you didn't know Allo." Mary's threat wasn't much, but it was enough, for Robert. Plus, she had spilled a name. "This interview is concluded, for now." Robert rose, followed by Finn. Robert nodded at the lawyer as he left. He could hear the question fluttering over his shoulder as he left, but kept going.

"Are you freeing my client?"

"Let's walk up the street. Can you get Vito? I'll go ahead." Robert went to the main level and out into the rain, turning south, his mind churning with what he had just learned. He entered the cafe, his head wet from the short trip, and ordered three Americanos from Yuko, retreating to the back of the room to wait. While he sat, he tried to figure out if any of the customers present were with the VPD. After a few moments and not any wiser, he was joined by his partners.

No sooner than they had sat when Robert waggled his finger at Finn. Finn was learning quickly what Robert's various hand signals meant and went over to the bar to fetch the steaming cups.

Finn returned. "I am sure you could patent your own sign language for caffeine addicted people, Robert."

"I've been thinking of it," he lied. "The lawyer must have convinced Mary that nothing had happened to her Andy. Or nothing public, at any rate."

"Who is Andy?" Vito asked.

"Andy could be the man behind all this mayhem. Robert tricked her into spilling his name. It shouldn't be too long before we know who he is. Then all we have to do is find him before he kills anyone else."

"Very succinct, Finn. It also appears that Mary is at least an accomplice to Anne's murder, if not the actual killer. She stupidly said as much. Although, in the absence of solid evidence, chances of charges are tiny, I would say." Robert again looked over the patrons. "You guys recognize any officers in here? Just wondering if the watch has started."

"Nope," Vito answered.

"Have any of the others from the squat been questioned yet?" Robert asked.

"Working my way through them. A feisty lot, for sure. One of them said that Mary slept up in the penthouse suite with her boyfriend, kind of like the queen bee. But we already knew that," Vito responded.

"It'd be good to find out what we can about Andy from them. And remember, some are users. They may be feeling a tad antsy by now."

Vito smiled, "They are probably unaware of Andy's darker side, so I'll go at them harder. Don't think we are going to able to hang onto them much longer, however."

"All the more reason to get this done sooner." Robert held his coffee cup as he re-lived the short interview he had just conducted. He was losing his grip on the case.

Finn spoke. "What if we released her and put a tail on her ass? Or even better, put a device in her clothing?"

Robert raised his eyebrow as he studied Finn. "We already released her once. Repeating mistakes is not in my playbook, hopefully. Although, to be honest, I've never checked my whole playbook. It might be in there, hiding."

Finn smiled. "Good coffee today."

"I need to go attend to some unfinished business when we're done here."

"Arnott Bay business?"

"Maybe."

Vito looked at the other two, curious as to what was going on. However, an explanation was not on offer. Robert got up and went over to have a word with Gilberto.

He returned to the table. "Andy hasn't been back, at least while Gilberto has been here." Robert checked his watch, drained his cup, and stood up. "Got to go. You guys take your time."

As he walked back down Cambie to his rendezvous with Sandra, he went through what he would say. Tough, yeah, that's what he needed to be. He hoped that he wasn't the sole reason for her trip to Vancouver, but he had a suspicion that it was, despite what she had told him. She had to be at least ten years younger than him. He wasn't paying attention to his surroundings as he made his way back to the station, concentrating on what he was going to say. He entered the empty lobby. He went up to the receptionist and asked if Sandra had returned. The reply was negative, so he went over to the sitting area and slid onto a plastic chair, waiting like a customer for some police attention.

Ten minutes later, Sandra entered the station, hair damp. She looked over and nodded, thankful that Robert had appeared as promised. He stood and pointed to the door. The rain had tapered off to something intermittent, which Robert was fine walking around in. What other people thought about walking in the rain was of little importance to him. If they didn't like rain, they probably shouldn't be living in Vancouver.

"The interview went well. Better than I expected, anyway. Staying with friends?"

"Yes. They live in Kits."

"Nice." They walked north, towards the Creek. "You realize that Arnott Bay was a one-time thing, correct?" He was pretty certain she was hoping it wasn't. "I have a family here. Well, not a wife, but two teenagers. My wife passed away a few years back. I won't deny that you were attractive to me, and..." Here he paused, "And you still are. I've always been a sucker for a sense of humour. But that is it, Sandra. It was a very unusual circumstance." He looked sideways at her, trying to gauge whether anything he was saying was making an impression.

Then he added. "The case that I was up on Raven Island about has only gotten worse, more dangerous, over the last weeks. I need to focus on it."

Sandra looked back at him, maybe realizing that the age gap was larger than she had first imagined. "I thought I'd try, Robert. And you were nice. It's not a common thing to find in men."

They reached the seawall. Rain had started up again. "Think we should head back." They turned and retraced their steps, stopping in front of the Cambie Street police headquarters, under a canopy. "Goodbye Sandra, and good luck. Not sure if I'll be up your way again. I'm staying away from water. I made a vow."

Sandra nodded, then reached over and kissed him lightly on the cheek. He grabbed her head with his right hand and kissed her back, on the lips, reluctantly letting go. She looked down, turned, and was gone, heading back south. Robert stood, watching her back, regret already starting to grow. He wanted to call her back. He could be a miserable bastard.

In Surrey, Rodney had made progress in understanding who the cast of characters were from the mayhem of the previous spring. From what he could tell, only three people were left alive at the farmhouse in Langley after the shooting had stopped: Detective Robert Lui, and two related civilians, one a gangster. Their names were Bobbi and Safa Atwall, brother and sister. Two dead gangsters were also found inside the house, a Ho Li-Fan who previously hailed from Hong Kong, and a Manny Dhillon — the infamous Manny. A pit bull, apparently tasked with providing concierge services, had also been found dead outside the front door, perhaps not fully conversant with the job requirements and dangers.

The preliminary statements taken at the scene pointed to a hostage drama that had been disrupted by Safa Atwall, who initially seemed to be the only person aware of the situation outside of the people in the room. No police had been called prior to the *dénouement*. Safa admitted to killing the dog, and the two men, who were in the process of torturing both her brother, and Robert. So far, Rodney had found nothing that could get Robert into trouble, so he kept reading. A couple of guns had been recovered at the scene, one of which Safa had brought to the party, doing all the damage with it.

Rodney skipped to the preliminary forensics report, which detailed the method of death for each victim, as well as commentary about whose fingerprints were on which gun. It was here that Rodney's pulse quickened. Robert's prints were found on both guns. Also, one of the guns was a match for a cold-blooded execution of a social worker earlier that spring. Safa's admission that she had killed all the bad characters somehow didn't ring true to Rodney. It was her brother who was the gang member, not her. So where did she suddenly gain all the moxie to get the upper hand on noted gangsters?

He sat back in his twirly chair and studied the view while he did his best to think things through. Information seemed to be missing, particularly in the forensic area. Nothing indicated that swabs had been taken at the scene, only interviews done with the surviving people. Had the details existed, then been deleted? Or had the information never been processed as per normal procedures because the dead were notorious wanted men? In his opinion, there is no way Safa could have taken out two gangsters. Robert must have been the one to pull the trigger, with this Safa covering up for him. Perhaps a meeting with Safa might be in order. He checked the notes again. No charges had been laid against anyone who had survived the ordeal; again, something smelled rotten.

He then went to the files about the victims. The more he read, the wider his eyes grew. This Manny was one bad mother if even half of the stories were true. He had heard a few of them, of course, but some of this was new information, kept close by the Gang Taskforce. He wondered if the gang Manny had headed was still active, and if Safa's brother was still a member of it. Perhaps caution might be in order.

# Chapter 22

The rain finally stopped Friday morning. It was as Tony had always predicted. Once the rain started, all you wanted was for it to quit, even if you were a Vancouverite born and bred. As Robert drove west to work, he puzzled as to how to move the investigation forward, barely paying attention to the cars passing him on the still wet pavement. He entered the underground area at Cambie Street and parked, listening to the roughness of the engine's idle before shutting it off. The car needed service. It was just one more thing that got shuffled to the rear when a case was consuming his attention.

He walked onto his floor, and was about to check in with Finn and Vito when Norma called him over to her desk. Ahh, maybe a breakthrough?

"A Deirdre called for you. Left a phone number. Desired a call back ASAP." That was it, and curt wasn't the word for it.

"I don't know a Deirdre. Do you have the number?"

She slid a small piece of paper over the desk, retracting her hand quickly.

"Thanks." He grabbed the slip and made for his office, foregoing his partners for now. He slid his coat off, hanging it on the rack, then settled into his chair and dialled the number.

"Hello?"

"Robert Lui, Vancouver Police. A Deirdre called me?"

"Oh, thanks for returning the call. Sandra is missing."

"What? Who are you?"

"A friend of Sandra Kour. She was staying with us while in town. She never came back last night. She said she was going to meet with you yesterday afternoon." Deirdre's voice rising, on the edge of hysteria.

"Have you tried her cell? She did meet with me, but we were done by half-past three."

"There is no answer when I call her. I tried yesterday several times, then this morning a couple of times. I also texted." Her voice gained another octave.

Robert was silent while he digested this. An unpleasant realization took hold. He had been sloppy again. "Okay, we will look for her. Stay tight and please let us know if she shows up, okay? Tell me her cell number. We can try a few things. Could you spell her last name for me?"

"Yes. Do you know what happened?" Deirdre asked, then spelled Sandra's name.

"No, but we'll find out. I'll be in touch, Deirdre." He took the number and name down.

Craps, craps, craps. This was not good. He went out to check with Vito. "Any luck with the identification of our young man?"

"Yes. His name is Andy Dhillon. No record of any arrests or interaction with the VPD."

Robert felt a chill travel up his spine. "Spelling?"

Vito spelled the name slowly.

"Shit. That's Manny's last name." Robert lapsed into silence, digesting the implications of this. "Check with the Surrey boys, and, if nothing, put it out to all the local cities. That girl I talked to yesterday afternoon has disappeared. I just heard from her friend. Never made it back to Kits. Get Finn. We need to see Thomas." Vito went over to grab Finn and the three walked over to Norma's desk.

"Boss in?" Robert asked.

"Yes, but...." The answer was enough. Robert brushed past Norma and knocked as he opened the door. A uniformed officer who he didn't know looked up in surprise from one of the guest chairs. Thomas stared at the three, startled at the impertinence. After an awkward moment, Thomas asked the officer if they could resume their conversation later in the day. The man got up and, as he passed the three detectives, he gave them the furled eyebrow look.

"That was pretty rude. This had better be good, Robert," Thomas said.

"Sorry. But we have a couple of problems suddenly."

"That you three can't solve?"

"A girl has been taken, I think. We collected Mary Tinlit a couple of days ago at a squat that boasted a bunch of demonstrators. A man who took part in the protest Tuesday was followed to it. Another young man who I now believe may be the prime suspect in our officer's deaths was also at the squat, but wasn't there when we busted it. We were after Mary."

The three settled into chairs before Robert continued. "Here is where it gets bad. Gilberto at the cafe said someone's been in there, asking about me. I took him a picture to confirm. It was our suspect. So, this guy must have been tailing me. The interrogation of Mary revealed his first name - Andy. They are an item. Vito ID'd the guy. His last name is Dhillon, same as Manny's."

Thomas leaned forward. "That doesn't sound good. And?"

"Yesterday, a young woman who I met up on Raven Island came to see me. We went for a short walk outside the station before we parted. We kissed just before she left. I expect that may have marked her. I just found out that she never made it back to the friends she was staying with in Kits. They called this morning. I think Andy took her, probably as a bargaining chip. I expect he thought Sandra was my girlfriend, or wife. I don't know."

"But this is a theory so far, correct?" Thomas looked perplexed. "You kissed her? I thought you and Norma...." He was obviously not current with the state of affairs in the station.

Robert stared back at Thomas. "Correct. On the theory part. But I've seen this Andy before, at another protest. He was staring at me like he knew me. Now I know why. We are getting the particulars on him. If he is related to Manny, then.... The VPD have had no interactions with him, until now. It's the girl I'm worried about."

"You want the force looking for both, I take it," Thomas said.

"Yes, if you could help make it happen?"

"Okay. Need pictures."

Robert stood up, the other two following suit. "I'll get them to you. We are checking on Andy's background. Thanks Thomas."

The three detectives rushed by Norma's desk, no explanation to her about their brusque entry into her boss's domain.

"I think we need to talk with Mary again." Robert looked at Finn as they walked. "Can you arrange it?"

"I'll let you know when it's fixed."

Robert went back into his office and sat. His first thought was that he was grateful that it wasn't his children who had been targeted. Then he mentally kicked himself. Sandra had done nothing to deserve what had happened to her. But perhaps he was being paranoid. So far, all he had were theories. He really didn't know where she was, or what had happened to her. The only connection between her and the events in Vancouver was Mary Tinlit. And this connection was tenuous at best. Mary and Sandra didn't know each other, as far as he knew. He called Deirdre back and arranged for a picture of Sandra to be sent to him.

Several minutes later, Vito came to his doorway. "The Surrey boys have a file on Andy. They say he is a half-brother of Manny's. Same father, different mother. No known gang affiliations, but he has a temper. Twice brought in on serious assault charges, but charges were dropped when the complainants didn't show up to make further statements."

"They weren't looked for?"

"Not successfully, it seems."

"Well, if he is a cousin of Manny, then sound moral character is probably not one of his defining traits. Manny probably had something to do with the disappearing complainants. We need to know where Andy can be found."

"I'll get back to you," Vito answered.

"I wonder if Mary knows this guy's real history?"

"Don't know. Probably too caught up in her own world. If Andy lies like Mary, then possibly not. I'll call Surrey again." Vito disappeared. More waiting. Robert stared out his window, willing something good to happen.

Then Norma came to his door, peering in, but not entering. "I'd appreciate some courtesy next time, before you go barging into Thomas's office." She was not smiling.

"Noted. Someone has gone missing. It felt important." He wasn't going to offer anything further on the matter. "I will try not to do that again, Norma," he added, as he watched her back disappear. It was early in the autumn for it, but a heavy frost, unannounced by any of the local weather personal, seemed to have settled onto the desk of Thomas's assistant. Robert was digging his own grave where Norma was concerned. Very successfully it seemed.

In Surrey, Rodney had succeeded in finding out Safa Atwall's contact information. Rodney was in his office, eyeing his view of South Surrey, not being harassed by his boss's assistant for a change. He dialled Safa's cell number. It rang for a while, then went to voicemail. He left a short message requesting her to contact him as soon as possible. Then he sent her a text, trying to up the pressure, identifying himself as an officer with the IIO and referencing the case of the previous spring, things he had neglected to mention in his voicemail. Satisfied, he left to go for coffee, skirting the assistant as he left the floor. That was something he had figured out how to do fairly quickly in the brief tenure at his new job.

Safa looked at her cellphone, noting the call and text from Rodney. They had arrived while she was in class, attending a course at the local polytechnic university. She was confused. Hadn't that case been declared concluded? And what was the IIO again? She recalled something about them the previous spring, but she had forgotten. She'd call her brother later in the day to see what his view was of this unexpected intrusion into her life. She prayed it wasn't more bad gang things returning after Bobbi had succeeded in extracting himself from the grip of the Two Tigers. The death of the gang's leader had made this much easier. That Bobbi's sister, Safa, had 'facilitated' Manny's demise helped to keep other gang members from considering any further contact with Bobbi. If he wished to leave, it was all fine with them. No one was eager to follow Manny's path to the afterlife sooner than necessary.

# CHAPTER 23

Back in Vancouver, Finn told Robert that Mary would be set up at two o'clock for her second interview. Finn wasn't sure whether her lawyer would attend. Mary was not one to deflect to people she assumed to be slower than herself, which seemed to be everyone. Robert drummed his fingers on his desk, not sure what else he could do until they had questioned Mary further.

His phone rang. "Yes?"

"It's Rory, in the basement."

"What's up?"

"You should come down here. Someone has left a message for Red Hammer."

"Be down shortly."

As Robert walked by the bullpen area, he signalled Finn to join him. He didn't wait, however, clattering down the flights of stairs as fast as he dared. He entered Rory's domain. The three other cyber cops were in the room. Otherwise, nothing had changed. They all stared at Robert.

"Rory?" Robert asked, as Finn caught up.

"Look at this. It's a message referencing a girl in the possession of Haida Guy."

"Name? Of the girl?"

"Sandra."

"Shit." He read through the rolling script.

"Yeah. He wants to make a trade, for Mary Tinlit."

"He obviously knows Red Hammer is the VPD."

Rory nodded. He looked up at Robert.

"How is the rest of the traffic?" asked Robert. "I would expect it to be diminished after the bust of the squat."

"Very few people participating now."

"That's a shame. How do we smoke this guy out? This is now a kidnapping, in addition to the murders." This was said as much to himself as to anyone in the room. Rory shrugged.

"Any other messages about Sandra, from anyone?" Robert asked.

"None."

"Okay people, thanks. Let me know if you have any brainwaves, or hear anything else." He looked at Finn and left the room, Finn trailing.

"Don't you think this is an opportunity, Robert?" Finn said as they entered the stairwell.

"Suppose. It's also a possibility that a few people will get killed. I don't think we need that."

"We could organize a swap, then grab Andy."

"Sounds so simple when you put it like that." Robert looked sideways at Finn as they strode back up to their floor.

"I know, I know. Okay, it may be a little more complicated."

Robert was thinking. "Do you suppose that Andy told Mary he is Haida? That would be something Mary would suck up like a lollipop."

"Perhaps. She seems to be so fond of lying that maybe she doesn't detect it when she is on the receiving end."

"We'll find out soon enough. I'm going for some lunch." The pair had no sooner arrived on their floor when Robert did an about face and left, heading for Cafe Paulo by himself.

As it was early, Robert had his choice of the paninis on display. He opted for a tuna salad. He retreated to the rear of the cafe with his coffee and tried to enter the mind of someone he had not met. It was not an easy task. Would this man kill again? And kidnapping a woman, seemingly innocent? Where were they? He must have a car. How would he nab someone without a car? He trusted that Vito would be scooping up every last scrap of information about their foe, things they could use to track him. Robert's nagging worry about his children returned.

Yuko called out, "I'm bringing your panino over soon, Roberto." He nodded back at her.

She came over. "Here you go, Robert. Are you okay? You look angry."

He shook his head. "No, Yuko, just thinking too hard — work stuff. Thanks for the panino." He smiled to smooth things over. His relations with the fairer sex definitely needed some attention, which he'd give, once this case was finished. At least, this is what he promised himself.

After a satisfying lunch and a long walk to clear his mind, he returned to his office, calling in Vito and Finn for some pre-interview preparation.

"I'm thinking of doing this one solo. What do you think? If there is no lawyer present, Mary will naturally believe that she has the advantage."

"I agree. We'll watch from the side room," Vito said. "We have found that Andy owns a car. A Subaru. One of those sports rally models — white. Word has gone out to all forces in the Lower Mainland."

"Nice work, Vito. I doubted he could take a captive without a car. Any word on a place of residence?"

"We have an address, attached to the car. It's being checked as I speak. Several officers are responding — Surrey Police."

The three detectives descended to the holding area, entering the side room to get a look at Mary before the interview. No lawyer was present. Mary was sitting calmly, staring at the sheriff stationed beside the door.

Robert entered the room and sat down across from Mary, laying some papers gently on the table.

Mary started, "Solo this time. Like, why is she here? Scared of me?" She glanced over his shoulder at the sheriff.

"Would you like her to leave?" Robert asked.

"Like, obviously." Mary replied, seemingly confused by the courtesy.

Robert wasn't under any illusion about gaining confidence from Mary but turned and nodded at the sheriff, who left the room quietly with a tilt of her head. He stared at Mary, who met his eyes without flinching.

"Andy." He was keeping it simple.

"What about him?"

"Last name?"

"Like, screw yourself."

"We need to locate Andy as soon as possible." He waited, then added, "To prevent any harm coming to him."

"What harm? You are the one who should be careful about harm." Mary was confident in how this interview was going.

"I don't know what befell Allo, but I shouldn't like to see the same thing happen to your new boyfriend. Friends are precious in this world." He was laying it on rather thickly. He could almost hear his fellow detectives laughing through the glass. Mary looked at him with a tilted head, eyebrows wrinkled. He could see uncertainty starting its burrowing. He remained silent for a full minute.

"Dhillon," he said.

Mary started, surprise impossible to hide. It was her turn to remain silent.

"How do you spell his last name, Mary?"

Before she could help herself, she had started. "D-y-l...." Then she stopped.

"Where do you think he is from, Mary?"

"I don't think anything. He is a Haida warrior. You are the one who like, needs to run."

"Mary, you might need to reconcile yourself to the fact that we seem to know more about your boyfriend than you do." Mary tittered at this fantasy.

Robert remained silent, studying her.

"D-H-I-L-L-O-N." He spelled it out slowly. "That is how you spell his last name. I doubt he even knows where Haida Gwaii is, let alone been there. He lives in Surrey."

"D-Y-L-A-N!" She spelled it out quickly. "Same as the singer."

Robert chuckled. "You mean Zimmerman, surely? Bobby took his stage name from a Welsh poet. Lord knows where Dylan Thomas got it from. Maybe his mother gave it to him. I think I've given you too much credit, Mary."

For the first time, Mary looked truly confused.

"How does it feel to be on the receiving end?"

"Of what?"

"Lies, Mary. Lies. Andy is a brother of one of the most disreputable gangsters in Lower Mainland's history, and that is saying something. His name was Manny. Recently deceased. I witnessed his death." He looked down and selected a sheet of paper with Andy's surveillance picture. He slid it over to Mary. "Picture of your beau, Mary, just to demonstrate we know what we are doing. Officers are looking for him now."

Mary glanced at the picture, and remained silent while thinking this through.

"Why do you lie, Mary? Are you afraid of something?"

Mary's eyes darted around, unable to meet Robert's for a change.

Robert wasn't one to let his advantage slip away, however. "What do you want, Mary?"

"What do you mean? Like, I want out of here."

"No. What do you want out of life, Mary?" He watched Mary's eyebrows knit together. It was obvious that no one had asked her this kind of question, recently, or maybe, ever.

"Let's assume for a minute that you didn't kill anyone. Why would you be hanging around people who did? It is not nothing, Mary, killing someone. Society always expects debts to be paid. Great lengths are gone to, to make sure payment is made. And payment is not nice."

"What do you want?" Mary seemed to be cracking, ever so slightly, as she tried to turn the tables.

"You are an intelligent woman. What do you think I want?"

"You want me to rat someone out."

"I wouldn't ask you to do that," he lied. "Your friend is spreading his wings. We've just learned that he has kidnapped a woman he doesn't even know."

"Why would he...?" Mary's face showed she realized exactly why Andy would do this. It was her true love, trying to free her.

"Yes, Mary. He probably believes he loves you and would do anything to pry you out of here. And you probably think you love him in return, as he apparently would do anything you suggest to him." Robert watched as Mary's face betrayed surprise at having her thoughts so easily discerned.

"This interview is concluded for now. You may continue to enjoy our hospitality. We will keep looking for Andy." Robert stood, opened the door and signalled the sheriff. He went into the side room while Mary was escorted back to her cell.

Vito's eyes were dancing as he looked at Robert entering the room. "That wasn't very successful, was it?"

"A waste of time. She learned more than I did. Not how interviews are supposed to go, I believe. I suppose we are not going to get anything further from Mary." Robert laughed to himself.

"Any word on Andy's residence yet?" Robert asked.

Vito checked his cell. "Yup. A condo in the middle of Surrey Town Centre. No one home and no car either. Does not appear that anyone has been there for a while."

"Work?"

"No known place of employment."

"Wonder if he does the gang thing as a means of getting by?" Robert asked. "I'll contact Bobbi. He might know. If Andy doesn't work anywhere, it's going to be tough to get info on him. Surrey understands to put a watch on his place, correct?" Vito nodded.

"Might be time to head downstairs again. Start a dialogue with this nutter." Robert was feeling desperation setting in.

"Okay, let's do it. The guy probably doesn't want to be looking after a girl for very long."

Robert could hear his landline ringing, so he went back into his office.

"Yes?"

"Walter Gray here. George's drill was definitely the one putting holes in the Beaver. We've charged Mr. Tinlit with mischief. He doesn't know how his drill escaped the property. Says he keeps a close watch on it at all times. Ha. But we've had to release him on a minor bail amount."

"Attempted murder charges?"

"Not likely."

"Have a pleasant weekend, Walter." He hung up. About as expected. "Okay, let's head down to Hades."

Up on the executive level, Norma van Kleet walked onto the floor and went up to Ranit's desk.

She smiled. "Could I have a word with you, Ranit?"

"Of course. What can I do for you?"

In the basement, the three detectives entered a partially occupied room, two people having left the premises, weekend and all. Luckily, Rory was feeling responsible and still scanning screens for misbehaving citizens.

Robert started. "Rory. Which site was this Haida fellow using to send the message to us?"

"The original site that we picked up on."

"Let's put the ball in his court. Tell him that we can make a trade. Ask him how he wants to do it."

Both Finn and Vito stared at Robert. "You're sure you want to do this?" It was Finn who asked.

"Calm down. We're not doing anything. This is online BS. I want to see what he does, how he reacts." Rory was watching the back and forth, not moving a muscle, waiting for a resolution, and direction.

Finn shook his head. "I guess. Okay, let's try this. He looked down at Rory." Draft first, before sending."

Rory's head swivelled back to his screen while typing up the brief message. Robert was impressed with people who could do this without looking down at their hands. He always needed to keep a close eye on his fingers. The detectives gathered near, reading the text over Rory's shoulders.

"Okay? Good to send?" Robert asked. The others nodded. "Let'er loose, Rory."

The three then stood around, waiting for a reply which, of course, did not come.

"Maybe he's out for an early dinner." Rory being magnanimous. After a few moments, it was obvious that waiting around wasn't helping.

"Can you do something so that you get a forwarding message to your cell when he replies? Don't think we want to hang out here until he decides to send us a message."

"Yup. I'll let you know." Rory tapped a few keystrokes and looked up at Robert. "Done."

"Thanks. Gentlemen, I am heading home. See you when he responds." Robert was completely done with the day.

# CHAPTER 24

The weekend passed slowly. There had been no message from Rory about an answer to the detective's online message, which Robert found extremely concerning. He spent most of the two days worrying about Sandra, and fretting about how to get his hands on Andy. He went into the station, for what, he wasn't sure, but didn't accomplish anything by doing that. He stocked up on groceries and made a few dishes to freeze for future emergencies. His children were mostly not around, carousing with their friends, he supposed.

When Robert arrived in his office Monday morning, sky clear, the day looking promising, two messages were laying on his desk. Mary wished to speak with him. Maybe she was feeling antsy about the lack of attention being paid to her. He ignored it. He suspected she would be shipped off to remand in Surrey anyway while bail was being discussed, the breaking and entering charge having been laid. The second note said that Sandra's cell phone had been found, Sunday evening, by a security guard in an alley behind the Tornado construction site. Nothing else was found after an extensive search of the area. The police had tried to ping the phone earlier, unsuccessfully. He'd call Deirdre later in the morning. Who left the messages was unclear, as he didn't recognize the handwriting. He walked over to Norma's station, where Norma seemed to have been replaced by someone looking suspiciously like Ranit.

"Where's Norma?"

"Good morning to you as well, Robert," said Ranit. "She is up on the top level."

"Doing what?"

"Assisting the Deputy Chief, Mr. McKnight." She smiled as her attention returned to the screen in front of her, her blunt cut bob swaying ever so slightly.

Robert's eyebrows knitted together. "Is Thomas in?" He started for his doorway.

"No. Don't know where he is at present. Anything else I can help with?"

"Guess not." He returned to his office, confused. Even to a slow learner like Robert, it appeared that chances of reconciliation with Norma were dead on arrival. She was from the north part of the Netherlands, a town called Assen where Calvinists ruled the roost. Despite many Dutch not practising any religion, Norma's family had gone against the grain, and were members of the Dutch Reformed Church. Robert was getting the distinct feeling that forgiveness and reconciliation were not number one and two on the list of attributes of that congregation. Of course, some effort on his part might be needed, but he had larger things to attend to at the moment.

In Surrey, Safa had followed up with her brother. He had no knowledge of anyone poking around in the previous spring's events. After Bobbi had been released from the hospital and custody, in that order, and enduring the investigation, he had found work with a small Punjabi developer in Surrey, through a friend. He was helping out while he learned the ins and outs of the business. He was also concentrating on staying away from his previous associates, making sure his break from the gang life held true and fast. Saffa decided to ignore Rodney. Of course, she had no idea how driven Rodney was by the idea of revenge.

Monday, mid-morning, Bobbi's cell chirped. He was in his tiny office, reviewing numbers that would tell the tale of whether a small townhouse project should proceed or be sent to the rubbish heap.

"Hello. Bobbi here."

"Hi Bobbi. It's Robert Lui calling."

Bobbi's heart fluttered ever so slightly. Shit. He'd only been out of the action for half a year, and any poking around in that history made him nervous. Not to mention that his present employment was probationary in nature, no screw-ups permitted.

"Hi. How are you doing?" Bobbi tried to be sociable, while hiding his fears.

"Fine. Yourself? What are you doing these days?"

He didn't need this social BS. "Why are you calling, Robert?"

"Looking for some info on Manny's family. I assume he came from somewhere, and that he had relatives, yes?"

"A safe assumption."

"I only ask because one of his close relatives seems to be making a nuisance of himself, and I wonder what you might know about him. Sorry to bring up the past like this, but we are slightly desperate. I assume you have heard about a couple of VPD officer murders recently?"

"Yes. Who is it you are asking about?"

"A half-brother, Andy Dhillon."

Bobbi went into his mental address book. "Yes. I remember a young guy that was talked about. Manny wouldn't let him into the business. Partly, it might have been an effort to keep his close family out of the action, but, on the other hand, I know he had his only full brother running guns out of Seattle. I believe the real reason was that Manny considered Andy a screw-up, which, considering what Manny got up to, must be something special. That could be the real reason he kept him out. There was also talk of religious mania."

"Did he do anything for the gang? It doesn't appear that he is employed anywhere. We're wondering how he gets funds."

"Don't know. Never met him. Manny probably gave him money. I didn't know the Seattle guy's name either."

"Other family?"

"Manny came from a big family, so lots of cousins around, I believe. Manny's father may have married Andy's mother, but I'm not sure. I don't know too much else about Manny. He didn't talk about his relatives much."

Robert considered this but didn't enquire further.

"I have a question for you, Robert, if you don't mind."

"Sure."

"A guy, name of Rodney Fister, has been harassing my sister. Do you know what it's about?"

"Rod was a detective in my office. Doesn't like me. He left to join the IIO. So not with the real police anymore. Sounds like he is trying to poke around Manny's death last spring. He'd like nothing better than to screw me over. I'm sorry he is bothering your family, Bobbi."

"She is ignoring him, so far. Don't know how much longer that will work."

"Rod is also new to gang work. Probably wouldn't be too difficult to scare him somehow."

"I'm out of that life, Robert."

"Just thinking out loud. Forget I said that. You don't know where Andy lived do you? We have an address on 138th Street, but it seems he hasn't been home for a while."

"Sorry."

"Can I text you his mug? Want to make sure we're talking about the same guy."

"Sure."

"Take care, Bobbi." He hung up.

Take care, Bobbi? Was he losing his mind? Bobbi had been part of one of the worst gangs in the Lower Mainland.

Things changed, Robert supposed. And his sister had saved both their lives. That was not a small addition to the equation. And now Rodney was fishing in closed waters. But Robert wondered if he had been out of bounds himself.

Bobbi considered what he had just learned, development numbers left by the roadside. Scare Rodney Fister? Despite what he had told Robert, there were still things he could do. Family was precious, and he valued his sister highly, especially after what she had done the previous spring. If this Rodney character was intent on getting involved in the Atwal's lives, then something might need to be done. His cell dinged, so he checked it. The picture Robert sent was indeed Andy. The eyes were as Bobbi remembered, those of a true believer. He replied to Robert.

# CHAPTER 25

On Cambie Street, just as Robert was preparing to head out for lunch, his landline rang.

"It's Rory. He replied."

"I'll be right down." As he swept by the bullpen, he signalled Vito, Finn seemingly absent. The pair walked down and into Rory's domain, right up to the back of Rory's chair.

"Where is the message?"

Rory rolled the screen a few times and brought it up.

**'Exchange to be at the PNE grounds east side of the Pacific Coliseum - 6:00 pm today. Only Robert Lui and Mary to be there.'**

Robert and Vito looked at each other. Robert shook his head. "No way. He has had all weekend to plan this, and now is giving us no time to prepare."

"I agree."

Robert said to Rory, "Tell him no. Make it Wednesday at six. We need some time to prepare. Let's see what he says."

Rory typed the reply and sent it. While Robert waited, he went over to the other youngsters, trying to fathom what they were up to. It seemed they were all looking at websites, none of which made any sense to Robert. A brave new world, he supposed.

Rory yelled. "He just answered. Not happy." Robert returned to read the message.

**'Would it be better if I just mailed pieces of Sandra back to you in the post?'**

"Tell him, no. Single word only."

"You sure?"

"Yes."

Rory replied, and the waiting continued. Robert started pacing, hands in his pockets.

"You're not going there by yourself." Vito stated it as fact.

Robert nodded. "And we aren't bringing Mary, either. This guy might, or might not, show up with Sandra. She is all the leverage he has."

Robert tapped Rory on his shoulder. "Write this to him."

**'Robert barely knows Sandra. Don't know what you think she means to him'.**

More waiting. Then, a reply.

**'We all know that isn't true, don't we? Wednesday will be fine. Looking forward to it.'**

"Sounds unhinged, don't you think?" Robert mused to himself. "And cocky. Don't think those two qualities go together very well." He looked at Vito. "Let's get some lunch and start planning this out."

Vito nodded. They thanked Rory and went back upstairs. "Chinese?" Robert asked as they hit the main floor.

"Don't think so. Let's go to this sandwich shop I dine at."

"Dine at? Sandwiches? Lead the way." He was grinning at Vito, and happy with the prospect of a new place to eat, or dine, as Vito so eloquently put it. They walked up to Broadway, Vito leading the charge. Instead of turning east, Vito headed west. After passing by place after place featuring cuisine from half the countries of the world, Vito stopped in front of a cafe simply named Bob's.

"Is there a Bob?" Robert asked.

"Not sure."

They entered. A counter ran down the length of the space, a couple of underage employees on one side, hungry customers and a loose collection of tables on the other. A cheesecake medley to stop your heart occupied half of the display case closest to the door, while baguette sandwiches lined up in the remainder towards the rear.

"Looks promising." Robert said. "I wonder how many just go for the dessert — forget the healthier food?"

"Their problem. Pick a baguette - it's on me."

"Get a raise?" Robert looked at the espresso machine sitting smack on the counter's centre, wondering if the help knew what they were about. "I'll spring for coffees after."

Few people seemed to stay after paying for their purchases, and no one was sitting in the rear, so it wasn't a bad place to talk business. They grabbed a table at the back after receiving their food.

"Let's get a couple of people out there immediately, scope out the area, and set a watch. I suppose this means the Tactical Group. You familiar with the place?" Robert asked.

"I went to the fall fair a few years ago. Don't really recall the outside of the Coliseum. They were dragging bulls around inside — I remember that. Large buggers," Vito responded. "The whole area might be semi-occupied, I would think, this time of year. No one is out there during the week in the fall. The ponies only race on weekends this time of year, and the rides are shuttered. I don't know how often the Coliseum gets used these days. Maybe Andy is holed up there?"

"Possibly. This sandwich is pretty good, Vito."

"I'm a sucker for a good baguette, put together properly."

"Think I'll add Bob's to my lunch roster."

"He was hoping you'd say that. He can contemplate retirement now."

"Don't know how we'll handle Wednesday, though. Requires some high-end thought."

"My specialty, Robert. Don't know about you, however."

The sandwiches were finished. "What'll you have?" Robert was ready to order dessert.

"Espresso — single, long."

"'Kay. Let's see how good they are here."

After finishing their coffees, which Robert deemed satisfactory, the pair strolled leisurely back to Cambie Street, enjoying the cool air and strong sun — weather that had slim chance of being repeated as October headed to its close. People had smiles on their faces for a change, but Robert didn't care. He was thinking about Sandra. Once back, they grabbed Finn, went to Robert's office, and started plotting.

A prosecutor called Robert Wednesday morning, complaining about pressure to release the mansion dwellers. Robert told him to please hold fast, he'd get back to him early Thursday. That afternoon, Robert was being prepped on what to do and not to do in the various scenarios likely to play out that evening.

Watchers tasked to the Hastings Park site late Monday had reported nothing in the two days they had attended. Tuesday, a few snipers had been situated high up on the Hastings racecourse stand's roof, and on the roof of the Coliseum itself. The duty was protracted, something that didn't sit well with the Tactical squad leader, not to mention the fellows freezing their behinds off on the roofs.

The team was in a large meeting room on a different floor. Robert was strapping on body armour. An oversized checked shirt followed, then he slipped on his shoulder holster. His smaller gun was already fastened to his ankle. Only the other detectives knew about it. He tried on the outsized anorak — not his, but borrowed from one of the beefier constables on the Tactical team.

"No blood on that, understand? It's my best and only waterproof jacket."

"Your concern and lack thereof is duly noted," Robert responded.

"I didn't mean...."

"It's okay. I know what you meant. Your jacket is important to you. I get it." Robert looked over to the woman officer donning her less than fetching coat. She already had her armour on.

"That fit, Patricia?"

"It'll have to do. Don't need anyone else seeing me like this, though."

"And I was going to take you out for dinner after we are done. Oh well." Robert grinned.

A quick search of female constables from the employee roster had turned up Pat, who made a passable replica of Mary Tinlit, as long as you didn't get too close. It was moments like these that made Robert realize the downside of an imbalanced police force, gender-wise. Patricia's home was in the traffic division, but it took only seconds for her to agree to this duty, even after the danger was graphically explained. Spiked hair, several shades of white and black, framed her face, so modifications were needed. She had watched video of the three interviews that featured Mary to round out her minimal preparations. Her gun was on her belt, at her back, hidden by the coat.

"I'm ready. Let's do this," Patricia said.

Robert was both impressed and taken aback by the eagerness. "They explained how dangerous this will be, correct?" He eyed Patricia with concern.

"Yes?" Patricia hesitated, then, "You mean, really dangerous?"

"That's what I mean. Two cops are dead. This guy plays for keeps."

"Oh." Some enthusiasm leaked out.

The Tactical leader continued with his instructions. "No one gets traded for anything, understood?" Nods all around. "We'll have a perimeter around the entire site. It won't be watertight, too large at one hundred and fifty acres. You'd need the army to help out. They declined the opportunity. Once the guy is spotted, fall back and let us do the rest, get it?" He was staring at Robert.

What a dork, thought Robert. Sounded like the Old West. He wasn't holding out much hope for Sandra with these cowboys running the show. "Sounds like a plan," Robert responded. A very bad plan, he suspected. There also seemed to be hint of no need for a trial if Andy was indeed spotted.

"Okay, let's mount up." The leader left the room, followed by some men sporting backwards facing baseball caps. Vito and Finn grinned at Robert. Robert wasn't feeling the humour, being the point man. Patricia didn't seem as phased by the mentality on exhibit. She suffered through this kind of stuff every day in traffic.

The sun had long disappeared when Robert drove an old ghost car onto the Hastings Park site just north of the Coliseum. He had dropped Finn and Vito on Renfrew Street, adjacent to the park, before entering. The vehicle had been selected for its obvious appearance as a VPD unit so that Andy could identify them. Evening had fallen and lighting was sparse as they drove to the east of the large arena. Vast expanses of dirty asphalt lay hidden from Renfrew's street lighting. This part of Hastings Park was more conducive to the wanderings of racoons and coyotes than humans. Robert slowed the car, and as he stopped in the deserted lot, a couple of people-sized bats walked by them, barely five metres away, heading east. He shook his head. "Is there a party going on here that we don't know about?" Patricia was peering out the windshield.

The car had its communications linked back to Cambie Street, where the Tactical leader was situated, calling the shots.

"What do you mean?" The leader asked.

"A couple of large bats just walked by us. Costumes, I hope. Hold on, here comes Donald Trump with what I'm guessing is a daughter, or wife?"

"What?"

"Who did the research on this location? Looks like some kind of Halloween thing going on here." Robert asked his microphone. Silence ensued. He looked over at Patricia, shaking his head. "It's almost six. We're getting out." More silence. Robert swore as he opened the car door. Patricia got out of her side, came around behind the car, joining Robert. They waited impatiently, peering into the darkness, heads swivelling around.

Robert realized what a bad situation this was. Andy could come out of anywhere, dressed in anything, and they'd have no warning. The snipers wouldn't know who to target either if it came down to protecting their lives. That's if they could even shoot straight after sitting for hours in the cold.

A couple of ducks walked by about thirty metres away, maybe Donald and Daisy, maybe not. The ducks ignored the officers, continuing their waddle east. Patricia returned to the passenger side, and both were about to open the car doors to leave the area when another costumed couple headed their way from the east — moving against the flow. What looked like Star Wars characters were slowly aiming for Robert and Patricia. One was dressed in a long flowing brown robe, Obi-Wan perhaps. And possibly Princess Leia beside him. She was wearing a veil. They stopped around ten metres away. Meanwhile, an intermittent flow of people continued to walk to the east from the north side of the Coliseum, travelling close behind the couple. This was getting worse. If Andy decided to start firing, there was no way they could respond in kind without endangering the public. Andy was also keeping the woman very close to his body, maybe realizing that other police might have him in their sights, waiting for an opportunity.

"Send her over." The man's voice was high, hints of broken glass in the inflection. His left hand looped through the crook of the woman's arm while resting on the hilt of a lightsaber. He moved from side to side, probably aware of being a target. His right hand remained hidden in his cloak. Robert suspected a gun was being trained on him.

"Let me see Sandra's face first."

"Not going to happen, Robert."

"Then we are leaving. Adios, Andy."

The Jedi didn't say anything for a moment, perhaps flummoxed that his name was known, then. "Wait. You knew my brother, correct?"

"Which one?"

Obi-Wan smiled. "Manny, of course. The one you killed."

Robert had had enough of the bullshit and opened his car door. A shot cracked, the slug hitting the car door at an angle, ricocheting off. Sounded to him like a SIG Sauer, if it was being fired through some ratty Jedi robe. Maybe Tony's. Robert was certain Tony'd be mortified to find out his gun was being fired at Robert. A second shot cracked, but it seemed to miss everything. He pulled his gun, crouching behind the door, but as he aimed, the couple retreated, making sure people were close behind them as they joined the growing throng heading east to Playland. Patricia had also dropped to her knee on the passenger side of the car and was taking aim. Some of the other party goers were looking back at the scene, perhaps wondering what the sounds were about.

"Don't shoot. Too many people," Robert yelled over to her. Patricia nodded and slowly rose, slipping her weapon back under her coat.

Robert got into the car and described the outfits to the team leader so the chase could start. Robert had a strong feeling as to the outcome, so he signalled Patricia to get in. They drove back around the Coliseum to the access point where Finn and Vito were waiting. Robert stopped, and they got into the rear.

"What's with the ding on the side of your door, Robert? I don't recall that being there a half hour ago." Finn asked.

"Got a bit frisky in there."

"They'll probably dock your pay to fix it, say you were careless." Finn chuckled. "So, they showed?"

"Yup. At least Andy did. Not certain who the girl was. She was wearing a veil. Dressed up as a Star Wars couple. Operational research needs some attention, that's certain."

"We can still hear you, Robert." The leader's flat voice came over the mic.

Robert leaned over and flicked a toggle, terminating the connection. "Assholes. Guess we're lucky we didn't get tagged in there. Last time I'm part of a Tactical Operation. We'll do our own research from here on in." He looked back at Finn briefly while driving. "I don't know if he figured out that it wasn't Mary with me. Didn't hang around." He looked over at Patricia. "How are you doing?"

"Okay, I think. Way more interesting than traffic."

Robert nodded as he concentrated on driving. "Andy only seemed concerned with shooting at me rather than anything to do with Mary. My guess is that they'll melt into the crowd and won't be picked up tonight. It was a long shot at best. At least we're in better shape than the car. Thanks for the effort, Patricia." He looked over at her. She nodded thoughtfully.

# CHAPTER 26

Fog had drifted into Robert's neighbourhood Thursday morning, rendering light tenuous. It was difficult to tell if morning had actually arrived. Robert took his time after the previous evening's adventure, arriving at Cambie just after ten. Ranit spotted him as he passed by the bullpen area and waved him over. "Thomas would like a word."

Robert stopped, staring. "So, this switch with Norma, it's permanent?"

"Fraid so, Robert. Anything else I can do for you?"

"Guess not. Be right back, Ranit." He went to his office to dump his briefcase and coat, slowly returning to Thomas's office, pondering what he had just learned. He knocked, entered and took the proffered chair.

Thomas fixed Robert with an intense stare. "How'd it go out there? Tactical didn't say much, other than that you didn't show up for the debrief. They want you suspended."

Robert, no longer bothered by this type of chatter, laughed. "Almost took a bullet because of their ineptness. Not going near those cowboys again. If they don't like it, tough." He waited, but Thomas remained silent. "I'm guessing they didn't apprehend anyone. Am I correct?"

Thomas nodded, still mute.

"It's my own fault, asking for their help. By the way, Patricia from Traffic was good. Didn't freelance. Anyway, this Andy Dhillon is our guy. The shots he took came from a SIG Sauer, by the sound of it. Tony or Archie's gun I suppose. Tony'd be pissed at the thought."

"I'll tell Tactical to stow their outrage and stay clear of you. They found a brown cloak and a toy lightsaber on the pavement, later in the evening. Cloak was ragged but seemed to have bullet holes in it. And they found one of the bullets after a search. They are checking the ballistics. One of the shots hit your car, I hear." Thomas paused. "I heard something else. That Allo fellow has surfaced from his coma. No lasting damage according to the medics, they think. But the word is that he is enquiring about his legal options. That's about it. Next steps, Robert?"

"Not certain. Need to talk with Vito and Finn. Thanks Thomas, I'll keep you apprised." He rose, but before leaving, asked, "So, what happened out there?"

"You mean, Ranit?"

Robert nodded.

"Beats me."

"I thought you ran this floor, no?"

"I thought so too. On reflection, maybe not. I've had a word with the Deputy Chief. He seems happy with the new arrangement."

"His idea?"

"The women cooked it up, he said. Just a wild guess here, but are you and Norma on the outs?"

Robert gave him the barest of nods, then turned and left. Sounded like Norma had sent her message — no longer interested. He eyeballed the pod farm as he went by. Both detectives were absent. He remembered something he needed to do regarding an overdue lunch. After arranging the meeting with Bernard, he sat, thinking about the previous evening's events. His desk phone rang.

"Robert Lui?"

"Speaking."

"It's Deirdre calling. I heard from Sandra this morning. She says she is fine. She met a relative last week and visited with him over the weekend. She said she lost her phone on the street somewhere, she doesn't know where."

"What? She says she is fine? Do you believe her?"

"I'm unsure. She sounded calm, but something seemed off. Thing is, her small bag is still here. Just a few clothes in it, I think."

"How well do you know her?" Robert was having trouble with this.

"Not that well, I suppose. We met a few years back here in Vancouver. Hung out, went to some concerts, ate well, drank. You know, fun stuff."

Robert didn't know, but the friendship didn't sound all that deep. "What do you do for a living, Deirdre, if you don't mind my asking?"

"I'm a chef at one of the hotels downtown."

"Right, thanks for the call, Deirdre. If you hear from her again, could you ask her to contact me?" He reeled off his cell number. "I assume she didn't leave a number."

"Correct. No number. I'll give her the message." She hung up.

In Surrey, Rodney was tired of being ignored. Safa was only the latest in a line of people not paying attention to him. His co-workers didn't seem warm and sociable, which he was fine with. All the people he questioned for his cases, however, didn't seem the least bit impressed with him, and gave him no information at all. Safa, he suspected, would be easy to intimidate, so he was going to try to strong-arm her. He was ignoring her brother's connection to the Two Tigers. He didn't know much of anything about Safa's life, but had one piece of information: her home address. This is where he went.

It was late Thursday morning, and anyone with half a brain would consider that perhaps, just maybe, Safa might be at a job, or learning something in an institution somewhere. Poor Rodney couldn't think tactically, let alone strategically, so he showed up at the front door of Safa's parent's modest stucco house in North Surrey. He rang the bell and rapped the wood door hard several times for added effect. After several moments, the door was opened, not very far, by a middle-aged South Asian woman clad in a newish saffron sari with a simple gold chain around her neck.

"Yes?"

"Is Safa home?"

"She is not here. Who are you?" She did not like the look of her visitor.

"I'm with the IIO. I need to speak with her, ASAP."

The acronyms flew right over the woman's head, splatting onto the wall behind her.

"Goodbye." She slammed the door closed.

Rodney stood silent a moment, then let his temper get the better of him. He started hammering the door with his fist. Inside, Safa's mother was frightened. She went to her husband in the kitchen, asking him to call Bobbi. Getting the police involved was absolutely a last resort.

"Yes?" Bobbi was in a meeting, but family trumped all so he excused himself, left the room, and answered his cell.

"There is a man hammering on our door. What should we do?"

"What kind of man?"

"White man." Bobbi could hear his father asking his mother for more details.

"IIO or something."

Sounded to Bobbi like Rodney was taking it up a notch. He responded, "Don't let him in. I'll make a call. He won't break in, don't worry." As he said this, he was worried. Who knew what this crazed cop would do? He called the Surrey Police. Robert would take too long.

Inside of thirty seconds a siren wailed in North Surrey, closing in on the Atwall residence. Rodney had stopped hammering, then heard the siren drawing closer. Did these people call the police on him? Shit. He bounded down the front steps, heading for his car. He got in just as the cruiser pulled up behind him. He knew enough not to budge. He lowered his window and waited. The officer took his time, checking things, then he exited his car and slowly walked up to Rodney, hand not on his gun.

"Licence, registration."

Rodney handed over the documents, waited a moment, then identified himself. "I'm with the IIO. Trying to get a witness statement."

The officer, who already knew Rod's affiliation, looked down at Rodney as he handed the items back to him. "This is how they taught you to do it? Hammer on a door and scare people? Not impressed. We have better things to do than attend dickheads making a nuisance of themselves." After the editorial comment, the officer retreated to his car, got in and waited for Rodney to make himself scarce. The officer knew that this address connected with a former gang member, checking all this before stepping out of his car. He wondered what the IIO were doing on the doorstep.

Rodney sat for a few minutes, feeling his anger build again. He realized that despite the officer's protest about better things to do, he wasn't leaving until Rodney moved along. He reluctantly started his car and slowly drove off, returning to the centre of Surrey.

Robert waited outside his noodle palace on Broadway, shifting from foot to foot. It was cooling down, the weather changing to something more in keeping with the end of October. He finally spotted Bernard, walking from the west, probably after getting off the train.

"Hey Robert, good to see you. We going in?" He pointed to the door.

"Nope. Heading west. I've found a new place to eat."

"Intriguing."

"That's one word for it."

They walked a few blocks, pausing in front of Bob's before entering. "This it?" asked Bernard, head slightly tilted. "Exotic."

"That's another word for it."

Once they had settled in at Bob's, Robert with a chicken salad baguette and Bernard choosing a vegetarian option, Robert started the conversation, cautiously.

"I've been watching some of your stories about the case."

"Riveting, aren't they? We are running thin these days. Heard there was some shooting out at Hastings Park last night?"

"Aimed at me, actually."

"You were there?"

"Unfortunately."

"Can you tell me what happened?"

Robert narrowed his eyes, gauging how much he could let out.

"We are on the trail of a cop killer. I believe he showed up last night. He melted away in a crowd, however. Do you know about the haunted houses out there this time of year?"

"I think I've heard about them. Never attended one, however."

"This guy knew about it. Used it to his advantage."

"You know who it is?"

"Think so. Can't say, though. Ongoing, yada yada."

Bernard smiled as he chewed. "It seems unusual not to have caught the guy yet. Am I correct? Cop-killers attract a lot of attention, usually lethal attention."

"New age, Bernard. A while back, yes, he would have been apprehended by now, or dead - take your pick." Robert watched as different help worked the espresso machine today, somewhat inept at it, in his estimation. "Case is complicated by an apparent connection to some protest movements in town here. My belief is that it has nothing to do with that. These murders are personal — that is my theory, so far at least."

"And the Bella Kind connection?"

"Still relevant. That is all I can say. Maybe you should fly up there, do a little light digging. It is quite a beautiful part of the province. If you find stuff, I will confirm or deny. On background, of course. And, oh yeah, stay away from floatplanes."

"Fair enough."

Robert felt he hadn't really told Bernard much of anything, so he related the bust of the squat in Shaughnessy. He wasn't sure when or why he might need Bernard's help again, but he knew he would at some point. It was just debt coinage that he was piling on the reporter. And Bernard knew it.

"Anything I can do for you, Robert?"

"How about eating a fat slice of cheesecake? I notice that your eyes haven't left that case by the door since we arrived."

Bernard nodded in assent, grinning.

"How is your arm, by the way?" Bernard had suffered injuries to it as a result of trying to help Robert with some research the previous spring. Questions not well received by the subject.

"It aches, but it seems to work."

"It's how career memories are made, Bernard." As he said this, he looked down at his right hand, the two smallest fingers not lining up with much of anything.

"Any flavour I want?"

"Dive in."

After Robert had paid, foregoing coffee for once, they split up at the Broadway station, Bernard going back downtown, Robert heading to the office.

# CHAPTER 27

Robert walked onto his floor and was immediately hailed by Vito. He rose and followed Robert to his office, closing the door behind him. Vito sat across from Robert, fixing him with a stern look.

"I've been doing some research, something we should all be more diligent at, I dare say."

This didn't sound promising. "And?"

"Haunted houses are a regular thing out at Hastings Park this time of year. Not hard to find out about, takes just the barest hint of initiative."

Robert nodded.

"This next piece of information is slightly trickier. You said the kidnapped girl is named Sandra Kour, correct?" He spelled the last name slowly, for effect, Robert judged.

Robert nodded. "Not sure she is still kidnapped or not. Just heard from her friend in Kits. Deirdre says Sandra is fine now, although she didn't sound convinced about it."

"That may jive with what I learned. I delved into Manny's family history, as much as I could, anyway. Guess what Andy's mother's maiden name is?"

"Oh shit, don't say it!"

"Kour. Looks like Sandra could be some kind of half-sister to Manny, or maybe a cousin. Haven't pinned it down yet, and I'm not sure we'll be able to confirm the relationship. Kind of puts a different light on things, doesn't it?"

It was one of those moments where life turns on its head.

"I don't believe this." He stared at Vito as he started re-examining everything that had happened up in Bella Kind from the moment he had arrived at the Arnott Bay Resort. He stood up. "Let's go. I need some joe to help me think. Is Finn around?"

"Don't know where Finn is," Vito said, as he stood up.

Ranit caught sight of the pair as they were on their way to the stairs. "Where are you two off to?"

"Out for a meeting." They didn't slow, opening the door, then disappearing. Ranit shook her head disapprovingly. Norma had given hints as to the behaviour of her new charges. This seemed to be firm evidence of it.

As Vito and Robert entered Cafe Paulo, Robert waved at Gilberto, then spoke to Vito. "I'm going to call Arnott Bay when I get back, see what they know." He ordered two coffees and headed for the newly favoured table at the rear of the cafe.

"You think you were set up from the start?"

Robert stared into the middle distance, re-living the moments at the lodge. "Sure, it's possible. But I don't think so. Sandra would have to be some kind of master actress, like an Oscar winner. I just don't think she is that good. Don't forget, we slept together the last night, and that was totally off script. I was supposed to be gone at that point."

"Finn mentioned something." Vito smiled. Yuko signalled from the bar. She seemed pressed. Several customers were waiting for their drinks. Robert went up to fetch the cups, nodding thanks at Yuko, and returned.

"She seemed genuine. Now I don't know for certain."

"It's what a good enemy does. Sows confusion and distrust."

"I suppose," Robert said, sipping at his drink. "Enemies usually aren't that well organized, I've found. Especially the gang-connected ones. If she is connected to the gang, that is."

It was Vito's turn to stare at nothing. "Should we make contact with Andy again?"

"Maybe not. Maybe I need to talk with Mary again. But first, I need to find out how long Sandra has been up at Bella Kind. I'm guessing, not that long. People move around all the time in that industry."

"Here, in town, sure. Don't know about up-country, though."

"She did hold down several roles at the lodge. Let's return to the core of the issue here. Is Sandra a willing or unwilling participant?"

"The million-dollar question, Robert. What's your feeling?"

"I'd say unwilling, but perhaps not in danger. Who is going to chop up their cousin? I mean, really."

"A crazy person, perhaps."

"Good point. Bobbi said this guy was off kilter. Don't forget, unfortunately, families are where some of the most horrific stuff happens."

"An uplifting thought, Robert."

"My specialty."

Vito looked at his cup. "What happened to Norma? I liked her. She was competent — a rarity these days."

"Up on the top floor," said Robert. "You can probably thank me for the change. We are on the outs, completely. I am an idiot. A moment where I should've said no, didn't, and fessed up about it."

"I'd like to argue with you, but your presentation is so cogent, it is without refute." Vito was grinning.

"Bugger off." He wanted to smile as he said this, but he couldn't. "Let's get going. I have a call to make."

In his office, Robert studied his phone, waiting for what, he didn't know. This month was turning into one of the worst Octobers in his career. He knew it was childish to hate a month. Traditionally, he had a profound hatred of November in Vancouver. It was cold, dark, and often rained for weeks on end as though it had nothing better to do. This October was valiantly attempting to nose into the lead. He was heading home after a couple of calls. Time to reconnect with his teenagers, that is, if they remembered who he was.

"Arnott Bay Resort. How can we help you?"

"Manager, please. Robert Lui, with the Vancouver Police." He waited. Seconds drifted into minutes.

"No sign of him. Anything else I can help with?"

"Your name?"

"Liz."

"Perhaps you can help me, Liz. Do you know Sandra Kour? Works there."

"Sure. We've worked together for almost two years now. She was supposed to be back here by now. She is kinda like my boss."

"Do you know when she started there?"

"Sorry, no. She was here when I arrived, though. Has something happened to her?"

"No, no," Robert lied. "I need the manager to call me with that information. Thanks." He recited his number, then hung up. He then called the RCMP. Walter Gray couldn't offer any further enlightenment as to the employment history of Sandra. Robert wondered why he kept asking for Walter's help. Perhaps he was a masochist at heart.

He was done for the day. He sat, pondering dinner. He texted Sophie, asking her what she felt like. Chicken - response a little too concise, but it was enough. He headed to the local grocer to pick up what he needed. Back to basics was where he was heading. Grilled chicken, roasted potatoes and green beans with an oil and garlic dressing.

He switched the car radio to the country station and raised the volume. He was listening to performers he had never heard of, singing stuff fit for the garbage bin. He fumbled for a CD while keeping his eyes on the road. He slipped an old Wintersleep disc in, and cranked up the volume to max, listening to the blood music that took him back to the last days of his wife's battle with cancer.

As he drove, his thoughts shifted to Sandra, still confused, but hoping that she was safe, wherever she was. He felt deep inside that Sandra was not part of the gang life, having dealt with enough gang members to know. Joining the Gang Taskforce had turned out to possibly be the dumbest thing he had ever done, career-wise. There seemed to be no end to the danger it had brought to his life. And not just his life, but those he loved, and close friends. Even when the bad guy is dead, relatives pop out of the weeds, seemingly hoping for revenge. His romantic life was no better. It was the kind of streak that made drinking very appealing.

He pulled into his carport, switched off the radio, listened to the roughness of the engine for a moment, then killed it. He sat, not thinking for a change. It was pitch black. The kids had not switched on the exterior lights. He wanted to stay here, in the darkness, where no one could find him, which is what he did, staring into the middle distance at nothing. Eventually the carport light flicked on. Robert looked over and saw Robin peering out at him, concern on his face. He should be concerned, Robert thought as he shifted and opened the car door, grabbing the groceries from the seat beside him.

He entered the kitchen. His two children were staring at him.

"You don't look as though you've lost any weight while I've been busy. That's a good sign. Do you remember who I am?"

Sophie tilted her head to the side. "You look like someone who used to live here."

"Well, I'm back. Grilled chicken with all the fixings tonight. Make way, I've got work to do. If you could set the table, that'd be nice." He went back out to the patio to get the fire going before prepping the chicken, foregoing a drink until the bird was on the grill.

The kids were still hanging around, probably to make sure their dad didn't disappear again.

"How are you, pops?" Robin asked. Nervously, Robert judged.

"I'm good. Sorry for the absences. The murder cases are oddly not solving themselves, so my attention is required."

"Are you making headway?" Sophie asked.

"Yes, I would say, dangerous headway. But let's talk about something else."

"How is Norma?"

"Bad topic, Sophie, I am afraid."

"Oh dear."

"Yes, that's what I thought. I have had better Octobers. How are Hallowe'en preparations at school? Is there a dance coming up?"

Robin answered. "Yes. I'm thinking of going."

"How about you, Sophie?"

"Same."

Robert looked over at Robin as he reached up into the cupboard for his whisky glass. "Hockey?"

"Lost once, that's it. NHL, here I come!"

Robert laughed as he smiled at Robin. "So, I can think about retirement soon? Excellent. If you could swing it, a large house in the Okanagan somewhere near all the other retired hockey stars would be just fine. Let's get these vegetables going. They're not going to prepare themselves." He had cut the chicken's backbone out, oiled it, and added salt and pepper. With the fire ready, he went back outside, spread the coals, then dropped the spatchcocked bird onto the side away from the direct fire and closed the top. He poured himself a generous glass of whisky.

The chicken came off the grill, skin a burnt sienna hue. Robert let it rest for a few minutes before carving. The roasted potatoes came out, and the beans were finished with the dressing. A mayo sauce waited patiently for the potatoes. The trio dined like gods. Nothing was spoken until the plates were empty, chicken bones laying naked. Robert was content, for the moment. Both teens seemed thrilled to be finally eating decent food.

"I'll clean up, you two." He stacked the dishes and slowly put them into the dishwasher after his children disappeared. Once the machine was started, he sat in the family area, considering his life. He watched a few minutes of a moronic TV program and decided to call it a night. He quickly passed out after his head hit the pillow.

Ringing broke his sleep. He looked over at the alarm clock, groggy — after three. Who would call him in the middle of the night? Not more bad news? He reached over for the handset. "Hello?"

"Robert, I need you." He heard a distant thump, then nothing. He looked at the handset, helplessly. It was Sandra's voice. He was awake now. He grabbed his cell, looking for Finn's number.

"What? You know what time it is?" Finn didn't sound pleased after finally answering.

"Can you trace a number for me? Call was made to my home number just a few minutes ago. It was Sandra and the message was short. I believe she's in trouble, despite what I thought earlier. She might have used Andy's cell, not sure." He then relayed the number that Sandra had called from.

"I'll get someone on it, Robert." Finn sounded more alert.

# CHAPTER 28

Robert woke from a fitful sleep early Friday, worried after the phone call, feeling as tired as he had when he turned in the previous evening. He lay there, puzzling how he was going to help Sandra when he knew so little. Maybe they could latch onto the phone and locate her that way, or locate Andy more likely. He swung his legs around and sat up, then remained sitting, as though that was it for the day. He had sat up. Mission accomplished. Darkness surrounded him. Maybe the sun was taking the day off again.

He shook his head — enough bullshit. He wasn't going to solve anything sitting in his bedroom.

He yelled. "You guys still here?" Silence. He supposed his kids had left for school early. Maybe they had joined clubs. He didn't know. He showered, then dressed, checking both of his pistols. Coffee was called for and he decided to make it at home for a change. He rooted around in the freezer for any bread available while the water boiled.

He called Finn again. "Any luck?"

"Not yet. You heading this way?"

"Shortly. Need to address my addiction first."

He made breakfast quickly, considering how he was going to tackle this without the backup of the Tactical Squad. Once again, he drifted to the tethered goat gambit. He took the toast out of the small counter-top oven, buttered it and added honey, a rarity for him. He felt that extra energy was called for. Bee's energy. He smiled as he chewed, the aroma of cocoa from the coffee filled the kitchen. He flipped on the radio. The CBC host was talking about the violence being visited on Vancouver, both from the police murders and the random attacks that were a daily occurrence in the downtown area. It seemed to be the usual trope, moan about the problems, rile up the listeners, and consult an 'expert'. He could only imagine what the other stations were making of the situation but didn't dare change the dial. Hearing those diatribes would only raise his blood pressure needlessly. He finished the coffee and headed out to his car.

Robert hadn't been in his office for more than a minute when Ranit called over to him. "Boss wants you, now."

He entered Thomas's office but didn't even get to sit down.

"They are releasing Mary Tinlit tomorrow morning. The breaking and entering charges are insufficient to keep her. And of course, her lawyer is suggesting she shouldn't have been kept inside as long as she has. There is talk of a complaint being brought."

Robert was thinking. "Craps. Tomorrow? Saturday? I need to get a couple of people down to Surrey to follow her."

"Seems reasonable. Better get that set up. But be careful. If there is a complaint, then harassment could be added if she figures out what's happening to her."

Robert turned and headed for the bullpen, looking for some of the same officers who had volunteered for the City Hall protest duty days earlier. He found one and dragged him into his office, explaining as he walked. "Here are the photos of the girl you'll tail, and the guy who we are really after. You figure out how many people and cars you need, but you need to get moving. She is being released tomorrow am, Surrey Remand. And don't let her find out you are on her tail, got it?" Then he added, "No need to let the Surrey Police know what you are up to."

The young officer grinned. It seemed that Robert had just made his week, maybe month, who knew? Robert admired the keenness. After he had left, Robert went over to check for Finn or Vito. Neither were present, so he descended to the depths, to see if Rory had any sharpish ideas.

As he walked down the stairs, he realized that Andy wouldn't know about Mary's release, for a while, anyway. Maybe he could arrange another meet. He had an internal debate about the stupidity of this idea when he had no back up, and no desire for any. He entered Rory's domain just as his cell burbled its inane noise.

"Robert here."

"It's Finn. Traced the number. Probably a burner. But we also have a number for Andy's phone. Got it from one of the wireless providers. Problem is that it is tied to the phone found at his place of residence. Not on him. He must have another one that he is using to talk to us on the chat group."

"So not totally stupid, is he? Give me both numbers. I'm with Rory. Let's see what our best and brightest can do." He ended the call. Rory looked up at Robert, hint of a smile growing. Robert wrote down the numbers, sliding the slip over to Rory. He studied it skeptically.

"Does this guy have any other connections that you know about? Someone he might get support from?" Rory asked.

"No. We don't know very much about Andy."

"Relatives?"

A slow agonizing grimace broke out on Robert's face. "Shit, his half-brother, Manny. Maybe that's where he was getting his succour and support. Problem is, he's dead."

"That doesn't mean anything. In fact, it would aid him, to hide behind a dead brother. Financially, and digitally, he'd be invisible if he was careful enough and things weren't wound up in Manny's estate like usual. When did he die?"

"Last spring, almost half a year ago. Maybe you are correct. Things may not be finalized." Robert studied Rory, staring down at him. Perhaps the basement wasn't the optimum place for this officer. Rory was feeling uncomfortable, Robert silent.

"Did I say something wrong?"

"I think you are in the wrong place, Rory."

Rory looked around, puzzled. This was the only room he had ever worked in as an officer for the Vancouver force.

"Forget it for now. Manny Dhillon." He spelled it out the last name. "Access the file and let's see what we have. I haven't even looked at it. Too close, I suppose. Not the best of memories."

Rory nodded. He had heard some of the stories. He scrolled through the labyrinth system, found the file, and started reading. Robert sat down, waiting for illumination. It took a while. Robert was about to stand up and leave when Rory started talking.

"The Two Tigers had a club, their headquarters, I think, in Surrey. Several other properties listed on the asset list in various locales across the Lower Mainland. No indication as to what happened to them. We have a phone number for the club. It had a tap on it last spring for a time. There are transcripts attached, in the file."

"Manny must have had a cell."

"Not listed. Let me enquire." Rory rolled over to his fellow denizens, gave an instruction, rolled back. "Shouldn't take long. I'll check the properties."

In the heart of Surrey, Rodney Fister wasn't in a quitting mood. He was still plotting how to get at Safa for a shakedown of sorts. From her file, he knew that she had been attending Kwantlen the previous spring, so this was where he would look. He called the technical university and shook a few branches.

It was after the lunch hour on Friday. Safa had finished her classes and was chatting to a friend as they ambled across the central courtyard at the Surrey Campus of Kwantlen, thankful that the week was over. They were laughing, planning, and thinking ahead to the Diwali celebrations starting in a couple of days, not paying attention to anyone else. Near the covered arcade on the north side, they almost bumped into a man who was standing in their way. Safa looked at him in annoyance, making to turn around him when he spoke.

"Safa Atwal?"

She looked back at his eyes. "Maybe. Who are you?"

"Rodney Fister, with the IIO." He pulled out an ID card and waved it in Safa's general direction.

She wasn't having any of this crap. "Let me see it."

Rodney reluctantly handed it to her. Safa studied it while the friend looked over her shoulder.

"Okay, what do you want?"

"Your friend can get lost."

Safa's friend wasn't the fair-weather type. She stood her ground, staring at Rod.

"If you have something to say, you better say it, or I'll call security. And you can do it right here." Safa knew enough not to move. "How'd you find me anyway?"

"Wasn't hard." It was a mild boast, but Rodney was still on the back foot, not expecting this kind of resistance from a young woman he thought he would easily intimidate.

"Last spring, you said you were the one who killed those gangsters."

Safa's eyes hardened. "I don't remember. Why?"

"It's not true, is it?"

Safa wasn't stupid. "I know they deserved what they got that day."

"Robert was the one who killed them, right?"

"And how would he do that? He was tied to a chair, getting his fingers broken by Manny."

Safa's friend was looking at Safa as if she had been transformed into a different person. She knew a few things about Safa's past and family, but this was new information, shocking information. Rodney looked perplexed, but Safa knew he wasn't going to quit harassing her any time soon. Finding her at Kwantlen proved that.

"Wait a minute." She pulled out her phone to call her brother.

"You're not calling the police, are you?" Rodney was leery after his experience at her parent's home.

Safa looked back at him. "No, my brother. He was in that gang, as you know. He'll help you out." She returned to her quiet conversation with Bobbi. The other two could not make out what she was saying. Bobbi had formulated a plan, not a very good plan, but it was all he could think of. It was time to put it into motion.

Safa ended her call. "We need to get up to the old club that the Two Tigers used. It's not far from City Hall. My brother will meet us there." She looked at her friend. "I'll call you tomorrow, Sonya, okay?"

Sonya looked uncertain, but deferred to Safa, who had always demonstrated good judgment. She nodded and moved off slowly, looking back at Safa and Rodney once or twice. She didn't trust the guy at all. He had an evil pallor to him.

Safa faced Rodney, told him the address. "I'll meet you there."

"No, you're coming with me. I don't want you disappearing on me."

"I am not getting into a car with you, under any circumstances, get it? As I already said, I'll meet you there."

They stood facing each other for a few moments in a stand-off, then Rodney relented. "You'd better show."

Safa nodded, turned and strode resolutely through the colonnade towards the north parking lot, her mind swirling.

In the basement of Cambie Street, Robert had re-appeared after stepping out for a quick snack. Rory had finished his appraisal of the various holdings under Two Tiger's sway earlier in the year. "They had four properties; two commercial or industrial sites in North Surrey along the river, the club in Central Surrey, and a hobby farm in Langley."

Robert knew about most of these sites, having visited and suffered some sort of trauma at a couple of them.

"Three of them have new ownership, leaving the club's status as undetermined." Rory wasn't finished. "Isn't there some kind of government agency that goes after assets of known criminals?"

"Yeah. Maybe not always successfully."

"I wonder what happened with the four properties then. Doesn't government usually move kind of slowly?"

"Tortoise-like would be their top speed. Some intervention perhaps by someone higher up the food chain? But the club escaped their clutches, so far?"

"Seems so."

One of the young women rolled over to Rory, handing him a slip of paper, then rolled back to her monitors.

"It appears we have a ping answered for a phone registered to one Manny Dhillon. Address of its location matches that of the club in Surrey." Rory smiled at his team's prowess. "Someone has been paying the monthly bills."

Robert looked around, then stood up. "Okay, let's go."

Rory looked back at him, uncertainty in his eyes. "You want me to go with you?"

"Yeah. You have your gun?"

"In a locker."

Robert stared down at him, eyebrows raised. "We need to scurry."

Rory stood, knowing this was a largish opportunity. But it also seemed a trifle hare-brained to be running off to Surrey without some basic planning or back up.

As if he could read Rory's mind, Robert was on his cell, calling Finn. He left a message when the call wasn't answered. He got the same result trying Vito, so he left a second message. "Looks like it's you and me. Get your gun and let's go. Meet in the garage." Rory stood up and helplessly grinned at his fellow cyber officers.

"Good luck, Rory." One of the women said, shaking her head. "Think you might need it." Rory agreed, but didn't tarry. He headed out to retrieve his weapon, excitement growing.

# CHAPTER 29

Robert was driving for this expedition, leaving Rory to study his cellphone intently. Robert glanced over. "What are you looking at?"

Rory looked up. "Got a plan of the building we're heading to. Always good to know what we're walking into, correct?"

"How'd you do that?"

"Can't say." Rory's eyes twinkled. They had been on the move for over half an hour. The car was speeding over the Alex Fraser Bridge, heading south, the brown river far below.

"You're going to need to guide me soon. I'll be heading east shortly, assuming we are going to the new city centre, correct?"

"Yup. Not far from City Hall. You'd think the mayor and council would be pissed at having the Two Tigers practically as neighbours," Rory said.

"They probably weren't aware of the notoriety of said club. On the other hand, maybe they did know about them," Robert mused. He glanced at his watch, the clock in the squad car seemingly inoperative. Almost two o'clock. His cell rang. He fished it out of his coat pocket, handing it to Rory. "Answer it, please."

Rory took the phone and listened. "We are just entering Surrey, should be at the club in about twenty or thirty minutes, Vito." He listened intently. "He wants us to wait for backup, Robert."

"We'll try. Tell him to get here pronto. He is the only backup I trust, and Finn of course."

Rory relayed the instructions, wincing as Vito swore at him. He looked back at Robert. "Not happy, it seems."

"Figures." They were driving east through a wasteland of single-family suburbia. At King George Boulevard, they would turn north, for a destiny that included violence, Robert was certain. "Ever done something like this before, Rory? Rescuing someone?"

"Is that what we are doing? Can't say I have, Robert."

"I rescued my son from a gang over a year ago, but this feels different. There was some rationality behind my foes last time. This Andy seems to have one thing on his mind, killing people, and he doesn't seem particular about who."

"Great." Rory glanced over at Robert, pretty certain of the answer before he asked, but... "Maybe we should wait for Vito and Finn. What do you think?"

"We'll park close by and do some scouting before we go in — give those guys a chance to catch up. Which street is it?"

"106 Avenue. Enchanting name. Must have been named after that famous Canadian explorer, 106. Turn right after we pass by City Hall." Rory's head was turning left and right, "Boy, there are a lot of towers here now. Where'd they come from?"

Robert laughed as they headed north, then slowed as he went through the intersection where 105 Avenue crossed.

"Who laid this city out?" He muttered to himself. "Next street, I assume?"

"Yup."

Robert turned right, slowed further as they passed by the club sitting on the south side of the street. It was a two-story building, set back from the street with a front yard featuring parking stalls, all empty, save for three cars, one of which was a white Subaru. A small strip shopping centre sat to the left, across the street from the club. Robert pulled into its lot, backing into a stall as far from the street as he could. He killed the engine. The two officers looked at each other, then focused on the building across the street.

"There is a lane running up behind the building." Rory said. Robert twisted, reaching into the rear seat, and brought a knapsack forward. Pulling a pair of binoculars out, he scanned the front of the club, looking for cameras. He saw one on each building corner up near the top of the walls.

"I'd expect this place to be well protected, gang headquarters and all. There are usually blind spots, though." He put the binoculars down. "That is one ugly building. Looks like they used the entire arsenal of cheap finishing materials."

"Are we on an architectural tour now?"

"There's a thought. One of those cars looks suspiciously like a police undercover vehicle. One of the others looks like what Andy supposedly drives. Let me look at the plans on your phone." Their heads came together as they perused the layouts on Rory's cell. A large room was the focus of the ground floor, with some service rooms at the rear, likely a kitchen with smaller storage and office areas. The second floor seemed similar to the main level. An enclosed foyer was just inside the front door. Exit stairs sat at each building end with another stair in the middle.

"Let's go, Rory. We'll range around back first." The officers exited their car, walking out to the street and then east, their eyes checking everything out. East of the club were a couple of old houses, their best years far behind them. Robert shook his head. Surrey had some growing up to do, he supposed. Although he recalled the same thing in Vancouver's Yaletown only a few years earlier — the occasional ancient home with rotting trims sitting forlornly amid looming condo towers as the area slowly changed.

They walked by a small private school at the street's end, then reached the lane, turned and headed slowly west towards the club, keeping to the edges of the pavement. Rory pointed up at more cameras mounted on the club's lane corners. Robert nodded. They both ran the last few paces to the building's back wall.

"I'm guessing that Andy might be a bit pre-occupied, so I doubt we'll be seen." He turned and hugging the side of the building, headed north to its front, Rory following. Robert peered around the front corner at the three cars in front of the building.

"That is definitely a city issue car. Wonder whose it is?"

"How we going to get in there, Robert?"

They heard a muffled scream from inside the club. It sounded faint, as though far away, but it also came from a woman.

"Sounds like we need to hustle. Maybe I'll try the front door, what do you think?" Robert didn't waste time waiting for an answer. He went over to the solid wooden door and tried it. It opened outwards slightly. He reached into his coat and took out his pistol, flicking off the safety. Suddenly, his conscience reared its head. "Perhaps you should wait here, Rory, for the others." He was pretty certain that Rory had no experience in what was sure to come. He also didn't need a flustered officer firing a gun wildly if things went off the rails. He winked at Rory as he disappeared through the door.

Rory was unsure what he should be doing. He stood against the wall, picking his cell out of his breast pocket. He dialled Vito. "Where the hell are you guys? He just went in, without me."

Vito swore. "Don't follow him, hang on and we'll be there soon enough. Five minutes tops."

Robert was in a small foyer. What looked like a cloakroom was off to his right. Did they hold soirees here? It seemed improbable. He stopped at the next door, listening intently. Nothing. He cracked it open a few inches. It was dim, only half-lit inside. From Rory's floor plan, it should be the large room. He re-checked that the safety was off and stuck his head in, his pistol barrel held high. The space looked empty. He walked into the room, listening intently. Nothing. He ventured slowly to the back wall, where a corridor led to the rear of the building. He checked a couple of doors in the hallway very carefully, pulling them open a crack. Nothing. The ground floor seemed deserted. He returned to the front room, looking at the central stairs. He shrugged to himself and headed up slowly, trying to be soundless. At the top landing, he faced another door. He didn't waste any time thinking, but opened the door, and slid through to a tableau of four people, one armed.

"Drop the gun, Robert. If you don't, Sandra will be onto her next life." Andy raised a gun, aiming at Sandra's head, a SIG Sauer, if Robert wasn't mistaken. Andy was staring a malevolent smile at Robert. Sandra's eyes were wide open. Robert doubted they could get any larger.

"Sure, okay. Let's keep calm here." He lowered, then dropped his weapon, hoping it wouldn't go off by itself.

"Why are so many people here? Is it a party that no one told me about?" Andy seemed amused.

Robert was surprised to be looking at Safa and Rodney. "What are you doing here, Rod? Take a wrong turn?" Rodney was bound with rope, sitting on the floor.

"Screw off, Robert."

Andy watched the interplay. "You know each other?"

Robert declined to answer this. Instead, he addressed Andy. "You may not know this, but Mary is being released from remand tomorrow." There was no reaction, so he continued, "So, why are you keeping your cousin, Andy? You usually treat family so badly?" He looked over at Sandra as he said this. She returned the look, achingly, it seemed. Andy didn't answer. He strode over and hit Robert on the side of his head with the flat of the gun. Robert saw yellow sparks briefly, then nothing.

Rory was standing by the club's front door, alone, afraid to venture out where he might be picked up by the building's cameras, focused on the parking lot. A car screeched into the parking lot, parking by the other three. A young South Asian man got out, staring over at Rory.

"Who are you?" Bobbi yelled over.

"Rory." He was nothing if not concise. "Who are you?"

"Bobbi." He walked closer.

"Vancouver Police Department," said Rory. There is a situation going on. You should leave."

"My sister is in there. I'm not leaving."

"Who are you?" Rory was confused.

"Robert Lui knows who I am." A hint of menace.

"Okay. I came here with Robert. He's inside, but I don't know what's happening in there."

Bobbi walked right up to Rory. "Maybe we should go inside."

To Rory, this sounded hesitant. He was fretting, chewing at his lip. He had heard nothing after Robert had slid through the door, and the other two detectives had yet to arrive. Should he go in? He was about to reluctantly venture inside when a VPD patrol car pulled into the lot at speed. Was it them? Detectives usually shunned the racy black and whites, but maybe speed decided things. The car lurched to a stop with a loud squeal and the passenger door opened. Finn jumped out, staring over at Rory and Bobbi.

"Where's Robert?"

"Still inside. I don't know what's happening. Haven't heard a thing in over ten minutes."

"That's it. I'm calling the Surrey Police. I don't care what Robert thinks of back up." He leaned back into the squad car and spoke to Vito quickly. Inside of a minute, the first patrol car of many pulled into the lot.

Robert slowly opened his eyes, one of them at any rate. His right eye wasn't working very well. That side of his head hurt like hell. He was on the floor on his back. He looked down the length of his body, which seemed shorter than what he was used to. Most likely it was due to his hands being tied behind his back and then to his ankles. Was this a hog-tying demonstration? He turned his head. Beyond Rod, who was similarly bound about two metres away, Andy looked to be working on a noose, using rope very similar to that found at two recent murders. Robert was curious as to what Andy was going to anchor it to. He couldn't see anything on the ceiling that might be of use, but he knew somehow that Andy had already figured this part out. What a crappy place to die.

Farther, against the wall, Sandra and Safa were standing, manacled together, and then to a bolt jutting out of the wall, as though people were regularly in need of restraint in this establishment. Who knows what the club members got up to when the gang was in full bloom. Both of them were looking at Robert, evidently relieved that he had gained his senses, but they seemed afraid to say anything. He couldn't remember seeing eyes so large, and so intent on him.

Robert tried to move and found a new source of pain — his ribs. Andy must have given him a good kick while he was down and out. At this rate, his ribs were going to be asking for early retirement. He tested the rope binding his wrists, but it was tight, no give. He involuntarily groaned. Andy looked over and smiled as he worked at his noose crafting.

"Good, you're awake. You can watch your buddy here swing first, before I haul you up." He continued tying the rope together. Robert looked across at Rodney, whose face had taken a battering, but he seemed conscious. His wrists were similarly tied to his feet, but in front of him, unlike Robert's bondage. He was sitting with his back against the same wall that the women were chained to.

"What makes you think you can come in here to my place?" Andy asked as he crafted.

"Thought the Two Tigers were the owners, not you."

"Things change."

Robert was trying to buy some time, hoping that perhaps Rory had either marshalled the calvary, or was making his way inside like a ninja. "Sometimes, but not ownership."

Andy dropped the rope and strode over, giving Robert a well-aimed kick at his already battered ribs. Sandra whimpered as Robert exhaled sharply and let out a low moan. "Maybe you should go first?" Andy seemed to be offering choices.

"No, I like the order you've chosen. Works for me." The words came out in rasp. He was having severe trouble breathing. A thought came to him. "May I ask you a question?"

Andy stared back at Robert, not moving.

Robert took this as a maybe. "Word on the streets is that you are a religious man, yes?"

Andy nodded as he smiled, seemingly pleased with himself.

"Is this how you celebrate Diwali?" He was appealing to his supposed mania.

Andy's eyebrows wrinkled as he thought about this. He didn't kick Robert for a change, but didn't answer either. He backed up and started tapping a tabletop next to him, staring at the floor. Robert couldn't see very well but sensed that he had hit a nerve.

Suddenly, a smile broke out on Andy's face as he looked back at Robert. "You have made a good point, but Diwali doesn't start until Monday. I think we're good to kill a couple of policemen before then."

Not the answer Robert was hoping for. Rodney groaned. But Robert wasn't done.

"Did you watch as Mary killed her architect friend?"

"My Mary wouldn't hurt anyone. You must know this."

"No — it's not obvious at all. Did she watch as you killed Anne?"

"She was there. I think Anne deserved what she got, according to the chatrooms."

Robert couldn't believe what was happening — a killer spilling the beans. Of course, it'd be moot if he didn't survive the next few minutes. He really didn't want another rib kick into the bargain, but decided to go all in. "Do you do Mary's bidding? Did you kill Archie Hamilton for her?"

Andy seemed to ignore him and went over to the table to select a wood yardstick. Robert started to worry about being beat further, but Andy reached up with it and poked a ceiling tile loose. He hit it again, and it fell onto the floor, breaking in the process. He did this again with two more tiles. Robert was looking up at steel joists in the dark ceiling cavity, the structure holding up the roof. Probably more than adequate to support a police officer or two. Wasn't Archie Hamilton found hanging from a steel joist?

"Did you kill my partner?" Robert wanted answers.

"He was too nosy."

As Andy was trying to throw the rope's end up and over a joist, not successfully, a loud voice was heard by everyone in the room. It was the usual command,

**'We have the building surrounded. Drop your weapons and come out with your arms in the air.'**

Robert would have laughed if his ribs didn't hurt so much. Andy was back to concentrating on his hangman's task, seemingly ignoring the plea. It was as if he didn't care whether he would be caught, if only he could kill a couple of more people. Finally, the rope caught and snaked over the bottom chord of the truss. He smiled, playing out the rope before grabbing the loose end.

Robert was desperate. He twisted his hands again, trying to loosen them. No joy, but in doing so, brushed against his ankle holster. He looked over at Andy, who was getting the noose ready for Rod's head. He wasn't paying any attention to Robert. Robert felt higher up, where the Beretta could be, if it hadn't been discovered. It was still there! How stupid was this supposed gangster? He shifted around slightly so Andy couldn't see him trying to extract the gun.

Andy was busy, dropping the noose over Rod's head and snugging it to his neck. He was sure of himself, his gun on the table, not within easy reach.

Robert strained with all his strength to reach the butt of the Beretta. It was just out of reach of the tips of his fingers. He tried to slide the holster down closer to his ankle. Andy was still not paying any attention, having cinched the noose tight. The holster settled an inch. Robert strained, finally able to touch the gun's butt. He angled his feet back around, where he could aim, a one-eyed, two bad fingers aim, but Robert hoped his training would kick in.

"Think you should stop now." His voice was low, deadly calm. He flipped the safety off with his thumb as he pointed the gun at Andy.

Andy had finished with the noose and looked over at Robert, laughing. "You want another kick?" His smile faded quickly when he saw the small gun pointing at him. Maybe he thought it was a toy. He lunged for the table where the SIG Sauer lay. Robert fired, his first shot missing Andy. Safa screamed as the slug hit the wall beside her leg. He kept firing, concentrating on his aim, hitting Andy in the thigh first, then the side of his chest. The Beretta didn't have a ton of stopping power, and when the second shot hit Andy's chest, it missed a rib. However, it didn't miss his right lung.

Andy staggered forward, blood starting its frothy pink exit from his mouth. Robert aimed as best he could and fired once more. He hit the torso again, wanting to be sure as Andy fell onto the table where his gun was, then the floor with a certain finality, blood leaking everywhere.

Safa was screaming. Rodney started smiling crookedly at Robert, the noose still tight under his chin. Perhaps the start of a beautiful friendship, maybe.

Robert looked over at Andy, who wasn't moving. A loud bang came from the main floor. Probably the police making their entrance into the building, a little late, but who was counting when the wicked witch seemed to be dead. He dropped his gun.

Safa started yelling, "Up here, up here!" Robert prayed the officers wouldn't throw a similar stun grenade into this room before making their appearance. He had had enough violence for the day.

He looked over at Rodney. "Guess you could get started on your report now, can't you? Officer involved shooting. I assume this is your case?" He returned Rodney's smile with a grimace, then laid his head back on the floor, totally exhausted, and waited for the calvary to arrive.

Robert woke, groaning softly. His side ached fiercely, the same area of his chest where a gunshot had cracked ribs earlier in his career. His head hurt worse. He rolled onto his good side, then sat up slowly, swinging his feet onto the floor. It hurt just to breathe. Morning hadn't arrived yet.

The whisky must have worn off, pain sharpening. He needed drugs. Was this what it felt like to get old?

He stood up and shuffled gingerly to his ensuite, flicking on the light. He studied his naked body in the mirror, dark blues and purples starting to spread across his chest, other colours sure to follow. His head wasn't any prettier. He opened the medicine cabinet door, studying the options. There was a vial containing pills from the emergency room he had briefly visited the evening before. After x-rays, they had told him his ribs were cracked, not broken. Pain-wise, it was hard to tell any difference. He selected a different plastic container, flicked two pills onto the counter, then two more. It'd take a half hour for the stuff to have any effect, but maybe the knowledge that the pills were in there would help before they kicked in. He swallowed all of them, chased by water.

He turned in the doorway and looked back into the bedroom. Was his life on repeat?

"You okay, Robert?" Sandra turned her head from the pillow, her large eyes opening gradually.

"Good, Sandra." He smiled at her. "It's just like Yogi Berra said."

"Who?"

"Yankee manager of old."

"What?"

"It's deja vu all over again. And I'm so happy it is. You feeling okay?"

"Better than you I expect, from your appearance. By the way, you look better with the lights out."

"Thanks, Sandra. I'm getting used to the abuse. Don't like it any better, but it seems to come with my job." He flipped off the light and returned to bed, sliding slowly and gingerly under the covers. He laid back with a soft groan, his hand reaching for Sandra's. He turned and smiled at her, light dim, but he could just make out her grin. She reached across with her other hand and laid it on Robert's stomach. There weren't many places she could touch him that didn't elicit a wince. Robert was finally content despite the pain and somehow knew Sandra felt the same way. He was pretty certain that he was in love.

# Chapter 30

Robert's October from hell was history. Monday saw Robert walk ever so slowly onto his floor, nodding at Ranit before heading to his office. It was a new month, and a new Robert, he thought to himself. More physically damaged and oddly happy, yet disturbed at the same time. He was pleased that the cop killer was dead, yet troubled that he had been the one required to kill him. Robert sat in his less than beautiful chair, studying the eastern skyline, waiting for the expected summons from Thomas.

Things didn't look promising on the work front. He suspected another suspension was on deck for him. Disregarding VPD protocol and poaching on Surrey Police's turf were just a couple of the infringements that would make their way onto his record. And this didn't include another roughing over by the IIO for the shooting death of Andy Dhillon, not to mention the possible pending legal action by Allo Foot. Somehow, even though he had little to do with Allo's release, having his name as the lead detective on the case would likely get him added to any case brought by Allo and his eager team. He knew lawyers liked to spread blame around, looking for assets to chase. Well, if it came to that, his car was all he valued. And he suspected that it was only he who thought The Silver Streak worth something. They'd be barking up a tree with no leaves, branches, or much of anything. His phone rang.

Thomas stared at Robert's face as he sat down in a guest chair. "Sorry to say this, but you really look like crap, Robert." The welt on the side of his head boasted a large range of the colour spectrum.

"Thanks. I feel just like I look, but also, I am happier than I've been in a long time. So, there is that."

"Suspended, with pay, Robert."

"You don't pussyfoot around, do you?"

"Expected something different?"

"Not really. But I didn't do too bad, did I?"

"No, you did great, Robert. One dead cop killer, and freed hostages with no injuries, excluding yourself, of course. You are on your way to legend status. But protocol is protocol, you know this."

"Well, this body is going to take a bit to heal, so I'm fine with it. I'll do some thinking."

Thomas looked back at Robert, not liking the last sentiment. He hoped Robert wouldn't do anything rash. "Any thoughts on that Mary character? She was released a couple of days ago."

"Well, Thomas, if someone has a boatload of time to spare, and has a commensurate amount of good luck, a case might be built for charging her with accessory to first degree murder. I'm sure she was the one pulling Andy's strings, but proof will be very difficult to find, particularly now that I managed to kill the one person who might have implicated her."

Thomas nodded thoughtfully. "Back burner stuff I suppose, however I'm going to keep the file open. I heard you left the hospital with Sandra, Friday evening?"

"Yes."

"And she is related to Manny?"

"Yes, but she kept a large distance from that side of the family. It was one of the reasons she ended up in Bella Kind. She wasn't having any of it."

Thomas mulled this over. "And what were Bobbi, Safa, and Rod doing there?"

"I think Rod was trying to strong-arm Safa into pinning the blame on me for Manny's death last spring. I'm not really sure why they ended up at the club, though."

Thomas shook his head. "You can leave your items with Ranit, and please take care of yourself, Robert. I'm here if you need to talk. You'll be back, don't worry. We just need to go through the motions."

"I will. Thanks Thomas, I couldn't ask for a better boss, really." He stood up with a soft groan. "Think I'll go up the street one more time." He nodded at Thomas as he left the room, then scanned the bullpen, looking for accomplices. Finn was it, so he beckoned him and headed for the door, Finn following.

"Seems to be a certain symmetry to my life, Finn," he said, as they descended the stairs.

"Coffee, you mean?"

"Well, sort of. Didn't this whole episode start at Cafe Paulo?"

"I believe you're correct. Symmetry. Sounds mathematical." They left the building, heading south. "Did they release Mary Tinlit?"

"Yes. Haven't talked with anyone doing the tail job, though. Water under the bridge. Somehow, I don't think any charges are going to stick to young Mary. Too clever, I think." They entered the cafe.

"Roberto! Did you walk into a bus?" Gilberto grinned, with just the barest hint of concern added.

"I have a difficult job, Gilberto. You know this. And sometimes, buses don't stop quickly enough. I believe I'll have a macchiato today." He looked at Finn, who nodded. "Make it two."

"Macchiato? Think I'll need to check my menu. You've never ordered this before, have you?"

"New age, Gilberto, new age. And that bad guy we talked about last week? Don't believe he'll be dropping by here anymore, ever, so you may relax." Gilberto nodded, knowing Roberto would have things covered.

Finn and Robert retreated to the cafe's rear and sat, waiting.

"So, everyone rescued, Robert. Promotion coming?"

"Suspension, actually. I'm going to do some thinking."

"Don't like the sounds of that." Carmelita came over to their table, gently placing their cups.

"Nice to see you are back, Carmelita." Robert said.

She smiled in return, did a twirl, and retreated behind the bar.

"No charges for Mary. What do you think she'll do once she finds out you killed her boyfriend?"

Robert stared back at Finn. "Hmm, hadn't thought that through, although it didn't feel like I had much choice in the moment. Yes, a trial might have been a better outcome for all involved, although then that asshole might have got off."

He shook his head. "I think she just might extend this whole thing farther. I don't know how, but I'm guessing I may need to keep my eyes wide open. On the other hand, psychopaths like Andy that will bend to your will don't come along every day." He paused. "As far as I know."

"What happened to Sandra?" Finn asked.

Robert looked down into his cup, as though the answer lay beneath the surface of the foam. "She's spending a few days with me before heading back up to Raven Island. She believes that I saved her life. Who knows, maybe she has something. I don't know where that crazy Andy would have stopped. When Andy took her, she thought everything was okay. Hadn't seen him in a few years and she thought they were just catching up. Then she couldn't leave and quickly figured out she wasn't going anywhere, but didn't know why. She had no idea he was as bent as he was."

"You mean?"

"Yes, I mean. Sandra will finish out her contract at Arnott Bay this winter, then return here in March. I'll head up there at some point soon for a visit." He smiled at Finn. "Once the pain dies away."

"What about her supposed gang connection?"

"She left Surrey quite some time ago, and had no connection to any of that." Robert answered.

"Somehow, I don't think the VPD will be as lenient in their assessment of the situation, Robert."

"Which is why I'll be doing some hard thinking, as I said."

Finn grinned in return. "Well, I guess she doesn't work for the VPD, does she?"

"Nope. And I believe I am truly smitten this time, as is she, apparently."

"Good for you. So, you are learning! Well done, Robert. But I thought you were staying away from water for the rest of your life."

"Apparently, I must make some exceptions to the things I say."

END

# About the author

Glenn Burwell was a registered architect who practiced in Vancouver, British Columbia, for almost forty years. He's seen all sides of the local development industry and how it affects the lives of people living in the region. This is his fourth novel. Robert Lui was introduced in *The Chapel of Retribution*, defended his family against gangsters in *A Sin Offering*, and investigated government corruption in *Greenside*.

Now retired, Burwell is working on more stories of detective Robert Lui, manages a small tomato and herb garden, and continues to keep an eye on the never-ending saga of housing problems in Vancouver.

You can contact Glenn and learn about his other books at the Somewhat Grumpy Press web site: https://somewhatg rumpypress.com/

Help independent authors and small presses by leaving a review at your favourite online retailer or review site, or sharing on social media.

www.ingramcontent.com/pod-product-compliance
Lightning Source LLC
Chambersburg PA
CBHW051319190726
48290CB00001B/219